VEILED
ROMANCE

Credits

Cover painting by: Zaman Zamani
Pictures: Faye Ershadi

ISBN: 1456425803
ISBN-13: 9781456425807
Library of Congress Control Number: 2010918147

Visit www.Simon-Writes.com to order additional copies
Email: SimonEbrahimi@gmail.com

VEILED ROMANCE

A PERSIAN TALE OF PASSION AND REVOLUTION

By Simon Sion Ebrahimi

They smell your breath,
lest you might have said I love you.
They smell your heart.
These are strange times, my darling.
The butchers are stationed at
each crossroad with bloody clubs and cleavers.

Ahmad Shamloo,
contemporary Persian poet

To:

Rabbi Scott Sperling,

With thanks

[illegible signature]

3/2014

ACKNOWLEDGMENT

Thanks to my wife, Nahid, the pillar of our family, who for all the years that I have been writing a multigenerational family saga (*Veiled Romance* being only the story of the last generation) has stood by me and given me support and encouragement every step of the way. I thank my daughters, Mitra and Maryam, and their husbands, Ramin and Amir, for their earnest guidance and the precious gifts they have given my wife and me, our grandchildren, Aria, Yasi, Cypress, and Jordan.

Although *Veiled Romance* is based on some true events of my life, all persons appearing in this book are fictitious and any resemblance of its characters to real people, living or dead, is entirely coincidental. Having said that, I raise my hat to Fred Feldman, the editor of any writer's dream and a great author and a caring friend. Although being taken hostage was what *I* had experienced, at times I couldn't help but wonder if Fred had been present in my office the day I was taken hostage.

This novel would not have been in your hands were it not for the noble support of Rabbi David Shofet, the spiritual leader of the Iranian Jewish community, and his conviction that the life stories of the Persian Jews must be preserved.

For their guidance and devotion, I am also grateful to my friends and critics, Guitta Karubian, Alan Ullman, and

Dr. Edward Sweeney who not only urged and encouraged me to unveil the *Veiled Romance* but also accompanied me on this long journey.

And last but not the least, my thanks to these friends and supporters who made this project possible: Jack Mahfar, Sion Mahfar, Daryoush Dayan, Yoel Neman, Sina Mehdizadeh, Mike Nazarian, Shahla Javdan, Nourollah Noorvash, Ezat Delijani, Barokh Shaheri, Iraj Shamouilian, Saeed Matloob, Amir Emrani, Shokrollah and Sima Baravarian, Ben Olandj, Ben Behin, Massoud Farahani, Mark Naim, Shahram Rabbani, and Nejat Ahdoot.

CHAPTER 1

January 30, 1980

It is my second night in this place. My cell is as dark and cold as a crypt. Yesterday morning, they took me, blindfolded, directly from the Central Revolutionary Committee and threw me in here. I pulled off the filthy cloth and waited for my eyes to get used to the semidarkness. Eventually I saw dust motes dancing in the narrow band of light filtering into the cell from a barred window at the top of the wall. Directly opposite that solitary window was a heavy metal door.

My cell is no more than ten feet wide by ten feet long. It is infested with cockroaches and the occasional mouse. The air is cold and damp. Shoved up against the wall beneath the window is an old, disintegrating mattress with a threadbare blanket. My sharp sense of smell, which I had always thought of as a blessing, has become a curse, for everything here smells foul—my own body and clothing, my sorry excuse for a bed, the air, and more than anything else, my *pasdar*—the member of the revolutionary guard—who is my jailer. I can actually sense him approaching from his skunk stench. That is the name I have given him in my mind, Skunk, although he has a name tag…Well, not exactly a name tag but a piece of fabric sewn to his jacket with “Zaki” handwritten on it. Skunk’s khaki camouflage revolutionary uniform is several sizes too large. He wears a canvas gun belt with a pistol in a flapped holster. He is short with a small head. Although he has a thick beard, only a few strings of whiskers curl above his lips. His eyes are tiny and yellow-brown. When he speaks, his high-pitched words whistle out from between the gaps of his mossy teeth.

I made Skunk’s acquaintance yesterday morning, after I spent an hour at the Central Revolutionary Committee while being interrogated by a mullah and a little, bearded man who acted as the stenographer at my hearing. When the hearing was over and my guilt—which was a foregone conclusion—was officially transcribed, I was blindfolded and transported here.

“What have you done, sister?” Skunk asked, sitting beside me as we made our journey. I fought back my nausea from riding blindfolded in the bouncing, swaying vehicle.

“Nothing,” I said as I felt his hand moving up my thigh. “I had a fight with this man who wanted to touch me.”

He swiftly pulled his hand away. “But you are an anti-revolutionary?”

“No. I’m an observant Muslim woman.”

He spoke no more. Finally, we arrived wherever I am now, and he threw me in this cell and locked the door. He returned perhaps half an hour later with a tray on which was a piece of bread and a tin cup of water. He put it on the stained, grimy floor. “Your breakfast. Sit down and eat, Sister Zahra.”

"Zahra" was the name given to me at the Central Revolutionary Committee by my interrogator, who also warned me that I was to forget my own name, that if I dared to even say it to anyone, including my pasdar, I would be executed. Obeying Skunk's instruction, I sat, gnawed on the stale hunk of bread, and listened as he laid out my circumstances.

"This place used to be one of the many hidden jails of SAVAK, the Shah's CIA, may Allah erase his name from the face of the earth," he began. "He had built hundreds—what am I saying?—thousands and thousands of these with the help of the Great Satan America and the filthy Jews' regime, the occupiers of the land of our Palestinian brothers. But now that we have been blessed with the first government of Allah on the earth, we are putting all the counterrevolutionaries, the sinners and the enemies of Imam Khomeini, in these houses converted to prisons. Especially whores like you. And soon we will start helping our Palestinian brothers to kick the Jews out of Palestine and..."

I nodded to humor him as I sat shaking like a willow tree in the wind.

"Get undressed," he abruptly ordered.

"What?"

"You're all *jendeh*, whores," he muttered, walking toward me. He unbuckled his gun belt and carefully tossed it behind him into a corner of the cell. "Yes, you and your mother and her mother were all prostitutes. Your mother is the bride of a thousand grooms, and your father, a faggot who sleeps under donkeys."

He began to fumble at his trousers. He seemed to be having trouble with his zipper. Despite my terror—or maybe because of it—I had the craziest impulse to burst out laughing, even though to do so would certainly mean serious physical injury or even death at the hands of this monster.

"What are you waiting for?" he yelled, charged toward me, and yanked off my hijab, my headscarf. He grabbed me by my hair and flung me onto the dirty floor, then straddled me and tried to rip off my shirt.

I screamed, clinging as hard as I could to my top. He put the palm of one hand on my mouth and pressed his other hand against my throat. "Shut up before I shut you up!" he snarled. With every word, he tightened his grip on my throat. "You can scream as much as you want, no one will hear you in this prison. Now take off your shirt, or I will kill you and leave your body here to rot!"

Unable to breathe, panicked, I cried out with my last exhalation, "*Allah fayaghfar men al yasha va yoazeb man yasha, va Allah ala kole sheian ghadir.*"

He lurched off me. "You know the verses of the Koran and you know them in Arabic?" he asked, sounding incredulous.

"And Allah forgives or punishes, for only He is the Almighty," I muttered the translation. I took advantage of his confusion to sit up and cover my hair with my scarf.

"But…but…whores like you have no right to even utter sacred verses!" he growled. Nevertheless, he moved back all the way to the door of the cell. "The holy words of our *Kalam-Allah* from *your* mouth?" He shook his head in disapproval as he lit a cigarette and took a deep drag. "That's a blasphemy. Where did they teach you this, in the Great Satan's CIA?"

"No," I replied. "I told you. I am an observant Muslim woman, and I pray—"

"Even though you have been to America, you know the Koran?"

"Yes." I folded the moldy blanket from my mattress to use it as my prayer rug. "Come to think of it, I haven't recited my morning prayer yet. I don't know Kiblah, the direction of Mecca. Which way is it, please?"

Looking dumbfounded, Skunk pointed to the door. I laid the blanket in that direction and sat on it in a prayer pose. "Allah be with you, brother. May I ask you to bring me a prayer seal this afternoon?" And before he was able to answer, I began my *namaz.* "*Ghol hova Allah ahad, Allah...*" And as I murmured my prayer, the genesis of finding a way to escape this dungeon began to take shape in my mind. The first thing I needed to do was ascertain the whereabouts of my jail. But how?

Skunk hurriedly retrieved his gun belt. As he fumbled with his keys to unlock the cell door I gestured that he should stay until I was done. He froze, as I suspected he would, for even one as ignorant as he would know it was a major sin to interrupt any prayer.

"I need to go to the bathroom, Brother Zaki," I said when I was done.

"Very well," he grumbled as he opened the door. "Follow me."

We left my cell for a long corridor dimly lit by three bulbs hanging from the ceiling. We passed another metal door like mine on my left and one on my right. Two more such doors were at the corridor's end. One I supposed was the way out of this corridor of cells. The other turned out to be the toilet.

"Go in," he said. I walked into the filthy place and he began to follow me in.

"Brother Zaki!" I said patiently. "'Tell the believers to cover their private parts. That is purer for them. Verily, Allah is all-aware of what they do.' That's from Al-Noor, chapter twenty-four, verse thirty." I stared at him obstinately.

"Shut your filthy mouth!" he yelled at me. I heard other voices—those of two other women—coming from the cells along the corridor

"Allah Akbar…There's another woman…Please be kind to her, Brother Zaki."

"You shut up too," Skunk cried, then turned to me and said, "All right. I will turn my back to you, but I am not going to let you shut the door."

And that is what he did.

CHAPTER 2

Leila Omid. This is my name. I'm the daughter of Aria Omid, who is my *pedar*, my dad, and Mitra Hormozi, who is my *madar*, my mother. Pedar is the son of Major General Bahman Omid, who was deputy minister of war to both Reza Shah Pahlavi and his son, Mohammad Reza Shah—the Shah—until over a year ago, in February 1979, when he was overthrown by the Iranian Revolution.

"At the time your mother and I married in 1953," I remember Pedar telling me, "I was a medical student at Tehran University. I was twenty-six and she, a nursing student, was twenty-two. Our marriage was not easy. My in-laws—who were from Jewbareh, the Jewish ghetto in Esfahan—were resolutely against their daughter marrying a gentile. They would say, 'A dove flies with a dove, and an eagle with an eagle.' I volunteered to pretend to convert to Judaism, but it wasn't good enough for them.

"Pretend, Father?" I asked.

Pedar smiled. "Don't get ahead of my story," he said. "Anyway, 'To marry my daughter,' your grandfather asserted, 'you have to be of Jewish seed...to have been conceived in a Jewish mother's womb.' And so, at the risk of putting my father's high military position in jeopardy," Pedar explained to me, "I gave them the shock of their lives. I told them that I was born Jewish.

"I swore your maternal grandparents to secrecy and then revealed my family's great secret: that my father, General Omid, was the great-grandson of Rabbi Hezekiah, of Mashhad. I explained how in the early nineteenth century, during the reign of the Qajar dynasty, the Jewish community of Mashhad was pressured to convert to Islam. Many Jews at first resisted, until the executions started. The elders of the community, Rabbi Hezekiah among them, told all the two hundred Jewish families that God would forgive them if they should pretend to convert to Islam, a faith they then pretended to practice. In the meantime, they took their true faith underground. Still indentified as *Jadidi*—new Islam converts—they named their sons Ali, Hussein, and Mohammad, but gave those boys secret Jewish names. They even went to Mecca and Medina on required Islamic pilgrimages.

"And all that while, within the basements of their houses, they made hidden synagogues," my father continued. "They bought meat from Muslim butchers, which they gave to their pets, and slaughtered the sheep and goats they bought on the sly according to kosher laws. They hid their daughters at home until they came of age and then married them to members of their own community. They lived under these harsh circumstances until the constitutional revolution in the early nineteenth century. In the meantime, a few daring community members rose to claim high government positions—overtly as devout Muslims. None of them, however, ceased their ties to Judaism. As would be expected, Jewish rituals fell away, but one thing they insisted upon: that their children should marry within their ancestral faith."

In counterpoint to Pedar's side of the story, Madar told me how her parents eventually came around to supporting the marriage, but they insisted on a Jewish wedding. How to marry the deputy minister of war's son according to Jewish tradition in Iran became the next hurdle. Again, my paternal grandfather, the general, came up with the solution.

"Your grandfather, the general, arranged for both families to go to London," my mother recounted. "There, we were married by a rabbi."

In 1957, two years after I was born, Pedar built a modest country house in Tabas, a small town on the edge of the Lute Desert near Yazd Province. Here, we spend most of our winter holidays, exchanging the cold of Tehran for the region's mild tropical weather. In the middle of Tabas is a source of fresh water surrounded by sturdy palm and willow trees. Wheat farms, vineyards, woods, and, ultimately, the vast desert extend out from this oasis, like the planets that orbit the sun. I remember Tabas so vividly. How when I was a teenager I would spend my afternoons by the oasis, gazing at the reflections of the willow trees on the surface of the tiny lake. I took long walks along the paths that snaked between the tall yellow wheat stacks and green vineyards, all the way to the outskirts of the village. There, I would sit and watch the silhouettes of camel caravans crossing the tawny sand dunes against the fiery backdrop of the setting sun.

My parents' priority for my two brothers and me was always education. Reward commensurate to academic achievement, as Pedar liked to say. And that was why when my parents sent me to America to study, they were adamant that I be admitted to a respectable university.

CHAPTER 3

Skunk came back this afternoon. He announced himself first with his stink and next by the sound of a key unlocking the metal door. I steeled myself to face my jailer once again.

"Ya Allah!" he greeted me, entering my cell carrying a big bundle. "A cot, a prayer rug, and a prayer seal," he said as he put the bundle down. Then he went out and came back with my meal tray, but this time, it held a loaf of soft bread, a metal cup of tea, and a bowl of some sort of soup.

"Your dinner," he said, in an unmeaning parody of an unctuous, room service waiter.

Out and in again he came with a plastic container. "Water," he said as he locked the door behind him. He unfolded the cot, laid the prayer rug on the ground with the seal at its top, and sat on the edge of the cot. Then he lit a cigarette and patted the cot, inviting me to sit next to him.

"Thank you, brother," I said, tightening my chador around my face and standing as far away from him as possible in the little cell.

"I said sit next to me," he ordered.

I did so reluctantly, positioning myself at the far end of the cot.

"This morning, I spoke to my mullah." He took a small Koran from his pocket, kissed it once, put it on his forehead, kissed it again, and then gave it to me. "Hazrat Agha"—His Holiness—"told me that firstly, because you are an observant Muslim, I had to take good care of you. That's why I brought you these things." He pointed to the cot and the rug. "He also said that it is written in Kalam-Allah that a woman's brain is half the size of a man's." He pointed to the Koran. "Secondly, Hazrat Agha said it has been written there that as my captive, if I have intercourse with you it will lessen your sins and in my divine life, Allah will compensate me for my work with"—he giggled as a child promised a candy—"a mansion in Paradise with seventy-two virgin angels and an endless flow of heavenly wine. Now, when I say angels, I'm not talking about ordinary females. These heavenly beauties, Allah Akbar, remain virgin no matter how many times you take their virginity."

Once again, despite the terror I was feeling, I also experienced the most insane impulse, given my circumstances, to burst out laughing.

"This is the merciful Allah that we believe in," he said, continuing his appalling sermon. "This is the Allah that people like you who have gone to America—Death to the Great Satan," he cried midsentence, his shrill voice rising, "know nothing of!"

I looked into his rheumy eyes and knew that, fortified with his mullah's religious justifications, he was girding himself to act again upon his carnal impulses, and he would try to rape me.

"So," he went on, "if you resist my attempts to rid you of your evil, it will be considered as sinful as blasphemy. However, if you do not resist, then, when you are in hell, you will be given less punishment for the virtuous acts I have directed to you. And as for the Allah-fearing men like me"—he looked at the ceiling—"we who have tried to rid the likes of you of their aberrations and frivolities, we will be rewarded in the high heavens as I described to you."

As I sat listening, I wondered where this seemingly illiterate man had learned such words as aberration and frivolity, but as he went on, I realized that he was but parroting his mullah—a talent rare in Skunk's species, considering his illiteracy. And that scared me.

"You see, up there"—he pointed heavenward—"Allah is busy with a lot of things. To whom shall he delegate part of his tasks, you ask?" He paused a few seconds and then threw his fist in the air. "To pious men like me!"

Now, with his lips pulled back and revealing his dirty teeth, he looked every bit a skunk sniffing what it imagined was going to be a delicious feast.

"You can't argue against that, can you?" he asked rhetorically, looking serenely confident that I couldn't dispute his mullah. "So, be a good obedient sister and take your clothes off," he said in a low voice, I suppose trying to sound sexy, as he moved closer toward me.

"Brother Zaki," I said as I thumbed through the Koran that he had given me. "I hate to disagree with your mullah, but as an observant Muslim, I know for sure that there are no references to virgins or palaces in paradise in this holy book."

I was almost certain about that, but how could I prove the nonexistence of something? Anyway, my primary concern was to repel Skunk's advances by some quotation from the Koran. I flipped the pages frantically and found what I needed.

"Here!" I exclaimed, holding up the book as I read the Arabic, and then its translation. "'Oh you who believe! You are forbidden to inherit women against their will; and you should not treat them with harshness.'"

The look on Skunk's face was a mix of fury and disappointment. He remained silent for a few seconds and then burst out. "Hazrat Agha is wrong, and you are right? You think I am so stupid to believe you?"

"I'm not saying His Holiness is wrong, Brother Zaki. He may not have noticed this. Please tell him to look at Al-Nesa, chapter four, verse nineteen."

"Write it down and give it to me," ordered my captor as he lit a cigarette.

I obeyed and handed him the piece of paper. Before he was able to say anything else, I said, "Brother Zaki, you told me that you had been active in the revolution. Why don't you educate me about His Holiness Imam Khomeini's teaching?"

He squinted at me in distrust. I could see that he was weighing the desire of fornicating against the pleasures of garrulousness.

"I know what you're doing," he spat. "I know you are playing with me. So don't think that I am telling you this because you have asked me. This is because I am obligated by my religion to show you the road to deliverance."

"Thanks," I said, followed by a sigh of relief.

Skunk lit another cigarette, sat back on the cot and began. "It was sixteen years ago that the Shah, the bastard, exiled our supreme leader the Ayatollah, may he live long until the hidden Imam reappears, to Baghdad…" He went on and on about how Khomeini did this in Najaf, that in Baghdad, the other in Paris.

His boring stories, monotonous voice, and my fatigue from what I had gone through in the past twenty-four hours must have made me doze. The next thing I knew he pressed the cold oily barrel of his pistol against my cheek, awakening me.

"You fall sleep on such a spiritual, revolutionary, and sacred story?" Skunk shouted.

"Forgive me, Brother Zaki," I said as I gingerly moved the gun away from my face. "I'm only a woman. I am very sorry. Please go on."

He holstered his pistol while warning me that he wanted one hundred percent of my attention. An hour later, he was back to Khomeini's exile to Iraq in 1964. Skunk talked and I listened dutifully as I sat on the ground away from him. Another hour went by and then he declared, "I have taught you enough for today."

I thanked him for his invaluable information and told him how impressed I was with his struggles and sacrifices for his cause. My compliment must have mollified him.

"I can be nice to you if you behave." He held his pack of cigarettes in front of me. "Go on, take one."

I don't smoke, but I was afraid to refuse his offer. But when I stretched out my hand, he snatched back the package of cigarettes. "A woman has no right to smoke, especially in front of men! You see? This is how the Shah, may the damnations of Mohammed and his posterity be with him forever, made prostitutes out of our women! At least in my village, even at the time of the Shah, we had full control over our women."

What the hell was I supposed to do with this lunatic?

"I swear I never smoke, Brother Zaki. You see, when I fell down to the ground, I hurt my back," I pleaded. "I thought it would help."

"That's good, that's good. Suffering rids you of your sins. Not all of them of course," he cautioned me, as he lit his cigarette, then exhaled smoke through his nostrils. "As I was saying, you women dressed like filthy whores. You went about shamelessly exposing your hair and your arms and legs, arousing innocent men. And as if that was not enough, you put cigarettes between your lips, as if to say to the men, 'Why don't you fornicate in my mouth?' Do you agree with me?"

"Yes, of course I do, brother."

Skunk scratched his head, which he did very frequently, spreading a cloud of dandruff in the narrow light that came through the barred window. "You have a lot to learn from me."

He stood and left the cell, locking the door behind him. Relieved, I threw myself on the cot, hoping to escape into sleep.

CHAPTER 4

I could not sleep that first night of my incarceration. By the weak starlight that found its way into my cell through the small barred window, I saw creepy phantoms of the mullah inquisitor in the Central Revolutionary Committee, the frightening glares of the pasdars standing guard behind him and Skunk holding his gun and hollering. Outside, in the distance, I could hear dogs howling in the still night as I wandered in my half sleep through sickening nightmares until a meager shaft of morning light found its way through the barred window and chased the ghosts away.

And along with the morning sun came the sound of a muezzin reciting "Allah Akbar," inviting the believers to start their morning prayer. Not that I truly preferred the muezzin's recitation to the creations of Bach, Beethoven, or masters of Persian music, but there was something peaceful and calming to take from the call, whether one was a believer or not.

I sat on my cot, embracing my knees, brooding over how I had come to end up here. Of course, the answer was as simple as it was timeless for a woman.

I had selflessly risked all to help the man I loved.

If only I had pen and paper, I thought, so I could write down all that I was going through…But like everything else in this hole into which I'd been thrown, Skunk was the only one I could ask for anything—including my whereabouts, which so far I hadn't had any luck getting from him. How about the other women incarcerated here, I wondered.

Of course, asking straight out was clearly out of the question. I would have to trick the imbecile into giving me what I wanted. Hours later, the key turned in my door and Skunk came in, carrying my regular breakfast tray. "I'm sorry, Brother Zaki. I have to go to the bathroom," I begged as he was putting the tray on the ground.

"All right," he said, shrugging.

Once in the corridor, I called loudly, "Good morning, sisters."

"Shut up." Skunk jumped as if he had been given an electric jolt. "Don't say a word," he shouted at the closed doors of the other two jails. "No one talks here to anyone! And let this be the last time you say anything to the other two whores here!" he yelled at me. "Now, go in," he ordered, pointing to the bathroom.

This time, to my utter surprise, he waited outside.

Back in the cell, I sat on the cot as he walked back and forth, playing with his whiskers. "You know," he said as he suddenly stopped walking, "I wanted to do you a favor yesterday by lying with you. But you are so stupid that you denied yourself the great blessing of salvation."

I suspected, of course, where this conversation was heading. I needed to divert it, and perhaps even turn it to my advantage.

"I learned so much from you yesterday, Brother Zaki," I began. "I'm sure there is so much more you can teach me. That's why..."

"That's why what?"

"That's why I've been thinking that I need to make notes of your teachings. Do you think I could trouble you for some paper, a pen, and perhaps some light? I again thank you, Brother Zaki, for your teachings. I promise to be as obedient as you want."

"How do I know you won't write counterrevolutionary things?" he demanded.

"Brother, I promise I will only make notes of all your teachings. After all, you are far wiser and learned than any man I have met. You have studied our religion much more than I have. You know so much. You can teach me so much. I want to make a note of your every teaching and memorize it all."

"Really?" There was a look of satisfaction mixed with suspicion on his face, but I could see his ego usurp his skepticism.

"I will think about it," he said finally.

I kept my poker face. He was not a smart man, but he had an animalistic cunning. I did not want to overplay my hand.

"And you promise not to write anything in praise of the Great Satan and the Zionist Jews?" he asked me as he stood in the doorway.

"I promise, Brother Zaki." I wondered what he would do to me if he knew of my Jewish roots and my family's ties to America.

"I will think about it," he repeated, swaggering out of my cell.

Within minutes, he came back with a bundle of paper, a few pens, and a kerosene lamp.

CHAPTER 5

Growing up, my brothers and I always had private tutors: English teachers, piano instructors, and dance teachers, just to mention a few. My parents were well to do and did their utmost for their children. So I had no complaints as a child, but I did have a guilty conscience. I knew quite well that so many needy people trapped in abject poverty populated my country.

Perhaps because of their own medical background, Mom and Dad had always hoped that I would become a physician. By the time I was fifteen, I granted them their wish that I would pursue that career. To me, the practice of medicine would be a good way to put into practice my altruistic caring and compassion for my people who were far worse off. Overjoyed with my decision, Pedar started his planning. In 1970, when I turned fifteen, he enrolled me in a summer school biology course at George Washington University. It was to be my first trip to America. I would stay with the family of Colonel Peter Novak, an American friend of my grandfather, the general. But before I left, my mother took me shopping. "You are going to America," she said, "and after all, you have to look decent in front of the general's friends. You also have to buy them some gifts."

It turned out that shopping was not the only thing on Madar's mind. The main purpose of this mother-daughter day out together was for her to reiterate the importance of sticking to our traditions, of—as women—protecting and preserving our virginity until we were married. She told me about her own wedding night, when she had spread her "virginity napkins" on the bed and then, afterward, she had given them to her mother, who had shown them to the women of the family to proudly declare her daughter's moral decency.

This was nothing new to me, for although I was born into a politically liberal family, I had been subjected to an extremely socially conservative Iranian upbringing.

Peter, his wife Debbie, and their nineteen-year-old granddaughter Suzan picked me up at Dulles International Airport, took me to their home, and showed me to my room. During the next few days, Suzan introduced me to the new world—my college campus, museums, parks, and malls. We toured the White House and the government buildings of the United States of America.

As a teenager from what was essentially a Third World country, coming to terms with the American way of life was a delicious challenge. I had read a lot about the United States and had seen so many Hollywood films. But the real America? The air tasted very different, and the skies—despite the old Persian saying, "Wherever you go, the sky is the same color"—were deeper blue. I felt instantly at home in America and thought that this land was where I should have been born: a country wonderfully free of the myriad inhibitions inherent in the Iranian way of life. Peter,

Debbie, and Suzan made me feel like part of their family, mitigating my homesickness. Peter was Christian while Debbie was Jewish, but thanks to the tolerance of American society, they had never gone through the hardship my parents had endured when they had fallen in love. And then there was Suzan who spoke openly to her parents about her boyfriend, with whom she lived. And how about her virginity? I wondered, but never had the courage to ask Suzan. In the meantime, Suzan and I had a lot to teach each other about our respective countries' peoples, customs, and culture. After her summer vacation, Suzan was going back to New York University, where she studied political science. She wanted to become a politician. "So that I can confront warmongers like Nixon," she said openly in front of Peter, her grandfather, a staunch Republican in addition to being a military officer.

But Peter didn't flinch. "That's your opinion," he merely said.

I found myself comparing the exchange to the time someone in Iran had criticized the Shah in front of my own grandfather, General Omid, and had ended up in jail. My grandfather probably wouldn't have put me in jail for shooting off my mouth like that, but still…

"Not only won't Nixon end the Vietnam War," Suzan went on, "he's expanded his aggression to Cambodia."

"One day," Peter said calmly, "history will judge Nixon as one of the best US presidents." He turned to me. "And the Shah as one of the best kings of Persia."

Suzan interrupted her grandfather. "The Shah was thrown out by masses of Iranian people and only brought back thanks to the meddling of the powerful CIA."

I couldn't help reacting emotionally to Suzan's unintended rudeness. After all, I had been born into a royalist family and I had grown up indoctrinated with pro-Shah propaganda. Suzan must have noticed my discomfort. She changed the topic, saying to her grandmother, "Doesn't Leila have lovely long eyelashes?" Then she started talking about her boyfriend at school—in front of her family! This was another thing that was unheard of in my part of the world. For a young girl to speak openly of a romantic attachment—I must say I was shocked as I admired Suzan's bravado for that.

And so, during that summer of 1970, Suzan and I bonded and became close friends. For the next two summers, when I returned to the United States to continue my studies, she came from New York to stay with me at her grandparents' house in Washington, D.C.

CHAPTER 6

It is my second night in this underground prison. I'm writing under the dim light of the kerosene lamp Skunk brought me. I have made quick notes of all I can remember of his reflections on women's "aberrations" and "frivolity," the ways of their salvation, and his ever-virgin angels, and put the sheets on the prayer rug so that he can see them when he comes back tomorrow. Having done that, I now write of the days of my life, and it feels so gratifying.

Does Skunk have the same feeling of contentment when he imagines drinking his heavenly wine and fornicating with his renewable virgins in the afterlife?

• • •

Soon after I finished high school in 1973, I sent applications to a number of colleges in the United States. Almost all of them accepted me, including UCLA, which was the school I decided to attend. Pedar was thrilled. Madar was also excited but sad that I was going away for a long time. My paternal grandmother wondered why I was not studying at Tehran University Medical School, saying, "Where your father studied also." And yet, General Omid, in his own typical military way, declared that he hadn't expected anything less from his granddaughter.

My academic success actually made headlines in the major Tehran dailies: I was the youngest Iranian girl ever admitted to a highly regarded American university. Accordingly, and given my family's high-up connections, I was awarded a royal audience with His Imperial Majesty the Shah of Iran and Queen Farah. My parents were overwhelmed, as was my grandfather. "I met with His Majesty only once on a very critical issue," the general told me with a mix of envy and pride. He commanded my mother to make sure I was dressed suitably for such a historic occasion, and announced that he himself would tutor me on how to conduct myself.

At seventy-five, my grandfather barely looked his age. He had a full head of dark hair and he was tall. He towered over the average Iranian male. Although he had passed the age of retirement, he was among the few top military officers still serving at His Majesty's behest. He looked spectacularly handsome and dignified in his military uniform. We lived in the compound my grandfather owned. He had built five houses for his three daughters and two sons, and one mansion for himself, exquisitely decorated with Persian carpets, velvet curtains, and French furniture. It was in his mansion's large front parlor while drinking tea, that my grandfather tutored me on how to behave in the presence of the Shah and the queen.

"You stand still at perfect attention until Their Majesties have entered the room," he said as he himself stood up to play the Shah. "Then His Majesty will nod to you, and that indicates his permission for you to step forward. Now, let's rehearse."

When my audience with the Shah and Queen Farah finally came around, the royal couple merely asked me a few cliché questions, which I answered nervously, and then it was over, almost before it began.

CHAPTER 7

January 31, 1980

It is the third day since I was incarcerated. I cannot keep track of the hours because they took away my watch, but I make a note of the date as the days pass.

I try to mitigate my despair and strengthen my resolve by reminding myself of the fifty or so Americans being held hostage in their embassy for almost three months by Khomeini's revolutionary guards. Yes, their living conditions were almost certainly better than mine, but they were still birds in a cage, just like me, and for far longer. If they could have hope of their eventual release—and I knew from news reports before I was incarcerated that they harbored such optimism—so could I.

I continue to deflect Skunk's sexual advances with quotations from the Koran and by blunting his passion with my sisterly admiration of his revolutionary zeal. He takes great pride in telling me that before the revolution he had been a garbage collector. Indeed, he smells worse than the commodity of his trade. First, he was a garbage collector, then a freedom fighter captured and tortured in the Shah's jails, and now a proud revolutionary guard.

Is my story of transformation any less strange, I wonder?

And if things could turn out well for someone like Skunk, then perhaps my ending will be happy as well. Anyway, I won't let my sadness and sense of helplessness overwhelm me. The Revolutionary Court could still very well sentence me to be stoned to death for my supposed crime, but for whatever time I have left, I will commit my memories to paper.

Who knows? Maybe, one day, someone will find them.

Perhaps even you, Cyrus.

• • •

In late May 1973, I called Peter and Debbie and gave them the good news about my admission to UCLA. I even told them about my audience with Their Majesties. Then I called Suzan to share my excitement. "You're talking to a soon-to-be doctor," I proclaimed and heard her joyous laughter at the other end of the line.

A month before I was leaving for the States, I got busy buying the essentials of Iranian life that might not be easy to get in America, like comfortable outfits with authentic Persian designs and *gaz*, a delicious Persian confectionary that Peter, Debbie, and Suzan relished. In the middle of all this, Pedar told me that my grandfather wanted to see the two of us in private.

"What for?" I asked my father.

"Don't you know your grandpa?" He laughed. "Perhaps he wants to give you some words of wisdom."

And so, on that hot summer afternoon, as my dad and I sat facing the general in his guestroom, my grandfather quickly got to the point. "During these summer classes that you took in America, did anyone talk to you about the CISNU, the Confederation of Iranian Students National Union?"

"Grandfather, I have spoken to one of their members only once, but the moment he began to badmouth His Majesty, I walked away."

"Good." The general nodded. "Continue to avoid them. These monkeys are after ending the monarchy of the Shah. Promise me that you will never, ever get close to these traitors."

I told him that I had no particular interest in politics and that I believed in His Majesty's greatness. What I did not tell him was that after having lived in America for some time and having witnessed Suzan's opposition to her grandfather's political inclinations, I didn't appreciate him telling me how to think.

Outside the general's mansion, Pedar told me that with the amount of reading that I did, he was surprised that I didn't know more about the CISNU. Then he took it upon himself to tell me about the genesis of the anti-Shah Iranian students' organization in the States and Europe. It turned out the CISNU had taken shape after the success of a CIA-supported coup d'état in 1953—known as Operation Ajax—when Prime Minister Mossadegh was overthrown and the Shah was reinstated in power.

As I listened to the tale of international intrigue, I felt embarrassed by my obliviousness to the political history of my country. I supposed that my contentment with being a member of a family that enjoyed the benefits and privileges of being close to the Shah had blinded me to the truth. Why else would I have so blithely accepted the notion that the Shah held power through the love of his people when he seemed to be nothing more than a puppet propped up by faraway masters who pulled his strings?

Pedar must have seen my disillusionment. "There is more to this story, which involves a family secret that I want to share with you, but you must swear that it will remain between the two of us."

"Of course," I said anxiously.

We sat on a bench in the compound near our house. Ali-Asghar, the general's gardener for as long as I could remember, was watering the flowerbeds of petunias, pansies, irises, lilies, and sage.

"Water the rest tomorrow, Ali-Asghar," my father called out.

The old man turned his sunburned face to us, smiled, and said, "Chashm Agha," which literally translated means, "I carry your orders on my eyes, sir." But before he walked away, he waved at me and said, "Miss Leila, I hear you are going to America to become a doctor like your father! May you be protected under the shadow of Allah."

"Thank you, Ali-Asghar Agha," I said waving back to him.

With the gardener gone, Pedar cleared his throat. "What I am about to say may shock you," he began. "Your grandfather, General Bahman Omid, is a CIA agent who had a major role in Ajax."

I lurched back, covering my mouth with my hand. This was the most shocking thing that I had ever heard in my eighteen years of life!

"Grandfather is a CIA spy?" I winced.

"My dear girl," my father said as he put his arm around my shoulder. "I was your same age and as shocked as you are now when your grandfather told me of his exploits. What I can tell you with certainty is that my father's affiliation with the CIA is out of his loyalty to the Shah and his country."

"A spy is a spy." I groaned. "How can I look at him as my grandfather anymore and not as a spy?"

"Not so quickly, Leila *jaan*." He caressed my hair.

Jaan, roughly meaning "my life," has always been my father's term of endearment strictly limited to those he really loves.

"Let me describe the circumstances under which your grandfather made this decision," Pedar continued. "If you put yourself in his time and place, perhaps you will better understand the reason why he did what he did."

I desperately hoped my father could say something to make this revelation seem less shattering. "Go ahead, please," I said, hugging him.

"I will do my best not to sound like a teacher," he said with a chuckle. "The 1919 Treaty with Britain, in effect, established a complete British protectorate over Iran. With the discovery of oil in the Persian Gulf also came British sovereignty over the oil fields of Khuzestan, which was opposed by Mohammad Mossadegh."

"Mossadegh who became prime minister in the fifties?"

"The same," Pedar said. "However, at this time, he was merely a young politician, one among many. In 1925, when your grandfather was a lieutenant colonel in the Iranian army, he was among a few military personnel the Shah's father sent to the US for training. That was where he met Peter Novak, a sergeant and a CIA operative—"

"Peter?" I exclaimed. "Peter? Suzan's grandfather?"

"Remember, Leila," my father admonished me, "in our family, you are only the third person who knows about this—the general, you, and me. I suspect Debbie and Suzan are not aware of Peter's involvement with the CIA."

"Sorry. This is almost too much information to absorb all at once. But go on please," I added eagerly.

My father nodded. "As you know, in 1926, the Shah's father, who was a charismatic soldier and a contemporary of Mossadegh, toppled the corrupt and ignorant Qajar dynasty with the help of the British, founded the Pahlavi dynasty, and became its first king—Reza Shah Pahlavi. He offered Mossadegh a cabinet post, but not only did Mossadegh reject the generous offer; he also objected to the Reza Shah's coronation.

"In the meantime, Reza Shah introduced many reforms and encouraged the development of industry and education. He pushed the mullahs back to the mosques, prohibited Islamic hijab—the wearing of the scarves and chador—for women, and gave the minorities freedoms. Jews came out of their ghettos and found their rightful place in the society—for that alone your grandfather would have pledged his unwavering allegiance to the royal bloodline.

"But Reza Shah was not flawless," my father continued. "For all his good intentions and instincts, he was an ordinary soldier who had no education or political acumen. He became intoxicated with power, and bit the hand that had fed him. As political tensions heightened around the globe due to events that would ultimately lead to World War II, Reza Shah abolished the 1919 Treaty with Britain. Then, panicked that the British might retaliate, he made his second big mistake and entered into a secret pact with Nazi Germany. He was also frightened of a military coup d'état, so he reorganized the army, incarcerated a number of military officers, and discharged some, including, guess who, Leila?"

"I have no idea," I said.

"General Bahman Omid!"

"You're losing me, Dad. Grandpa is so loyal to the monarchy!"

Pedar shrugged. "Generally, when a politician makes a mistake, not only does he not admit it, but he also tries to cover it up with what will turn out as a bigger mistake. Knowing that your grandfather was a staunch advocate of the West, Reza Shah, who was cozying up to the Nazis, evidently felt he had to fire him. At that point, your grandfather, who knew of the Nazis' skill in hunting and exterminating anyone who had Jewish blood, was more frightened for his family and for himself than angry with the Reza Shah. At this point, he contacted his friend Peter Novak and shared his concerns. Soon, General Omid was called to the American Embassy in Tehran, where, since he came highly recommended by Colonel Novak, he was offered the position of a CIA intelligence officer.

"Now Leila jaan," Pedar leaned back to regard me, "Given the circumstances, what would you do if you were in his place?"

"I think Grandfather made the right decision. But I'm still curious to know what our patriarch has done as a CIA agent."

"First and foremost, he remained devoted to the royal family. When the Allied forces occupied Iran in 1941 to protect the oil fields from the Germans, they exiled Reza Shah to South Africa, and replaced him with his son, Mohammad Reza Shah Pahlavi. With the West back in the saddle, your grandfather, General Omid, was reinstated by the new Shah to his previous position as the deputy minister of war."

It was getting dark. Madar came to the patio and called out, "What are you two doing out there? It's time for dinner."

"Let's go inside," Father said. "Another time before you leave, I will tell you the rest of the story."

CHAPTER 8

Today marks my eighteenth day of incarceration.

I say it to myself the way I've been told the television anchormen say it on the nightly news reports in America in speaking of the American hostages: "Today is February 15, 1980—and the eighteenth day of captivity for Leila Omid..."

Thanks to a copy of the Koran that Skunk gave me, I have so far managed to ward off his sexual advances. I have studied the book and made notes of useful verses to deter him. In these eighteen days, every time I have heard his key turn in the lock, I have grabbed the Koran and pretended that I have been busy studying it.

Skunk is not all that stupid. Last week, he ordered me to recite my daily prayers, and to his disappointment, I was able to do so smoothly. Then I asked him to lead the morning and evening prayers when he came here. He agreed, and I could see how pleased he was to do so.

But this morning, "his elephant remembered India," as we say in Farsi, and he resumed his efforts to have sex with me.

"*Sigheh*"—temporary wife—"that's what His Holiness recommended," Skunk said, referring to his mullah. "Sigheh is not rape," he asserted as he walked toward me. "Not when first you give your admission: *Zowajtuka nafsi fel muddatil ma'loomati 'alal mahril ma'loom,* which means: I marry myself to you for the known period and the agreed-upon dowry. After you say this, I will say: *Ghabelto,* which means 'I accept,' and then you will become my sigheh."

"And you will take me home to live with you as your wife?" I asked, pretending naïvety.

"No!" he hollered as he stood face-to-face with me. "You will stay here, where you deserve to be, and you will be my sigheh. Now repeat after me: Zowajtuka…Say it!"

His breath smelled like vinegar. In my mind, I was hunting for a helpful verse, which would not surface, for he kept on yelling, "Zowajtuka…Say it!"

"Wait!" I screamed at the top of my lungs, risking punishment but buying me time to think. He stood staring, clearly shocked by my audacity.

"Do you have any idea what you are talking about?" I demanded as I struggled with my memory of the verses. "Do you know what the Koran says about this?"

"What?" he demanded angrily.

"It says…It has been written in Kalam-Allah…And I was reading it last night…"

And suddenly what I needed popped into my mind. "It says, 'If you attack a woman, your sexual forces will be of no avail to you!'"

Frustrated that I had checkmated him once again, Skunk threw me on the cot and stood over me. "You have been to America, and whoever goes to America is fucked by the Great Satan."

I began to laugh, despite my terror. The way Skunk pictured America was probably an island filled with whorish or helpless women, and the Great Satan—who he perhaps imagined like King Kong—mated nonstop with every one of his sex slaves.

"What are you laughing at, you piece of shit!" he bellowed as he pulled his belt off his waist, wrapped it around his hand, and lashed me across my legs. And as I was screaming in excruciating pain, he raised the belt to whip me again. I jumped, grabbed the copper water jug on the breakfast tray, and threw it at him. The jug missed his head, slamming against the wall behind him, showering Skunk. His eyes widened as water dripped from his beard down his torso. The belt fell from his hand as he sat on the ground and lit a cigarette, inhaled, and coughed profusely. "Get me some water," he ordered. I rushed to the jug that had landed upright on the ground and still held some water, poured it into my cup and handed it to him. He gulped the water, took a deep breath, and went on smoking. I sat down facing him.

"You see what you have done to me?" he moaned like a child begging for attention. "Why don't you let me be nice to you?"

Although the word *nice* in Skunk's vocabulary was synonymous with rape, this was a good chance for me to find out where I was being held.

"If you want to be nice to me," I said coquettishly, "why don't you take me out for some fresh air?"

"You do this to me"—he pointed at his wet jacket—"and you…I swear to Allah, if I didn't have this asthma, if I had the energy, I would get up and lash you to death."

And so, Brother Skunk rejected yet another attempt of mine to find my way out of this horrid place, but in exchange, he had betrayed his physical flaw—asthma.

"You need some fresh air, Brother Zaki. Come on. Let's go out for a walk," I offered brazenly as if we were buddies.

"What am I supposed to do with you, madar jendeh?" he screeched—calling me a mother whore. "Walk with a whore like you on the city streets and make a monkey of myself?"

"All right," I exhaled noisily. "Then I have an idea." I changed the subject. "I see you are interested in America and how men and women do things there. After all, as our Imam Khomeini has promised, we will conquer the world. The sword of Islam will go to faraway lands, to America, for example, and there you, my benevolent Brother Zaki, as a flag holder of this divine movement, when it comes to women, you will need to know how to make them yours."

Skunk crawled back and leaned against the wall behind him, clearly intrigued by my nonsense. Before he could object, I launched into a spur-of-the-moment, stream-of-consciousness fairy tale of how life was in America. "There are girls, there are boys, and then there's the Great Satan…" I began in my most soothing once-upon-a-time voice.

After several hours of nonstop nonsense about America, Skunk took his leave, and I returned to my memoirs.

• • •

It was only three days before I left for America. Between saying good-bye to my friends and family, I had been nagging my father to tell me the rest of his father's story about his involvement with the CIA.

One evening after dinner, Pedar asked if I would like to take a walk in the gardens to finish what we were talking about.

"Are you telling her the story of the one thousand and one nights?" my mother grumbled. "The girl is leaving in a few days, and we all want to spend time with her."

"We are having a father-to-daughter talk, Mitra jaan. You can have her to yourself the rest of the time she is here," my father reassured Madar as we walked out the door.

The afternoon heat had given way to the pleasant northern breeze that was characteristic of Tehran's summer nights. Walking hand in hand with my dad, I felt a twinge of premature homesickness as I contemplated leaving my cozy nest.

"So?" I said, breaking the long silence.

"We are going to miss you, Leila jaan," my father sighed, as if he had read my melancholy thoughts concerning leaving the only home I had ever known. "But I'm looking forward to the day you will come back as an American doctor."

"Thank you, Dad."

"So, where were we?" my father said, abruptly changing the subject. "Ah, we were talking about how Operation Ajax came about. Let's begin in the latter part of 1951, which was a year of many upheavals in Iran, mostly instigated by that constant thorn in the royal family's side, Mohammad Mossadegh. He was, at this point, a member of Majles—the Iranian Parliament. He had the support of the clergy, who were struggling to regain their influence over the Shah's secular government. With their backing, Mossadegh was able to intimidate the Shah into allowing him to become prime minister. A few months later, in January 1952, Harry Truman was the president of the United States and Mossadegh was the prime minister of Iran."

My father shook his head, smiling. "I remember how my mother and I were waiting for your grandfather to come home for dinner and when he came in, I'd never seen him so angry."

"'These Americans are crazy!' he roared as he slammed a copy of what turned out to be *Time* magazine upon the table. 'Mossadegh the Man of the Year?' he demanded of my mother, as if the poor woman had ordered this. Mother shook her head and went into the kitchen as the general thumbed through the magazine in anger," pedar recollected.

"'I'm looking for...trying to show you...here!' your grandfather said to me. 'Look at the other candidates, for God's sake! Dean Acheson, President Dwight Eisenhower, General Douglas MacArthur. But no! They pick this clown who is ruining my country as their Man of the Year. How these naïve Americans don't see that Mossadegh is a Soviet agent is beyond me!'

"I made the mistake of telling the general that the most newsworthy were chosen by *Time* magazine as the Man of the Year," my father explained to me. "Hitler and Stalin, for example, but all I did was throw gasoline on the general's fire."

"Does it not surprise you how the CIAs of the world tend to hire short-tempered people like Grandpa?"

"Who am I to evaluate the CIA's decisions?" Pedar asked rhetorically. "Leila jaan, the reason why I tell you this is to help you understand Mossadegh's international prominence and how his influence led to the disastrous Iranian nationalization of the oil industry. In the absence of the British petroleum industry experts, oil production came to a virtual standstill. What's more, in retaliation, Britain imposed an international embargo that prohibited the purchase of oil from Iran, froze the Iranian assets, and banned export of goods to Iran.

"To placate the people, and make himself their champion, Prime Minister Mossadegh declared Britain an enemy and cut all diplomatic relations between the two countries. Supported by KGB, he instigated huge rallies in Tehran in support of the nationalization of the oil industry, and in this, he was backed by the fundamentalist ideology of a mullah whose name is Khomeini, I think..."

My father shrugged. "Anyway, your grandfather proposed to the CIA that Mossadegh should be removed from his post as prime minister. The CIA agreed and the initiative was code named Operation Ajax. By early August, Operation Ajax began with the Shah dismissing Mossadegh. Mossadegh refused to yield. There were days of fierce rioting, but the royalists ultimately prevailed. Mossadegh was sentenced to prison, and the Shah negotiated contracts with a Western nation oil consortium, the results of which have greatly helped to bring about the national prosperity we now enjoy."

"Wait a moment, Pedar," I said. "I know your opinion about the Shah, but do you consider Mossadegh a genuine patriot or not?"

"I think—and this is my personal opinion—he meant well, but his interests and our personal interests were not aligned, so I'm glad he was defeated."

"And why would the West be so interested in our country?"

"Our oil, our strategic value in the region, and of course the desirability of having a pro-Western government as embodied by the Shah."

"Bet my grandfather the CIA agent got a nice raise out of all this."

"I do not need to defend your grandfather to you, young lady," Pedar said calmly. "Please remember that at the time, the KGB and the CIA were both active in Iran, and I'm glad the general chose to associate with the latter."

On Friday, June 1, 1973, I left Tehran for America. I arrived in Washington, D.C., and stayed a week with Peter and Debbie, and of course Suzan, who had flown in from New York. For the four of us, this week was like a pleasant family reunion, with only one exception: every time I looked at Peter, I couldn't help but wonder if his family knew he was a CIA agent.

Then Suzan accompanied me to Los Angeles and helped me rent a small apartment near the UCLA campus. "I want you to live comfortably and independently," my father had told me before I left Tehran. "So, rent an apartment of your own, and don't worry about the cost. I can afford it."

Suzan and I spent another week touring the city and its suburbs, and then it was time for me to begin my summer courses.

In the months to come, I came to know many students on the UCLA campus—intelligent girls and boys of all nationalities and walks of life. But more than anyone else, I became friends with a young woman approximately my age named Sedi, an Iranian student in the College of Civil Engineering who helped me overcome my homesickness. To her credit, the first time we met, Sedi told me that she was affiliated with CISNU and on a mission to recruit Iranian students to join the movement. For a while, I defended the Shah and his father, harping upon their positive deeds as Sedi argued with me by recounting the damage they had done our country.

A few days into this exchange, I told Sedi that I was tired arguing with her. That was when she surprised me. "We can still be friends with opposing viewpoints, can't we?" she said, and I agreed with her. So, despite the general's advice, I became friends with someone in the CISNU. Then, one beautiful fall day, I bumped into Sedi on campus.

"Listen," she said as she hugged me, "do you like *fesenjan*?"

"Of course," I said as I imagined my mother's fesenjan, the mouthwatering Persian dish that is a blend of pomegranate juice, ground walnuts, and duck, served on a bed of steamed rice.

"I'm going home to cook fesenjan. Join me for dinner?"

Dinner that night at Sedi's place was delicious. Afterward, we had tea and watched the news on TV, which was filled with stories about how the Organization of the Petroleum Exporting Countries, OPEC, had proclaimed an oil embargo in response to the US decision to resupply the Israeli military during the Yom Kippur war. The TV showed long lines of drivers waiting in their cars at gasoline stations to fill their tanks at hiked-up prices. The Shah, who had suddenly become outspoken about the Middle Eastern oil resources, was also part of the news story.

"The West can't continue to increase its energy use, pay low oil prices, yet sell inflated-priced goods to the petroleum producers in the Third World," the television showed him saying at a press conference. The Shah, ruler of the world's second-largest exporter of oil, went on to say that the oil prices were going to continue to rise.

"This once-obedient servant of the West has suddenly become arrogant and unruly," Sedi said as she stared at the television.

I was about to ask Sedi if the Shah's anti-West policies had changed her mind about him.

"This is what happens to all dictators," she said. "At one point, they think of themselves as untouchable. This idiot is doing what his father did and it will cost him his crown. I bet you, sooner or later, the Western powers will get rid of him."

I thought about my grandfather's machinations on behalf of the CIA to manipulate internal events in Iran—just like Sedi was suggesting—but, of course, I said nothing.

"Listen, my dear," Sedi was saying, "someday, members of the CISNU will be instrumental in replacing the Shah's dictatorship with a freely elected government. If you'd like to help, just let me know, and you can attend a meeting.

CHAPTER 9

March 1, 1980

"Once upon a time, there was a ruthless sultan who married a girl each evening and had her killed in the morning..."

This is how I remember my grandmother, Maryam, telling me the first story in this ancient group of tales when I was a little girl.

"With the Sultan intent on killing innocent women, the brave young woman, Shahrzad, vowed to stop the brutal king's killing spree by marrying him. That first night, she tells the sultan a charming story that goes on to the early morning hours, but the insightful Shahrzad leaves the tale unfinished, promising the king that she will tell him the ending the following night. The next night, she finishes the old story and begins a new one, again ending the evening with a cliffhanger of an ending. With this trick and with the magic of her stories, which last a thousand and one nights, Princess Shahrzad ultimately tames the feral and coldblooded king, and the killings are no more..."

Two weeks have passed since I last wrote about Skunk. I have been imprisoned for thirty-two days.

And for the last two weeks of my incarceration, this princess named Leila, reeking from the lack of bathing, has been telling stories to her Sultan Skunk about America where the Great Satan lives. Unbelievably, the trick seems so far to be working. He has made no more carnal advances toward me.

"Dear Brother Zaki," one such story begins. "The Great Satan is not the only a creature in that strange place. Of course, they have leaders like Jimmy Carter who is the son of the Great Satan and a slave of the Israeli Zionists."

"Death to America! Death to Israel!" Skunk shouts on cue, throwing his fist in the air, but he truly hungers for more juicy stories.

"Tell me about girls and boys and what they do together, sister. Oh, they are sinners! I have seen in American movies that they were showing at the time of the Shah—may he burn in the fires of hell and may Allah forgive me for my sinful act of watching such blasphemous pictures. I still can see the unmarried, half-naked girls on the beaches as they grabbed the boys by their arms and—"

"Those are movies," I said, pretending like I don't see his hand in his trousers pocket, as he plays with himself. "Those are movies that the Great Satan exports only to the God-abiding countries such as ours to tempt the innocent believers to commit sins."

Thankfully, he took his hand out of his pocket to do another fist pump in the air as he roared, "The Americans are filthy dogs!"

I needed to keep him distracted from pawing at me, while I searched for a way to escape this place. Worst of all, I was running out of stories.

"Have you ever danced, Brother Zaki?"

"Allah forbid, no! It is non-Islamic."

"But you see, brother, in many Iranian Muslim tribes, men and women dance—of course, keeping their distance from each other. If you decide you want to learn dancing, I will be happy to teach you."

Skunk smiling shyly, locked the door behind him when he left.

• • •

In early 1974, a few months after coming to America, I joined the CISNU. My decision was neither hasty nor uncalculated. Instead, it was a difficult one. Sedi and I referred to it jokingly as the fesenjan conversion, for it started that night with dinner at Sedi's house. After I heard what the Shah had dared to say against the West on Sedi's TV, I became more curious about the politics of my country. Inevitably, I also began to weigh my royalist political convictions instilled into me by my family against the reality of what was going on in Iran.

I went to a few CISNU gatherings and found what was being said very reasonable. The moment of decision, however, came the day I enumerated to Sedi the Shah and his father's achievements, such as recognition of the woman's right to vote, prohibition of the hijab, the creation of a secular state, and the establishment of schools to educate the masses. Most important, I told Sedi, was the Land Reform

Law of 1969, when His Majesty distributed all the crown lands he owned.

"His Majesty's father, my dear," Sedi answered, "was a simple soldier who, as they say, 'didn't have a star in seven skies.' So, where do you think these so-called crown lands came from?"

"Well..."—I hesitated—"actually, I don't know."

"They'd been seized!" Sedi said, shaking her head at my naïvety. "Wherever Reza Shah went and saw properties that he liked, it was enough for him to say, 'It's beautiful!' Next day, the owner was forced to transfer his title to His Majesty's name. Fearing revolt among the peasants, his son, the Shah, felt obliged to return to the people the land his father had seized. No, Leila, he didn't do it out of the goodness of his heart. It was his fear and self-interest that led to this seeming benevolence."

Sedi's authoritative stance on the subject, combined with my dissatisfaction over the war America was waging in Vietnam and the Shah's endorsement of America's aggression in Indochina, was enough to tilt the balance. And so I became actively involved with CISNU.

A few days after Sedi had invited me to dinner at her place, I called to thank her for her hospitality.

"What are you doing tonight?" she asked.

"Not another fesenjan party?"

"No, no. The Zionists have a gathering in a hall on Hilgard and I was wondering if you were interested in going with me. The speaker is an Iranian Jewish student and my friends and I are going to grill him!"

She went on and on as grandma Maryam's words rang in my ears. "We are not God's chosen people, but rather his sacrificial lambs." I wondered why Sedi was so angry with... my people?

"Are you there?" Sedi called.

"Um...yes, I am."

That evening, along with Sedi and a group of her comrades, I went to this gathering at a hall adjacent to a synagogue on Hilgard Avenue near our campus. As Sedi had asked, we arrived early and got to commandeer the front rows. Soon the hall was full and people were still coming in.

A young rabbi of the synagogue took the podium to introduce the speaker. "In his last speech, we found Cyrus's knowledge of Persian Jewry and the history of our people in Iran so insightful that we have invited him once again to further enlighten us on this very interesting subject."

The speaker walked up to the podium. He was very tall for an Iranian, almost as tall as my grandfather, the general.

"Greetings, Salam and Shalom," the speaker began in a soothing and captivating voice that took me back to my childhood, listening to the professional announcers on Radio Tehran. He wore a navy blue shirt and beige slacks. His hair came down to his wide shoulders, his cheekbones were pronounced, and his chin was strong. All in all, I thought he was as handsome as a movie star. I was sitting in the front row, next to Sedi, just a few steps away from him. As his deep blue eyes scanned the room, I felt like he was looking deep into my soul.

"Today," he began, "I will be talking about life in Jewish ghettos in Iran, but before that, I would like to give a short background on the historic ties between the Persian Jews as a minority and the majority of Iranians.

"Sometime around 530 BC," he went on, "Cyrus the Great freed the Jews in captivity in Babylon and offered them the opportunity to become his subjects. So, we have been country-mates for over two thousand five hundred years."

A heckler in the audience shouted, "We are lucky you haven't thrown us out of our land, as you are doing in Palestine!"

There was tumult as other hecklers, including Sedi joined in, shouting that the Zionists were occupiers of the Muslim lands.

The rabbi tried to bring the situation under control, but to no avail. Soon the guards rushed in, surrounded us, and as they were guiding us out of the hall, I heard the speaker's voice. "That lady there!"

I turned around. He was pointing at me. "I know that young lady. She can stay if she wishes."

The crowd turned toward where I stood. "Me?" I asked, and the speaker nodded.

"You know him?" Sedi said, gazing at me.

"No. But I want to listen to him. I'm interested in what he has to say because..."

It was on the tip of my tongue to reveal that I was a Jew. I said instead, "I just want to hear what he has to say."

"Traitor!" someone called on his way out.

I shrugged as I walked back and took my seat. Now I felt awkward, for I was the only one sitting in the front row.

The rabbi called the meeting back to order and asked the speaker to continue.

"So, as I was saying, twenty-five hundred years ago, Cyrus the Great, the Zoroastrian emperor of Persia, freed us from captivity in Babylon and gave us equal citizenship in his land where, for thirteen-hundred years, we lived in peace and prosperity. But, after the Arabs conquered Persia in the seventh century AC and imposed their religion, discrimination and persecution against religious minorities heightened. As a result, Jews were driven into ghettos. I was born in one of these ghettos—Jewbareh, on the outskirts of Esfahan, the second-largest city in Iran…"

I was stunned. This is where my mother had been born. Did this man really know me?

"Jewbareh, the ghetto where I lived until I was fourteen." He sighed as he combed back his hair with his long fingers. "My ghetto was a complex of centuries-old houses in irregular shapes and sizes that resembled the stooped demeanors of their inhabitants. These houses were built alongside the sudden curves of the Alley of Eleven Twists, a narrow dirt path that meandered like a snake from one end of the ghetto to the other, with a few other pathways that branched off the main alley. Every house had to have a short front door—a historical indignity imposed by a degrading law meant to be a constant reminder that no Jew should enter his house with his head up. When you put your foot on the soil of Jewbareh, you stepped into an ancient, still living, village. Here, even time was ancient. It had stopped many centuries ago…"

He spoke, but no matter how hard I tried to listen to him, his blue eyes—which I felt were more focused on me than the crowd—were ever so distracting. Are you related to my mother? I was itching to call.

"As a minority," he went on, "Jewbarites came to resemble the inhabitants of a small island engulfed by a sea of potential enemies, especially the neighboring Keshe nomads who, in times of calamity such as famine, would intensify their savage raids on the ghetto. The Jewbarites had lived through this more than once, often enduring the same suffering as their forefathers. No tangible barriers or fences, common in many European Jewish ghettos, surrounded this small, impoverished community of fewer than one thousand people, but it was fortified by walls of hatred and prejudice. This is where my maternal ancestors lived, I thought, as Cyrus spoke, and somewhere even worse, my paternal forefathers had been forced to convert to Islam.

"Jewbarites conducted their own small businesses alongside the shops owned by Muslims who sold items such as dried fruits and fodder which were not forbidden by kosher rules. Along the Alley of Eleven Twists you could see a few kosher businesses—butchers, cookeries and a bakery. Dairy products such as yogurt and cheese were all homemade. There were tailoring and haberdashery shops as well. As part of Shiite ideology, non-Muslims—especially Jews—were subjected to a wide spectrum of ill-treatment, among which were raids on their ghettos, beatings, thefts, rapes, the kidnapping of children, pogroms, and at times genocide. In the best of times, they were allowed to go out of their ghettos and buy from Muslims as long as they did not touch items that they might purchase. However, they were forbidden to engage in any other transactions whatsoever outside the ghettos, except in faraway, isolated villages. Muslims, on the other hand, were by law permitted to have businesses in Jewish ghettos."

I found myself shaking my head. He noticed and, pointing at me, he asked, "You have a different view?"

"I…uh…" I felt like I was hypnotized.

"Yes?"

"Well"—I swallowed despite a dry throat—"at least these days, things are not as bad as you are describing them."

"No, they are not now." He stressed the last word in an angry tone, but then he seemed to get control of his emotions, for he smiled a lovely smile. "Of course, Reza Shah—who came to power in 1925—and then his son, Mohammad Reza Shah, were the first of Persian monarchs since the invasion of Arabs to give relative freedom to the Jewish people. But what about the oppression that my people endured for centuries before that?" He stared at me, his blue eyes glowing. "We have a past that must not be buried, and here, I have to give a small example. One of the many stories I heard from my grandfather, if it is all right." He paused, still looking at me, as if asking for my permission. I nodded involuntarily.

"My grandfather had been a teenager when the third year of famine had hit Esfahan in the 1890s, and this is how he described the events of the time.

"In this year of famine, Jewbarites had to make room in their alleys for the Keshe intruders, who came in waves and raided the ghetto. Such incursions happened so often now that these vicious predators—themselves suffering from famine—had become virtual inhabitants of Jewbareh. If you and your family survived the initial wave of violence, it was only because you had given the nomads everything you had, and the question now was how you would survive the next attack. The starving Jewbarites, at the mercy of the violent Keshe, had no voice with which to cry and no tears to shed. They had become numb to fear. It was as if life had been drained out of them. The angel of death had spread its wings over Jewbareh. Those who survived the attacks of the nomads and mandatory conversion to Islam were still potential victims of cholera and plague. Infants, sucking on dried breasts, died of starvation in their mothers' arms. As they dropped to their deaths like autumn leaves in the wind, people became victims of the human vultures that killed in the name of Allah. Soon, the alleys' walls became stained with the blood of those with little or nothing for the nomads, and the streets were littered with the corpses of their victims.

"Now"—Cyrus exhaled loudly, shrugging his wide shoulders—"if this doesn't tell us that what we, the Persian Jews, have endured has not been the same, if not—in many ways—worse than what the European Jews have undergone, what else does? Perhaps that's why, when in my country, anyone addressed me with 'you Jews,' even if they did not mean it in a derogatory sense, I would walk away from them forever. And come to think of it, I would do the same thing even now."

Although, I have to admit, I was more immersed in this man's beautiful eyes than his story, I could not help but empathize with his rage as he went on declaring that the Persian Jews had equal, if not more, claim to the culture of their homeland. He praised his Muslim countrymen who lived alongside his people in peace and amity, and spoke of his ambitious dreams of a day when Iran would become a formally secular state.

And as soon as the question-and-answer session was over, I stepped up to the podium and stood facing him. "Do you really know me?"

"Well"—he smiled—"I do know my audience. Actually, I would love to get to know you. So, would you let me have the pleasure of having dinner with you?"

Of course, I clearly told him that I would not go to dinner with a complete stranger. I was here in the States to study, to become a doctor, to go back home and marry in accordance with my family tradition. I was no ordinary American girl who did things that were indecent in my culture—things like going out with men. Even American girls wouldn't go out with strangers…

"You haven't been here very long, have you?"

"Just a few months."

"I understand," he murmured as he wrote something on a piece of paper and handed it to me. "Here is my phone number, just in case…you know."

I don't know why. I just grabbed the paper with a shaky hand and hurried away.

The next morning, I was about to leave my apartment to go to school when I heard someone pounding on the door.

"Quick," I heard Sedi cry. "There's a fight between our comrades and the Shah's loyalist students."

"Why would I want to go to a fight, Sedi?" I asked as I opened the door.

"First, you owe me an explanation why you stayed back last night, but that can wait. Now, don't be so timid." Sedi laughed. "It's not a real fight, just a confrontation!"

She took my arm and pulled me along with her to campus, where I soon found myself in the middle of a war zone. The CISNU leaders were handing out broomsticks and bricks to their members. Sedi grabbed a makeshift baton and ran into the crowd.

I stood there, watching in astonishment, appalled at the way the two factions were screaming and cursing and beating each other…

Next thing I remember, I was in a bed with an excruciating headache, unable to open my eyes.

"Aaraam," said a man with a familiar voice. "Aaraam."

It was a Farsi word that means "be calm" or "relax."

"I struggled to open my eyes and see who was speaking. I saw a hazy figure, but the light hurt so much I had to close my eyes again.

"Where am I?" I murmured.

"You're in the UCLA Hospital and you are fine," he said.

"What happened and who are y…" I was out of breath.

"Aaraam," he said again as his voice echoed in my head. "Just rest. You were hit in the head by a brick. The ambulance brought you here. Don't worry. The doctor says you will be fine."

"Who…are…you?" I asked, still unable to open my eyes.

"Just rest," he insisted. "We will talk later."

"What time…?" I pointed at my wrist.

"It's five o'clock in the afternoon, on Friday. You've been out since yesterday. Ah, good afternoon, Doctor."

"Good afternoon, young man," another man said. "How's your cousin doing?"

Cousin? I thought as the doctor checked my pulse. I had no cousin here.

"She's doing fine. She seems pretty conscious. She's been trying to talk."

"You're one lucky young lady," the doctor said. "Both to be doing so well and to have such a caring cousin. This young man hasn't left your side since they brought you to the hospital.

"Doctor, when do you think she will be released?" the man asked as I felt the hand of a nurse under my neck, raising my head, helping me take a pill.

"In two to three days if everything goes well," the doctor said, and then addressed me. "Young lady, the pill you just took will help you rest."

Who was this man pretending to be my cousin, I mused, and then I slept…

When I next awoke, I could slightly open my eyes without experiencing pain. I turned my head and saw the blurred image of a young man who I assumed had to be my so-called cousin sleeping in a chair with his head drooping so that his long, dark brown hair covered his face.

"Your neck must hurt," I whispered.

He jerked awake, brushing his hair back behind his ears. I still could not see his face clearly, except for a pair of blue eyes I knew from the night before. Maybe the drugs they had given me loosened my inhibitions, but the first words out of my mouth were, "Who gave you those deep blue eyes?"

"My grandfather, 'Blue-eyed Isaac.'" He chuckled. "I'm glad you are feeling better," he said as he took my hand.

Then he stood and stretched. I narrowed my eyes and this time I could see him. He was wearing a pair of worn jeans and a short-sleeved navy blue polo shirt. "Can I ask you a couple of more questions, please?" I said.

"Of course," he said gently. "But why not wait until you feel better?"

"You're the same—"

"Yes. Cyrus."

"And you are my cousin?"

"Really, I didn't know how else to introduce myself to these people."

"I'm sorry. What time is it?"

"Six twenty-six in the morning, Monday, January 14, 1974."

"Friday, Saturday, Sunday, and Monday," I said, counting on my fingers. "Don't tell me you've been sitting here next to me all this time?"

"My pleasure," he said, scratching his unshaven beard.

I was speechless.

When the hospital released me, Cyrus brought me home. Once I was settled in my apartment, he asked me what I wanted to eat.

"Listen, nice man," I said. "You have been more than kind to me, and I really appreciate it. I'm still confused about why exactly, but I'm thankful. However, I think you've done enough. You look so exhausted and need to rest. So—"

"The doctor said you should not be left alone for a day or two."

"Oh, he did? All right. I will call a friend to come and stay with me."

That's when it came to me. Where had Sedi been during all this?

"Can't I have the pleasure of being your friend who takes care of you?"

"You're such a nice man, Cyrus, and I'm sure you are being considerate. But, as an Iranian, you have to know that I cannot and will not allow you stay alone with me in my apartment, Here," I wrote down my phone number and handed it to him. "You can call me. Now please go and take care of yourself."

Once he was gone and I was alone in my quiet apartment, it finally dawned on me that a brick had hit my head.

And a pair of blue eyes had pierced my heart.

CHAPTER 10

I awoke to pounding on my apartment door.

"Who is it?" I shouted.

"Why don't you answer your phone?" I heard Cyrus's voice on the other side of the door. "You've been asleep a day and a half. I've been calling you…"

"Give me a few minute, please," I said as I struggled out of bed, dragged myself to the bathroom, and stood in front of the mirror. This was the first time I'd seen myself since the accident. My forehead was swollen, and I had black stitches across my brow. Big purple shadows surrounded my red eyes.

"I was just worried about you," I heard Cyrus say from outside. "It's OK. I can come back later."

"Don't," I said on impulse. "Just wait a couple of minutes, please."

Hastily, I washed my face, put on a long housecoat and rummaged through my closet for my ski hat, which I pulled down to my eyebrows. I thought about applying makeup, but it seemed a lost cause. I rushed to open the door, even as I chided myself for being so obviously eager to see Cyrus again.

He came in wearing black pants and a white shirt, his arms filled with grocery bags. He was freshly shaved, and his long dark brown hair was combed straight back. His eyes were as bright blue as the desert sky at noon.

"I look terrible," I muttered as Cyrus brushed past me.

"It's a beautiful day out there," he said on his way to the kitchen, where he began putting away the groceries he'd brought. "You are going to take a shower, and we will step into the splendor of this fantastic day."

"I'm not ready to go out," I began.

"Certainly you are," Cyrus insisted. "And to make up for all the days you have starved, I'm going to take you to this place downtown that has the best steak in Los Angeles."

I got as far as the shower, but as I studied my grotesque forehead in the bathroom mirror, I couldn't imagine exposing myself to the world. "Sorry, I'm not going out," I shouted from the bathroom. "This thing on my forehead looks so gruesome, Cyrus."

"Thank you," he called back.

"For what?"

"That was the first time you said my name."

I started to laugh. "You are really something!"

"Just come out, please. I promise I will make you look like Natalie Wood before we walk out the door."

What the hell was I doing? I thought as I popped two painkillers from the stash they'd supplied me with at the hospital, took a quick shower, dried my hair, put my ski hat back on, and came out. He was leaning against the wall with a long scarf in his hand. I came closer and touched it. It was a finely handwoven tapestry, clearly very old but in perfect condition.

"Come close," he commanded, and I did what he said like a goddamned zombie, coming so close that I could feel his breath on my face, so near that I thought—I feared or did I hope—he would hold me in his arms and kiss me. Instead, he gently placed his hands on my shoulders and guided me to a chair, where he removed my hat, gently pushed my hair behind my ears, and wrapped the soft scarf around my forehead, covering my injury.

"Where is this scarf from?" I asked, struggling to distract myself from his closeness.

"My mother inherited two things—her name and this scarf. She gave it to me for good luck."

He helped me to stand and walked me to the mirror. "Tell me if you like what you see."

I couldn't believe how skillfully he had covered every bit of my injury.

The day was pleasantly warm and the sky clear. I was sitting next to Cyrus in his charcoal gray Volkswagen, driving on the freeway to downtown LA, listening to "This Land Is My Land." As I listened to Peter, Paul, and Mary's optimistic, peaceful lyrics, I wondered why the Iranian students at UCLA couldn't talk about their differences instead of throwing bricks at each other.

"What's on your mind?" Cyrus interrupted my thoughts.

When I told him what I'd been thinking about, he replied, "If you want, we will talk about this at lunch, but for now, just enjoy the day. You need to relax, Leila."

"But I'm already very relaxed and eager to hear what you think."

"OK. My answer is simple. Civility and respect for your opposition's viewpoints is something that Iranians have never learned. We don't practice it in our own country, so why should Iranian students know how to practice it here?"

That shut me up for the rest of the way. Half an hour later, we were sitting next to each other in Pantry Café, a beautiful restaurant that Cyrus told me had been established in 1924.

"And Americans consider this place historical." He laughed. "Whereas we Iranians consider any place less than two thousand years old contemporary. But I assure you, historical or not, the food is excellent."

He was right about the food, and I told him so.

"One other great thing about this place is the noise," he shouted into my ear. "It brings people close together."

So much about this man I didn't understand. He was handsome beyond description and had self-confidence and a great personality. Clearly, he was also well-to-do. He seemed to have everything going for him. Surely he had no problem meeting women. Why had he gone out of his way so much to look after me?

"Because I was there and saw it happen to you," he said, his beautiful blue eyes growing serious. "I also saw how your so-called comrades ran away to leave you on the ground. They went on with their political demonstration as though nothing had happened. I don't want to scare you, but the way you fell, I initially thought that brick had killed you."

I struggled to hold back my tears of relief over my miraculous narrow escape.

"Are you OK?" he asked, studying me.

I nodded, forcing a smile. "Tell me about yourself."

"Where do I begin? Let's see. I was born in 1952, in Jewbareh, as I said in my speech. My father is a fabric seller; my mother, a midwife."

"So is my mom," I said excitedly. "She is"—but then I suddenly realized that I should not give away her religion—"she's a nurse, I mean. Sorry, go on."

"Well, I lived in Jewbareh for the first fourteen years of my life after which we moved out of our ghetto to Esfahan, where I finished high school. In 1970, I was sent to America to become a physician according to my parents' wishes."

I couldn't help laughing.

"What?" Cyrus asked.

"This is exactly what my parents want for me. And that's what I'm studying to be."

"As I see it, this is your choice," he said. "In my case, I decided I didn't want to become a physician. That's what my parents didn't know, and I didn't tell them until I got here."

"How did they take it?"

"They were upset, of course. On the phone, they screamed at me, threatened that they would cease my allowance. But when I told them that what I wanted was to be a doctor of economics, then they gave in. 'We wanted him to be a doctor; he's going to be one,' my father said to my mom. 'And let that be that.'"

Over coffee, I asked Cyrus if he was a Shah loyalist, adding, "You seem to admire the Shah and his father for being kind to the minorities."

"Leila jaan." He sighed, and I was thrilled by hearing Pedar's term of endearment for me coming from Cyrus's lips. "All I care about," he went on, "is the prosperity of our people. I hate politics of destruction, and that's why I keep my distance from both sides of this controversy. Both factions are irrational. And that is the result." He pointed at my forehead. "As long as violence and hatred rule, we will not have a democratic government—or a decent government of any kind—in Iran."

Sedi showed up at my apartment a week after the incident. She claimed that she had only just heard about my injury, and while she was sorry it had happened, she went on to say, "This is a small price we pay for the freedom of our country."

"Will you do me a favor, Sedi," I said when she had exhausted herself rambling. "Leave and kindly close the door behind you."

"It must be that Zionist Jew you have fallen for," she snarled at me on her way out.

After Sedi left, I called Suzan and told her what had happened to me.

"Do you need me there?" she asked, obviously concerned. "How about my mom? Are you sure you're doing fine? Jesus Christ, what's with your people? I mean, throwing eggs and tomatoes is one thing, but bricks?"

"As a famous Persian poem has it," I said, "'We should've been given two lives: To gain experience in the first and to experience the gains in the next.' With that brick, I had learned the lesson of my life—to break away from these crazy zealots."

"A brick has hit your head and you are reciting poetry for me? You need to be taken care of. I'm coming to Los Angeles."

"Don't, dear. There's this nice young man…I mean…"

"Really!" she exclaimed. "A nice young man! Tell me about him. I'm all ears."

"No. It's not what you think. How can I put it?"

"Whichever way you like. Just go ahead and don't be shy. Why the hell are you so embarrassed to tell me about this guy who is taking care of you?"

"OK." I chuckled. "This is how it all started..."

A half hour later, I wrapped up my story by telling Suzan that in the few weeks that I had known Cyrus, we had become very close and although we were both busy studying, we always made time to see each other. I also told her that we had a lot in common, things like our academic achievements in Iran and...

"Leila!" she scolded. "You're driving me crazy. Enough about intelligence and academic achievement! Tell me about him. Begin with his looks!"

"Oh, that!" I giggled. "How can I describe him? Imagine Warren Beatty. Wait a minute. Is Warren Beatty Jewish? Because this guy is. His hair is long. And he's very tan, and he has a deep voice, deep blue eyes. I can't begin to describe his eyes..."

"Oh my God!" Suzan screamed into the phone. "You love this guy!"

"No—"

"Bullshit!"

I was silent.

"What's the matter?" Suzan asked, her tone now totally serious and concerned. "I didn't mean to upset you."

"Oh, don't be silly," I said. "But how do I explain to you—an American girl who has grown up with the idea of having a boyfriend—how what you suggest is so unimaginable for me, for someone coming from my culture? Since I've come to Los Angeles, Cyrus is the first man I have ever gone out with—actually, the only man I'm not related to with whom

I have ever even become friends. We have not gone beyond holding hands and the occasional rather platonic hug."

"Is it your decision to remain faithful to your ancient traditions?" Suzan demanded. "I know it's a big leap, but welcome to the twentieth century, Leila Omid!"

"And I'm not going to take that big leap, for I know it will make me end up in a big mess. Thank God, Suzan, he's from my culture, understands my limitations, and acts gentlemanly."

"Well, if it is your decision to play Mother, May I? forever, and this man doesn't mind it, then go ahead and deprive yourself of the most pleasurable gift of nature. If you want my advice, here's what you have to do. Change your standoffish attitude, doll up, and get him. That's all."

For my next date with Cyrus, I dolled up, determined to examine Cyrus's power of self-restraint. After all, if he was as attracted to me as I was to him, then he would hold back his carnal desires and just love me for who I was. I wore my tightest jeans and a dark blouse with the first couple of buttons provocatively left undone. He showed up on time with a bouquet of roses. He was wearing a light beige suit and turquoise blue shirt that highlighted his eyes.

"Why don't you come in?" I said, my voice shivering.

Before I knew it, he put his arms around me and held me tight, and for the first time, we kissed. In retrospect, it must have been a clumsy kiss, because for sure this was my first time. Then, in my mind's eye, I saw, like an army of my guardian angels, the stern visage of my grandfather, General Omid; my mom beating her chest; and my dad shaking his head...

I pulled back, wiping my lips with the back of my hand. I was vividly shuddering.

"What is it?" he asked.

"No, Cyrus, no! We…I mean I…I can't do this and I will not. Let's be just friends, if it's OK with you..."

"But what is wrong with being friends and—"

"Please, Cyrus. Don't even go there."

"All right, let's have a deal. You want to be friends. I respect your wish and won't go beyond whatever pleases you. But I'm in love with you and I expect you to understand that."

Dizzily, I staggered and Cyrus held me in his arms.

CHAPTER 11

We are in love, something I'm experiencing for the first time in my life, I wrote to Suzan. We have become the trellis and vine, as my father used to say to describe his paternal affection for me…

I was just sixteen when the desert's beauty inspired me to write a poem I titled "Trellis." It went:

You're a grapevine
With branches spread like the wings of an eagle
I'm the trellis under your cover
You have me absorbed into you
And claim that you're leaning against me?
I adore your branches
Your leaves
Your glittering grapes
And the wine of your intoxicated eyes

I suppose there's the soul of a poet in every Persian. I remembered it like it was yesterday how, when I'd shared my poem with my father, he'd said to me, "This is so beautiful, Leila jaan. I'll tell you what. Let the word *trellis* be our secret word between us, for how you and I are entwined like a trellis and a vine by our love for each other. Whenever I am sad, you can remind me of our affection just by saying the word, and I will do the same for you."

In time, it became a game between my father and me, this trick of making other abstract words our code to symbolize our feelings about ourselves and other people, places and situations. But first, was trellis—derived from my poem.

Cyrus and I spent all of our spare time together during the next few weeks, and as on a bright, sunny day in late February 1974, we were sitting by the window of Fred's Café on Westwood Boulevard, sipping coffee, I asked him, "Have you heard the rumors the CISNU is spreading on campus? They are saying the Shah's regime is on the verge of collapse, and they are encouraging the membership to go back to Iran."

"I doubt the West would let the monarchy fall," Cyrus said. "The West has too much at stake in that part of the world."

"How about what ordinary Iranian citizens have at stake?" I asked. "People like us, I mean?"

"This is a difficult question, or series of questions," Cyrus mused. "I am grateful to the monarchy for giving us rights. Do I think the Shah is a better option for our country than these CISNU revolutionaries? Absolutely. On the other hand, is the concept of a monarchy sensible in this day and age? No. It is irrational and archaic. However, when the people are illiterate and incapable of coping with democracy, autocracies are born and the most charismatic and imposing of the contenders win, until they make a suitably bad mistake. Take the shah's decision to exile Khomeini because he had dared to criticize His Majesty's policies. This was absolutely a mistake, for Khomeini, from his exile, is attracting massive fanatic Muslim support from those who hate the Shah's dynasty due to its social liberalness. But as a Jew, you can guess whose side I'm on concerning that particular issue."

"Don't talk like that, Cyrus. You are an Iranian first," I said steadfastly. I longed to tell him that I was also a Jew, but my family had sworn me to secrecy due to my grandfather's important position in the Shah's government. "I know that for the first twelve centuries, since Cyrus the Great freed your ancestors from Babylon and gave them Persian citizenship, they lived a relatively prejudice-free life with the Persian Zoroastrians..."

"Wait a minute," Cyrus interrupted. "You seem to be a scholar concerning Jewish life in Persia. Where has my beauty acquired all this knowledge?"

I couldn't hold back anymore. I prayed that my parents would forgive me as I shared my family's great secret.

"Cyrus, I am also Jewish."

Cyrus stared at me. He actually looked angry.

"Are you making a joke, Leila?"

"I'm not. I'm telling the truth."

I quickly filled him in on my family's ancestry. By the time I was done, he was relaxed and smiling.

Reaching for my hand across the table, he squeezed it and said, "So, I can call you a Jew now?"

"Jewish," I teased, correcting him. "Call me what you wish, but never stop loving me," I whispered, gazing into his eyes as blue and deep as the Pacific.

"You're maybe a Jew, but thankfully, in our country, you have never lived openly as a Jew and have no idea what it is like." Cyrus said.

"Why don't you enlighten me, please."

We left the café for my apartment, where he told me the story of his childhood.

"Gholam-Ali and I became friends in an unusual way," Cyrus began as we sat on my sofa and held hands. "It was my first day at Shams—Sunshine—High School, my new school after my family moved from Jewbareh, my ghetto, to Esfahan. The classroom was packed. The benches, made for three people, each seated at least four students. I looked around. There was a bench in the last row where only three students sat. I proceeded to sit next to them when they shouted, 'There's no more room,' followed by the taunt '*najes.*'"

Even after all these years, I could hear the rage that still lived in him concerning the memory.

"I'm sure you have heard the word najes," Cyrus said.

"It means filthy and untouchable," I said.

"And it means that whoever and whatever comes into physical contact with an infidel is also najes," Cyrus said. "I remember how no one would sit next to me—let alone befriend me. In the history of this Muslim school, enrolling an infidel Jew had to be the most ungodly act. I missed my old school in Jewbareh, where I had lived the first fourteen years of my life. There, among my own kind, I was not najes."

As Cyrus spoke, his beautiful eyes darkened in pain. "You can stop here if this bothers you," I said, squeezing his hand, but he shook his head and went on.

"As I said before, I guess you haven't had any such experience in your life." He sighed.

What could I say? I had never dreamed of enduring such suffering.

He stared at a family photograph on the wall, of my parents, my two brothers, and me, all of us looking happy and prosperous in my grandfather's compound.

"Anyway, the schoolyard was where, at lunchtime, students gathered in groups to eat their midday meals brought from home. Wary of trying to join the others, I sat apart in the schoolyard. On that first day, I opened my lunch-cloth and was about to begin eating when I saw Gholam-Ali towering over me. He was one of my three classmates who had called me najes that morning.

"'Hey, Jew!' he taunted. 'What are you eating? Dog shit?' and before I could answer, he kicked me in my side and I collapsed in pain. 'Listen to me carefully,' Gholam-Ali said. 'As long as you stay in this school, this is how you are going to be treated. Go back to your Jew rat hole. You're not welcome here.'

"As he began to walk away, he turned to point his finger at me and snarled, 'One more thing. If you complain or say a word to TabaTabai or anyone else, I swear on my mother's grave, I will kill you.'

"Who was TabaTabai? Shortly after we had moved out of Jewbareh, my father, *Baba*, proudly introduced me to a man he referred to as his friend, Mr. Seyed Mohammad TabaTabai, the principal—the Aghai Modir—of Shams High School. My father described him as a fine gentleman who didn't consider Jews to be najes.

"'You won't believe it, but TabaTabai even shakes hands with me,' Baba announced so triumphantly that you would have thought Hitler had shaken the hand of a rabbi. Anyway, on the day Baba enrolled me in Shams High School, he took me directly to TabaTabai's office, where I met him for the first time. He was a tall young man with a commanding presence in his elegant navy blue suit, snow-white shirt and the dark red tie. He wore a thick mustache, one that at the time had come to be known as the Stalin style. I noticed how my father was standing with his shoulders stooped and was rubbing his hands together, the very essence of meekness that was so typical for my people in the ghetto.

"'I have one small concern, sir,' my father murmured. 'If I'm not wrong, my son is going to be the only Jewish student in your school and—'

"'Stop!' TabaTabai commanded. Then he turned to me, grabbed my shoulders with his oversized hands, and looked me straight in the eye. 'If anybody ever bothers you, come to me immediately.'

"If my father had bowed any lower, his nose would've swept the floor. Oh, Leila, how I wanted to run away that day."

Cyrus stared up at the ceiling as he continued his story. "Back home after that first day at my new school, I must have looked miserable, because Baba wanted to know what was wrong with me.

"'Nothing,' I said, not able to look at him. My mother—*Mani* as we called our mothers in Jewbareh—said, 'It's only his first day at this new school. He has to get used to it.' What could I say?

"The next day at lunch, Gholam-Ali showed up again with another one of our classmates and beat me, and the day after that, three of them attacked me. Three days went by, three days of physical and mental torture I endured as the only Jew in that godforsaken Sunshine School.

"Then came my fourth day at the school. My submissiveness had not only emboldened Gholam-Ali, but also his pals, whose numbers were increasing every day. And they knew what they were doing. They only struck me in the torso and legs, so my bruises would not show. What I feared most was the next day, Friday, which was the public weekend in Iran and the day Baba took me to *hamam*—the public bath—for my weekly wash. That was when my hidden injuries would be revealed. And so there I was on that fourth day, Leila. I was all alone in the schoolyard at lunchtime, and I saw Gholam-Ali and his gang approaching. You know what? All at once, the fear left me. The closer Gholam-Ali and his pack of goons approached, the more I felt throbbing anger coursing through me.

"'Hey, Jew!' the bully said, but before he could finish, I threw a punch that landed on his nose. He staggered back. Awed by what they were seeing, his followers stepped back also as they watched blood shooting out of Gholam-Ali's nose. With his eyes wide open in astonishment, Gholam-Ali wiped at his nose, looked at his bloody fingers, and snarled, 'See what you did, you najes son of a whore!'

"Encouraged by his reaction, his gang tightened their circle around me, but Gholam-Ali shouted, 'Wait! I will take care of him.'

"Balling his bloodstained fists, he charged at me and threw me to the ground. I quickly got to my feet but he knocked me down again. I was sure he was going to kill me. No matter how hard I tried to fight him, I was no match for his strength. Again he attacked, but this time as he came at me, I kicked out hard, catching his knee. His leg buckled, and for once, he was the one who ended up sprawled on the ground. Ali's friends gathered around him, trying to help him get to his feet, and then turned their fiery gazes at me. 'You filthy Jew! You will pay for this!'

"But then the boys stopped their cursing. They were staring past me. I turned to see what they were looking at and saw the silhouette of TabaTabai against the early autumn sun.

"'*Farrash Bashi*!' TabaTabai called out to the school groundskeeper. 'Bring me *tarkeh*!'"

"As part of his job, Farrash Bashi soaked bundles of tarkeh—switches, essentially—in a pot of water, so they would always be on hand to be used to inflict corporal punishment on unruly students. Gholam-Ali was the first to complain. 'This najes Jew kicked me in the knee, Aghai Modir,' he moaned, clutching his leg. 'And first he punched me in the nose!'

"TabaTabai folded his arms on his chest, looked at all of us, and roared, 'The najes Jew did this to you?' Gholam-Ali's friends cheered; I began shaking. Was this the man who assured me that there was no room for prejudice in his school? Then Farrash Bashi came running with a bundle of dripping switches. The groundskeeper selected one from his bunch and came toward me menacingly—when the principal grabbed his wrist and pulled the switch out of his hand and said, 'Let the pleasure be mine.'

"Emboldened as TabaTabai walked toward us, Gholam-Ali began recounting my vices. 'Aghai Modir. This najes Jew…'

"The switch whooshed through the air to slice Gholam-Ali across the stomach. He screamed in agony and fell to his knees. His friends meanwhile were staring shocked and wincing as TabaTabai splintered a second and then the third switch across Gholam-Ali's back, until my tormentor was writhing in the dirt and begging for mercy.

"But Aghai Modir was not about to stop. Then, Leila, I did something that to this day, I still don't understand. I threw myself on top of Gholam-Ali, so that when the next stroke landed, it landed on my back."

Cyrus became silent. I was struggling to hold back my tears, to no avail.

"I'm sorry to have upset you, Leila," he whispered.

"My God! Those bigots! Oh my poor Cyrus!" I exclaimed. "What you have gone through leaves me speechless. Your tolerance is beyond me, especially your strength in putting the past behind you and concentrating on the great future ahead of you. But go ahead, please," I said.

"So on that terrible Thursday afternoon, as I walked home with my clothing stained with Gholam-Ali's blood, I fretted over what was waiting for me.

"'May I sink into the earth,' Mani cried when she saw me. Examining me, she now quickly observed the past week's bruises. 'May his hands fall off, whoever did this to you!' Then she set to work cleaning and bandaging me.

"When Baba arrived home that evening, he demanded, 'Did TabaTabai see this, and if so, what did he do?'

"I told Baba what had happened, and he was more pleased about the principal's brutal punishment of Gholam-Ali than concerned about my condition. Mani, meanwhile, advised me, 'You must become friends with your new classmates.'

"Of course, that point of view represents our people's historical submission to fate. Jews are supposed to submit to every indignity and like it. I wondered then, did my mother even realize that Gholam-Ali and his gang saw me as najes and that there could be no hope of friendship with them?

"'Do you want me to speak with the principal?' my father asked.

"'No, Baba. Please don't, Baba. Everything is fine, Baba!'

"It just goes to show you, you never know what's going to happen. Noticing how desperately I begged him, Baba didn't speak to TabaTabai and I became friends with Gholam-Ali. Don't look so surprised, Leila. I did. It was a few days after our schoolyard fight that had been interrupted by the principal. It was lunchtime and as I sat on the ground with my lunch in front of me, Gholam-Ali approached me—this time alone." Cyrus grinned. "His nose was still bruised and swollen and he was limping, so I was pleased to have done him some damage. He just stood there looking at me for a few moments. Behind him stood all the other students, clearly eagerly awaiting another fight. On impulse, I pointed to the spot next to me and said, 'Why don't you sit down?' He looked at the crowd behind him and then he sat down next to me. He opened his lunch, bundled in a ragged cloth.

"'Cyrus,' he began, but then he trailed off into an uncomfortable silence.

"'It's all right,' I told him.

"And from that day forward, we were friends, more or less. Actually, we were friends within reason, given the circumstances. For instance, that first day we sat together to eat, I noticed that his lunch was nothing but a piece of bread and a few slices of onion. For lunch, I had the previous night's leftovers from Mani's delicious dinner. I wanted to offer him some, but I didn't dare."

"Why?" I asked, perplexed.

"Leila jaan, I was najes, regardless," Cyrus said.

CHAPTER 12

March 8, 1980

Day forty of my incarceration. In the past few weeks, I have created a pretend relationship with Skunk. I have acted toward him as if I cannot wait until I can get out of here and marry him, reminding him that he can sleep with me only when we are married, for I am a virgin. Meanwhile, in my effort to reconnect to the outside world, I have attempted to convince him that my father can help both of us go to America.

Skunk came into my cell this morning with a novel idea. "*Last Tango in Paris,*" he announced to me. "Do you know this film?" He then proceeded to summarize for me in explicit detail the goings-on between "that guy with the butter" and "the whore."

I don't know if I should thank or curse heavens for that movie, because it turned out that my dangerous but idiotic jailer wanted to learn to tango!

"You will teach me how," he ordered.

I was scared, wondering whether he had the butter on his mind. To think I had to stand close to this bastard smelling of garbage and teach him how to tango, of all Allah's forbidden dances...

Keep your distance, I reminded myself as I began this pathetic class. Lest you stimulate him sexually.

Tango! Here we go! I hummed the song "Bésame Mucho."

Move it, Brother Skunk, my master dancer. No, not all that close to me, you idiot. Yes. This is better now. Just move, but don't come near me. Now two steps to the right, one to the left or the other way around. Whichever. That's right.

"I have to step away to watch your feet," I told him, disengaging from his fetid embrace.

As Skunk held his imaginary woman in his arms and shuffled his boots across the dirt floor, I stepped back and sat on my cot.

"One, two, one," I repeated until finally Skunk tired himself, sat by my side and said, "Next time, you will teach me pasodoble!"

Lord Almighty. Where the hell did this self-proclaimed messenger of Allah learn the names of these dances?

"Of course," I said, wondering how long I could remain in this cage before I went literally insane.

• • •

Nowrooz, the Persian New Year, which is also known as the Thirteen-Day Spring Festival, begins on March 21.

Nowrooz of the solar year of 1353—March 21, 1974—was nearing for me at UCLA, and I couldn't help but think of the excited preparatory tumult that was going on back home. My parents were likely making arrangements for the feast with a thorough bout of spring-cleaning. By now, our Persian carpets had been hung outside and beaten, the furniture had been polished, and the windows washed. Ali-Asghar, the gardener, would be prepping the flowerbeds blanketed with pansies, which were Pedar's favorite. My mother was probably fretting over how to set her Nowrooz table, or more specifically how to set her table as to outdo her friends. For sure, the table decorations would include goldfish in a crystal bowl, antique silver candelabras, and most importantly her *haft sin*—seven items starting with the letter *S*.

There was *sabzeh*, wheat grown in a dish, symbolizing rebirth; *samanu*, a sweet pudding made from wheat germ, for prosperity; *senjed*, the dried fruit of the oleaster tree, which stands for love; *seer*, garlic because of its curing properties; *seeb*, an apple for health; *sumac*, berries, radiant as sunshine; and *serkeh*, vinegar for tolerance.

Nowrooz was the season when I was most homesick, as were many of the Persian students on campus. And so we decided to do our best to create our own Nowrooz at UCLA by organizing a potluck party on the Persian New Year Eve. The Sunday before Nowrooz, as Cyrus and I were walking along Venice Beach, I told him that I was looking forward to celebrating the New Year with him at the students' gathering.

"Sure," he muttered hesitantly.

"What's the problem? Don't you want to go?" I asked.

"Of course I do, but what I'm going to tell you now might surprise you."

"Let me guess," I said as I turned, stood in his way, put my palms on his chest, and squinted. "Those blue eyes have trapped another girl whom you are taking instead of me."

"You are quite right," he said somewhat firmly. "And that's why I was wondering if you would be kind enough to let me borrow from you…let's see"—he pulled at his earlobe—"perhaps your long, curved lashes and luminous brown eyes…your lovely figure that—"

"OK, I got the message," I said and kissed him. "So, what's the surprise?"

"This will be the first time I will attend a Nowrooz celebration!"

"Of course you are kidding me."

"Of course I'm not. You see, because of the atrocities committed against the Jewish community in Esfahan, the Jewbarites have come to consider Nowrooz a Muslim feast. They celebrate the name of Cyrus the Great who saved them from captivity in Babylon, but they are reluctant to recognize Nowrooz as a national holiday." Cyrus shook his head. "It hurts me that for you this will be a joyous occasion, while for me it will be a mixed blessing because of the trauma my people have endured. Why can't we all live in peace together, Leila?"

"The utopia we all long for," I responded. "You know what, Cyrus? Since I have known you, I can't stop comparing my childhood with yours. How would I feel if, as a Jew, I had been born and raised in a ghetto, had been considered filthy, and subjected to such hurt and resentment as you have suffered?"

"That's the exact same observation Professor Rossi made to me," Cyrus said.

We were sitting on a bench, watching the sunset. I thought about what Cyrus had told me about Isabella Rossi, an Italian economics professor guest lecturing at UCLA. Professor Rossi was helping Cyrus with his thesis, and interested in Persian history and the Iranian traditions.

"Why don't you invite Professor Rossi to the Nowrooz party?" I suggested.

And so, on the night of the Nowrooz feast, Cyrus introduced me to Professor Isabella Rossi. I was startled by her tall, blond beauty and by her intellectual voraciousness as she ceaselessly probed me about every bit of the festivity.

"*Vel nemikoneh*,"—she doesn't let go—I whispered to Cyrus, who struggled not to laugh. Eventually, another of her students appeared, and Cyrus and I managed to break away.

"What the hell is she doing, teaching economics?" I asked him as soon as we were clear. "She is a beauty queen. I'm sure she would make much more money acting or modeling."

"You have to be her student and listen to her. She is so brilliant you forget what she looks like," Cyrus said.

As the submission date of his thesis got closer, Cyrus and I saw less of each other. For the next few weeks, we got together mostly at Fred's Café for a quick lunch or an early dinner. He told me how far he was into completing his thesis, I told him about my studies, and then we parted. However, we decided that for our summer holidays, we would spend a few weeks touring the West Coast.

On May 30, 1974, a date now seared into my mind, I was walking across the campus in the early afternoon when I saw Cyrus and Professor Rossi sitting underneath a tree on a blanket, holding hands.

There was a picnic basket between them along with a bottle of wine.

And they were holding hands.

I watched them for a few moments as they raised their glasses to toast each other. I watched and trembled with hurt and anger. I was shaking. To keep my balance, I held on to the tree that was hiding me from their view and turned my face away from the scene. I did not want to see them. Let the little demon—be it love or hate—that was shredding me deep inside do its utmost.

For an instant, I contemplated rushing over to confront Cyrus. But no, I would not. I had my dignity. I would go home. I would be OK. If he preferred his professor to me, so be it. As far as I was concerned, that was the end of my relationship with Cyrus.

Back in my apartment, I lay on my bed and tried hard to not be emotionally devastated. I reminded myself that from my grandfather, General Bahman Omid, I had inherited military discipline and from my parents, the stoicism to weather life's storms. But no matter how hard I tried, I felt like I was going to crumble into a million little desolate, heartbroken pieces.

I had to talk to someone. Suzan, of course, who else? I dialed her number. She wasn't home. I redialed repeatedly with no luck. Time went by—one hour or two, I guess. I remember it got dark. I was lying curled up on my bed with the phone beside me, willing myself to get up and turn on the light so that I could try Suzan's number once again. As I was dragging myself to the edge of the bed, I heard a knock on the door and jumped.

The second knock came and Cyrus called, "Are you there, Leila?"

I remained mute.

"Leila, it's me. Cyrus. I've been looking for you all day."

I said nothing.

"Well, if you're not home," he said in his teasing voice, "then I will wait here until you come back."

How the hell could he tell I was in here, I wondered as I got up, turned on the light, walked to the door, and pulled it open to confront him.

"Leila!" he began. "I didn't want to call. I wanted to tell you in person—"

"Stop!" I shrieked. "Don't you dare touch me!"

He turned pale. "What's the matter?"

"What's the matter? The matter with me is that I saw you with your Italian lover! How come you are too busy for me but have plenty of time to picnic with her?"

"Ah, now I get it." Cyrus chuckled. "You think you saw me cheating on you. May I come in and explain?"

"No!"

"OK. I will say it here. What I wanted to tell you in person was that Professor Rossi and I finished working on my thesis today!"

"Cyrus," I said, so angry I could barely get the words out. "I saw the two of you! In the park! You were holding hands," I cried. "I'm sorry, Cyrus. I understand your position. The fact of the matter is that, although I am bound to my traditions and believe in sticking to a 'decent behavior'—that is, not to sleep with anyone but my husband, you are a free man and have sexual needs. Yet, I think, if you really loved me—"

"Wait a minute. Holding hands?" Cyrus repeated, looking puzzled. "Of course not. We were not holding…Jesus Christ, Leila! Don't you know these Italians? She holds students' hands when she talks to them. That's all it was. I love you, Leila. For all the time that we have known each other, have I ever complained about our sexless relationship? Now, can I come in?"

He sounded genuinely irritated, but I was out of my mind with jealousy and hurt, and so the pain inside of me made me say something inexcusable.

"You Jews have a handy excuse for every trick you play, don't you?" I spat. "Do you really think the whole world is stupid enough to believe you?"

Oh my God! The look in Cyrus's eyes as he absorbed my obscene remark! Before I was able to apologize, he was gone.

For the next couple of weeks I tried to contact Cyrus, but he avoided me. Although I was not convinced by his story about why Professor Rossi had been holding his hand, I felt compelled to apologize for my senseless anti-Semitism, made even more nonsensical by the fact that I myself am Jewish. I went so far as to visit Cyrus's apartment, where his roommate, Hamid, repeated what he'd told me on the phone: that Cyrus was out, busy getting ready to defend his thesis. "Sure, I'll give him your message," Hamid assured me.

A week later, Hamid called me with the news that Cyrus had successfully defended his PhD thesis, had gotten a job, and had moved to New York. And no, he had neither Cyrus's New York phone number nor his address.

For days and weeks after that, I walked around in a gray fog. What if I had been wrong about Cyrus? Of course, the damage was done either way, but I had to know if I'd been justified in my outrage—not to suggest that there could be any excuse for the terrible thing I said to Cyrus.

There was only one way to know. I had to talk to Professor Rossi.

I checked the campus bulletin and saw that she was giving a seminar on the economic politics of oil. I attended, sitting in the back of the auditorium. She was wearing a stylish red suit that showed off her movie-star figure. Besides her astounding beauty, sweet, authentic accent, and beyond my intense jealousy, I found her lecture very interesting. This again brought back memories of my asking Cyrus how he tolerated the boredom of dealing with economics and finance and his response that he found it intriguing, logical and interesting. Entangled in these thoughts, I raised my head to see myself alone in the empty lecture hall. The seminar had finished and I was sitting there alone, glued to my chair.

"Hi there!" Professor Rossi called out as I approached her at the podium. She was putting her notes and charts together, packing her briefcase. "Is there anything you want to ask me?"

"Yes, Professor," I said as I walked to the podium. "It's perhaps a very stupid question."

"No question is stupid," she said. "Wait a minute. Have we met?"

"Yes, Professor. At the Iranian—"

"But of course," she exclaimed. "You're my prize student Cyrus's girlfriend!" She stepped down and reached out to take my hand. "Cyrus was always talking so much about you. But I'm certain you know how much the young man loves you. He called me last week to thank me for my help with his thesis. He told me that he was enjoying job at Jenkins Brothers & Associates in New York. I guess he has told you that it is one of the largest firms of financial consultants and certified public accountants in the world? As a matter of fact, I told him that I will be sending him an invitation to my wedding in Rome next July and that I was expecting him to come..."

Finally I pulled my hand free of hers. "I saw you and Cyrus in the park," I blurted out. "You two were holding hands!"

Professor Rossi stared at me. Then I could see the light dawning in her eyes. She began to laugh. "How old are you, my child?"

"Twenty," I said.

"And, of course, you are from Iran and grew up in Iranian society with no inkling or notion of Western societal behavior."

"What are you getting at?" I demanded, now angry with myself for starting to cry in front of this woman who had stolen away my love.

"Oh, no, no, no," Professor Rossi said, soothing me as she saw the tears rolling down my cheeks. "Look, I've just finished a long lecture and I have no energy to give another speech. So here's what's what: Cyrus loves you, I love my fiancé, and nothing happened between us. Trust me and don't cry."

I rummaged through my purse and found a tissue. "I'm sorry," I managed to say as I dabbed at my tears.

I realized now what Professor Rossi had so accurately surmised. If I had seen what I'd seen between Cyrus and the professor in Iran, it would have meant something far more meaningful and intimately significant than what I'd seen taking place in public, in broad daylight, on the UCLA campus.

How could I have been so naïve?

So provincial?

So dumb!

In America, holding hands meant nothing. I should have known that, even if, in my country, it was tantamount to being engaged.

"You are most welcome to accompany Cyrus to my wedding," Professor Rossi said. "Give me your address and I will add you to my guest list!"

And, of course, as she told me all this, she had resumed holding my hand.

CHAPTER 13

It is March 15, 1980. Forty-seven days have passed by since my incarceration.

I can't sleep and I eat very little, for I have no appetite. Even if I feel hungry, I cannot stand what Skunk brings me. And I truly stink. I haven't washed since they brought me here. At times, I hallucinate, seeing out of the corners of my eyes things flitting and flying across my cell. Knowing my parents, I am far more concerned for them than I am for myself. I picture my father pacing up and down our living room. "I told her to leave. I told her to go back to America," I hear him lamenting. And I hear my mother weeping for me.

Last night, I lay awake wondering how I could manipulate Skunk into letting my parents know I'm still alive. For all the money that they spent on my education, for all the time that I wasted studying "crisis control and management," I owe it to them to apply what I have learned and find a way to reach out and communicate with them.

I examine everything around me: my filthy, pestilent cell; the cot; the door; the barred window. What else? What do I hear? There is the faint but incessant noise of the other prisoners, whom I have never seen, coming from the far end of the corridor, nearer the bathroom. What else is there? Anything else?

No, only Skunk...He is my only means of reaching the outside world.

This morning he arrived at my cell late, but in a euphoric mood. "Today, Sister Zahra, we had the first elections of our dear Islamic Republic." He threw a newspaper at me. "See? The whole country is out voting!"

I looked at the paper, the first I'd seen since my imprisonment. It showed photos of demonstrators with their fists thrown into the air as they carried anti-Mojahedin slogans.

Iranian Mojahedin were members of an Islamic socialist organization founded in 1965 and devoted to armed struggle against the Shah's regime and Westerners. They had killed many proponents of the Shah and a few of the American military and civilian personnel who served in Iran. As Khomeini's movement began to gain momentum, he'd used the Mojahedin as a tool to overthrow the Shah, but the Ayatollah tightened his grip on power, he declared them Monafeghin—seditious sinners who deserved to be annihilated. In retaliation, apparently, the Mojahedin had turned their guns against the Khomeini regime.

"Very interesting, Brother Zaki," I said. "Nice pictures. Yes, they're all out voting. And what is this about the Mojahedin? I thought they were followers of Imam Khomeini."

"They were all pretenders, who are full of Western education and godless Western ways. Those faggot intellectuals wanted to steal our revolution. That's why all of us revolutionary guards have been ordered to take over their offices and erase their name from the face of the earth. They are cheaters, just like you are," he grinned like a dog with its tongue hanging out. "Every time I try to get close to you, you come up with something crazy to fool me."

I had to abort this discussion. "I always disliked the Mojahedin because—"

"You see? You try to change the subject to fool me. Do you think I'm stupid? One day you frighten me with quotations from Kalam-Allah; the next day you tell me Hollywood stories, then about the girls and boys in America, that Great Satan. Who do you think I am—a donkey? Every time I leave you, my balls ache. And don't talk to me about my wife. She is the mother of my children. It is her duty to take care of them, and it is your duty to take care of…no, it's my duty to rid you of your sins. This is what all other pasdars I know are doing to sinful sisters like you who are in their custody."

"But I thought we were going to practice pasodoble today and discuss how we would go to America and convert those infidels to Islam?" I managed a fake smile.

"And this time I have a better idea. From now on, every time I come here, first we do the act of making you less sinful, then other things."

"Well, according to—"

"Don't 'according to' me. From today, everything is according to Brother Zaki," he snarled. "Now open your legs."

Were we back to square one?

"But you are my brother," I said, supplicating.

"No, I am not your brother and don't worry. Last night, one of my pasdar brothers told me that although masturbation is forbidden in Islam, as long as I did not touch you or see your bare skin, I could do it. You are wearing trousers, just open your legs and leave the rest to me."

Disgusted but relieved. That's how I felt. If my filthy pants turn him on, so be it. I opened my shaky legs. He loosened his belt, put his hand inside his pants, fixed his eyes on my crotch, and began manipulating himself.

I closed my own eyes, wondering how long I was going to be trapped in this cage with this animal.

• • •

My days after my encounter with Professor Rossi were made blue and gloomy by my regret over how I had acted toward Cyrus—and the inexcusable slur I had hurled at him.

After I told Suzan about my breakup with Cyrus, she asked, puzzled, "But doesn't he know that your mom is Jewish?"

"Yes he does. And he comes from the same ghetto my mother comes from. But Mom's parents moved to Tehran when she was a child and they opted not to live an open Jewish life. Cyrus was born and raised in Jewbareh for the first fourteen years of his life. You had to be there, Suzan, and listen to him, and feel his emotional trauma when he spoke about—just to mention one case—what he had gone through as a Jewish boy in a predominantly Muslim school."

"But if he loved you—"

"Listen to me, my dear. I have thought a lot about this and quite honestly, I don't blame him for being so upset with me for what I said—especially and not despite the fact that I am of Jewish descent myself."

"Never mind," Suzan said. "This is what I want you to do. Get over Cyrus. Kick him out of your system, find a real boyfriend, and be a real girlfriend to him in the American way.

Come to think of it, it is possible that Cyrus left you out of sexual frustration. You don't know men, Leila."

Over the next few days, Suzan called me frequently, always repeating the same advice. What she did not seem to get—or I was unable to make her understand—was that the gap between our two cultures was grander than the Grand Canyon.

And then came a call from my father. As was his way, he got straight to the point. "I had a call from Suzan. She told me about the breakup between you and Cyrus. What a great girl. She's so concerned about you, Leila jaan. So are your mom and I. I'm sorry that your relationship didn't work. You are young, beautiful, and intelligent. You have a great future ahead of you and plenty of time to find the right man."

All that week the calls continued to come from Suzan, my father, and my mother. There was even a call from Suzan's parents, but none from Cyrus.

After a while, I stopped answering the phone. And then one night, as I sat in my apartment, my eyes fixed on a textbook and my thoughts drifting, I heard a knock on the door. I looked at my watch. It was nine o'clock. Was it Cyrus? "Who is it?" I called.

"Leila jaan, it's me," my father called out.

I opened the door and threw myself in his arms.

"It's almost one year since I have seen you," he murmured, hugging me.

"I'm so glad to see you," I said. "But why are you here and how come you didn't let me know ahead of time?"

He rubbed his unshaven beard and said, "Trellis. Remember? I'm here because you need a shoulder to put your head on."

And I did.

In the days to come, I would learn that it was not only his shoulder that he had to offer. He wanted me to meet Amir, a cousin of my mom's brother-in-law who was medical student at USC. I had seen him at family gatherings but had never spoken to him.

"Amir is such a decent young man," Pedar began. "He comes from a family we know well. We have known his parents for a long time. A few months ago, he came home for his summer vacation. His mom and dad threw a party for him and invited your mother and me. Apparently he's doing so well..."

My father went on to say that I had to move on from Cyrus. "You can't return the water to the river once it's ended up in the ocean," he quoted an old Persian proverb. "And, if I am your trellis, lean on me, trust me, Leila jaan. This young man Amir will soon be a doctor and return home. He has told his parents that he is seriously looking for an Iranian girl to marry after he finishes his studies here. His parents know you very well and are begging you to meet their son so that the two of you can get to know each other better."

"Better? So, the deal is sealed?"

"Nothing is sealed. Just meet him and go out a few times, I'm sure you will like him."

Yes, the deal was sealed. By the time my father left two weeks later, Amir and I had met, not because I had gotten over Cyrus or because I was looking for a substitute for him, but because I felt obligated to honor Pedar's wish. After all, my loving father had left his busy clinic behind and had travelled all the way from Tehran to Los Angeles only to soothe me, and I hated to let him go, feeling that he had not been able to resolve my problem.

At twenty-eight, Amir was five years older than Cyrus. He was not as tall and wore his jet-black hair cut short. He had an innocent round face and a thin mustache on his long upper lip. A jacket was an integral part of his attire. He cleared his throat every time he spoke, and he spoke only of medical subjects when we were at dinner or when we were walking together. Whether he wore a tie or not, his abundant chest hair overflowed his collar. And his eyes…well, they were not blue.

I had gone out with him three times in four weeks and he was still calling me, "Leila Khanom"—Miss Leila. He was so uptight that he didn't even hold hands with me. He was almost irritably polite. A typical date was Amir arriving in his Porsche convertible at my apartment, where he rang the bell but never came upstairs. Then he would take me to an expensive restaurant, talk about USC, ask questions about UCLA, compare the two, segue inevitably into a discourse on his medical studies, bring me home, and then good-bye.

Oh well, for a while, as long as it kept my parents happy, I was OK with it. But as time went by, the reality that I was in love with Cyrus, not this well-behaved poor soul, hit me hard. Every time Amir brought me back home from an expensive dinner, I missed Fred's Café—with its delicious sandwiches and warm conversation with Cyrus—more. And then, one night I had a strange dream. It took place on the large patio in my grandfather's backyard. General Omid was there in full military attire, as were my parents—Pedar in his physician's white cotton coat and Madar in a nurse's uniform. There were others, as well, whom I couldn't recognize. My grandfather saluted me, declaring that I was of the daughter of the deputy minister of war and that I had to be resolute and strong. Pedar took my hand as we sat by the trellis in our home in Tabas. In the distance, the desert shimmered and towering palm trees swayed in the temperate breeze. Then my father whispered in my ear, "Be strong and follow your heart..."

I woke up from this dream with a plan.

Suzan was going to be my accomplice. She would call Jenkins Brothers & Associates and make sure that Cyrus was working there and get his extension number for me, so that I could call him.

"I'll help you," Suzan said. "But from what you have told me, Cyrus is likely so upset that he would hang up on you. We have to come up with a better tactic. Let me think."

An hour later, Suzan called. Together with her boyfriend, John, an attorney, she had come up with a clever plan. John's law firm, genuinely unhappy with its CPA firm, was looking for a larger, more reliable one. He personally knew one of the senior partners at Jenkins Brothers & Associates. The scheme was for John to hire Jenkins Brothers & Associates as his firm's accountants and to ask that Cyrus be assigned to the account.

In a week, they had implemented the plan. "From this point on," Suzan told me, "John and I have to be very careful not to betray anything. As far as Cyrus is concerned, we don't know you. In the meantime, my dear, as I've said, you must be patient."

During this time, Professor Isabella Rossi's wedding invitation came, along with a schedule of her economics seminars, on which she had penciled a note: "In case you're interested." I was interested in the subject she taught, and I made time to attend her lectures. Before very long, I was fascinated with the subject of economics—to the extent that I faced the question of whether I truly wanted to continue my studies of medicine. What finally tipped the balance and got me to switch my major was the invitation I received from Professor Rossi to assist her in her research for a paper she was writing on the socioeconomic situation in Iran. I jumped at the chance, and soon, due to her mentorship, decided that what I wanted to be was a certified public accountant.

In the meantime, Suzan and I were in regular touch. By July 1975, her boyfriend, John, and Cyrus had become friends. Anxious to meet the object of my affection, Suzan had John arrange for the three of them to have dinner together.

"He's a great guy," Suzan told me, after meeting Cyrus. "Now I understand why you are going crazy about him. He's perfect for you. Why don't you come stay with us for your Christmas break? That way we can set up a meeting between you two at our Christmas party."

I was excited and apprehensive concerning Suzan's invitation. I missed her and wanted to see her, and of course, I wanted to see Cyrus, but what if he did not accept my apology?

Immediately I booked a ticket to New York for December 20. I spent the next few months fretting over the moment when I would see Cyrus and enduring my dates with Amir, in order to keep my parents content. I had concluded that Cyrus or no Cyrus, Amir was not for me. The shame of it was that he was such a nice man, and I hated myself for using him to keep my parents happy. But the mere thought of the moment when I would again see Cyrus on my Christmas break, although laced with anxiety and expectation, kept me going. I would beg him to forgive me, and he would. I would tell him that I had spoken to Professor Rossi, that she had invited me to her wedding in Italy. I would ask Cyrus if we could go together. I would also tell him I had changed academic programs, thanks to Isabella Rossi, and that I was not going to be a physician, but a CPA. To make him understand how much I loved him, I would transfer from UCLA to New York University. And...

Then, on a Monday evening in late November, I received a call from Suzan. As soon as I heard her voice, I knew it was bad news.

"Really, I don't know how to put this to you, but as a friend, I can't hold back. It's very confidential, very client-privilege stuff, so if you talk to anyone about it, and I mean anyone, John will face disbarment. Now promise me on the life of your parents that you—"

"I will, I will. What is it?"

"About ten days ago, this middle-aged Iranian guy contacts John to hire him as his attorney to sue Cyrus for having an affair with his wife," Suzan began. "It turns out the husband had hired a private investigator who took some pictures of Cyrus with the wife in a restaurant. John told the husband that the pictures don't prove his wife's infidelity and that, here in America, you can't sue a man for having an affair with your wife."

Suzan paused. "Are you OK? Tell me to shut up whenever you want."

"Don't be ridiculous, Suzan. We are talking about my life." I was grateful at least my friend couldn't see my tears. "Go ahead, please."

"Yesterday John was reading the Sunday paper and saw that the husband had killed himself. I looked at the paper.

The guy's name is Piran, and his wife, Bita. Does it ring the bell?" Suzan asked.

"No. Go on, please."

"Well, that was when John told me the whole story. We talked about it, but whichever way we put the parts of this puzzle together, we couldn't figure out what was going on. So, this morning John calls Cyrus's office to talk about it with him, and found out that Cyrus had returned to Iran for personal reasons."

"Personal reasons?" I repeated, "I just don't understand."

I didn't want to make the mistake of jumping to conclusions like I had with Professor Rossi, but if Cyrus was innocent of all that Suzan was telling me, why would he run away like this?

I felt wounded, let down, and determined to get over Cyrus. The first step would be to make a symbolic new start… I rented a new apartment so as not to be in physical surroundings that would remind me of my lost love. I even changed my telephone number.

CHAPTER 14

March 21, 1980

The first day of Nowrooz. No seven *S*'s, no goldfish. Just me, the four walls of my cell, and Skunk.

"Under directions of Imam Khomeini, we have begun to erase all traces of the Great Satan's cultural influence and replace it with Islamic values," Skunk announced to me this morning. "Accordingly, Nowrooz, this fire worshipers' feast, will be forbidden. Is that not excellent, Sister Zahra?"

"Yes, it is," I answered as I lamented the loss of sanity in my land. How can I tell Skunk that the Persians have celebrated this Zoroastrian occasion for thousands of years? How can I explain to this ignorant creature that Zoroastrians are not fire worshipers but that to them, fire is merely a symbol of light and righteousness?

• • •

In early 1977, Amir became a doctor, and as he was about to return home, he proposed to me. It put me in an odd position. With Cyrus out of my life, over time, Amir had taken a special place in my heart—the heart that once belonged to Cyrus. Once belonged? No! Despite his disloyalty, Cyrus was and would remain a part of me. But besides this dreamlike fantasy, there was a real world with a fine and decent man who had waited so long for me. When I told him that I had to finish my studies before I left America, he said it was fine with him and that he would go home and wait for me.

I was caught in a tough situation. How could I learn to love someone who had been match-made for me? "Love comes. It's nothing to be learned," says a Persian proverb. With Cyrus, love came with his blue eyes. With Amir, I had learned to admire his decency. But was he the man I wanted to marry? I was not sure. In the meantime, keeping him waiting for me was not fair.

"Why don't we do this, Amir?" I'd suggested a few days before he left. "Go back home and establish your medical practice, but don't postpone your decision to marry because of me. If you find a better match than me, then go ahead and marry. After I return, if you are still available and interested in me, then we will resume our friendship and see what will happen."

To my utter astonishment, he agreed. This whole relationship had begun as a deal and dealing with it "as a deal" was not inappropriate.

And so I returned to Iran on December 1, 1978, as a certified public accountant, with a master's degree in economics and finance. All the while, of course, I had followed the political turmoil in Iran, but being in the actual midst of the situation was a far cry from watching it on television. As my parents drove me home from the airport, Madar excitedly told me how she had prepared the guesthouse for me.

"You will have your privacy, Leila," Pedar added. "We understand that you are an adult now."

"Thank you both," I said gratefully. "It is good to be home."

We passed demonstration after demonstration in the streets, masses of my livid countrymen shouting slogans against the Shah, America, and Israel. As he drove, Pedar told me that Khomeini was recording anti-Shah speeches on tapes, which were being smuggled into Iran from France. Thousands and thousands of these tapes had been copied and distributed free of charge among the mass of demonstrators.

"Things are worse than what I thought," I said.

"Don't worry," Madar responded. "It will all go away. The Shah is backed by America, after all."

I did not see it that way, but I kept my mouth shut so as not to upset my mother. It was clear to me that events were spiraling out of control. Since 1953, when the Shah had regained his throne with the help of the CIA, street demonstrations had been outlawed. That here in Tehran there could be thousands of protesters openly shouting anti-Shah and anti-American slogans at the top of their lungs was unreal—and an omen that the dam was about to break and those who were with the Shah would be caught in the deluge.

After a few days in the city, I was desperate to escape the tumult. My parents agreed with my suggestion that we spend some time together at our desert home.

"How about asking Amir to join us?" Madar suggested.

Since his return to Iran, Amir had been in touch with my parents. Not only had he not found himself another girl to marry, which I had been hoping he would, but he had even talked to my parents about *khastegari*—officially asking for my hand to marry him—as soon as I returned. He even discussed his plans for the wedding, for, according to Iranian tradition, the groom paid for the wedding.

"Please don't, Madar," I said, pretending not to notice her look of disappointment "I want to spend time with my family only—you, Dad, and my brothers."

"Does he know that you—"

"That's a good idea," Pedar said, cutting her short in a commanding tone. "Family only!"

Once settled into our desert home, I enjoyed looking out at the dunes and the palms and willows and remembering my childhood days here at this otherworldly oasis! Not much had changed since I had last been here. As always, Tabas was warm and soothing and the majesty of the desert was so intoxicating.

All too soon, we had to return to the hornets' nest that Tehran had become due to political strife. After my five years of study in America, settling back into my homeland required many adjustments on my part. As if this was not enough, Amir called. Evidently, my mother had given him the news of my return, and the poor soul didn't even complain that I had not gotten in touch with him. "I miss you, and my parents can't wait to meet you."

I told him that I was busy settling down and finding a job and that I would call him soon.

Did he say no? Did he say what was wrong with having a dinner or a get-together in between? Did he insist on seeing me? No! He simply agreed. That's how Amir was. To him, life was methodical. To him, it made perfect sense that I would want to get organized before I saw him. Why couldn't he be a tiny bit passionate, like Cyrus? Persistent and even demanding?

Trying to distract myself from my melancholy, I visited with friends and family and began looking for a job. I also spent much time with Bijan—a dear cousin who has always been like an older brother to me. Bijan was in his midforties, and had degrees in psychology, philosophy, and Persian literature from Tehran University, just to mention a few. He spoke English fluently but with a heavy accent, for he had never been abroad. If you asked him why he had never married, he would point to his vast library and say, "Here is my harem! Every one of these treasures can keep my company for hours on end."

When I told him that I was looking for a job, he said, "I work in an accounting firm and I know they will grab you up. It's a prominent international firm of economists, financial advisers, and certified public accountants."

"Sounds good," I said.

"What's even better," Bijan added, "is that the firm's senior partner and I are close friends. Like you, he is also an American-educated CPA. Cyrus is..."

"Wait, did you say Cyrus?"

"Why, yes," Bijan replied. "Do you know him?"

"Do I ever!"

I suppose I always knew that in returning to Iran, I would inevitably run into Cyrus, especially since both of us were going to be in the same city and in the same profession. I had endlessly imagined the encounter. I had stockpiled an arsenal of cutting putdowns with which I would dismiss him. But to work in the firm where he was a senior partner was out of the question.

"Are you all right?" Bijan was asking me. "You look pale."

"I'm fine. Listen, cousin, what I really want is to work for the government as opposed to a private firm, so I can have some influence on the political situation."

"As you wish," Bijan said. "If you don't find a suitable job, let me know."

My efforts to find a government job failed. As it turned out, due to the turbulent political scene, no government agency was hiring.

"I still don't understand why you are not interested in working for an international firm of accountants," Bijan said after I'd told him about my job-hunting failures.

"I know Cyrus from America," I confessed to my cousin. "For personal reasons, I don't want to work for him."

"Were you romantically involved?"

"Yes," I admitted. "But it's been long over."

"Ah, then everything is fine," Bijan assured me.

"How so?"

"Cyrus has been married to his lovely wife, Roxie, for over a year," Bijan said.

I couldn't hold back my tears.

"Oh, my dear cousin," he said, soothing me. "Look, I'm sorry about your romance, but times are difficult and a job is a job. Let me introduce you to Farid, whom I also know. He is the partner in charge of human resources."

It took me awhile to reconcile with the fact that I had lost Cyrus, but Bijan was right. I simply couldn't turn away from an excellent professional opportunity because of my romantic history with Cyrus. And so, on December 20, 1978,

I consented to an employment interview with Farid, who eventually hired me as a group supervisor.

With over five hundred employees and an imposing building down the street from the American embassy compound, the Tehran office of Jenkins Brothers & Associates was mainly engaged in external auditing of large corporations with international investors. My first day at work, Farid escorted me to my desk, one of many in a large, open office space on the ground floor. I settled in among my co-workers, who were mostly men and women my age. Some were laboring through piles of papers and files; others were discussing politics.

"Hello and welcome!"

I swiveled in my chair to see a young woman smiling warmly.

"I'm Farnaz."

"I'm Leila." I returned her smile and shook her hand.

"Welcome on—"

"Are you Leila?" a man shouted, interrupting Farnaz.

"Yes," I said calmly.

"What? I can't hear you!" he yelled. "Speak up and answer!"

"She did," Farnaz said, coming to my rescue. "Not everybody is like you and screams instead of talking, Ali."

While Farnaz and this Ali character were having their exchange, I looked him over. He was of average height, but broad shouldered with a light-brown complexion and curly hair. Despite his suit and tie, he had a roughhewn demeanor, like that of another of the many Iranians named Ali I knew—Ali-Asghar, my family's gardener; Colonel Ali-Akbar, my grandfather's administration officer; Ali-Naghi, the grocer on our street corner.

Looking at this fellow, one had to think he would be equally at home pushing a hoe in a field as pushing papers in an office.

"All right everybody," Ali shouted. "Leila Omid is our new colleague. She is a CPA from America. Say hello to Leila from America."

As the others called out their greetings and welcomes, Ali commanded that I follow him to his office. Does this man know how to say please, I wondered, as I trailed him into his office and sat in the chair in front of his desk? He studied a chart and said, "I think the most suitable place to send you would probably be one of our American clients. How about General Metals?" he asked himself. "The job is halfway done. Our employee there is shorthanded because he is supervising two jobs at the same time. I will have him brief you. All right?"

I didn't respond. Clearly this fellow's query was rhetorical.

Abruptly he looked up at me and frowned, staring at my legs. "No, that won't do at all," he muttered. "Your skirt is too short," he snapped.

"Excuse me?" I said shocked. "Are you telling me that you dictate what your employees should wear?"

"Yes, I do."

"And what's wrong with this skirt?"

"It's too exposing."

"You've got to be kidding me!"

I had been raised in an open-minded family. What's more, I had just returned from the America that was imbued with the ideology of the feminist movement. So that this backwoods chauvinist might tell me what to wear was beyond belief.

"You keep your opinions about my clothing to yourself!" I said, stalked out of his office, and went directly to see Farid.

"What's wrong with this Ali?" I demanded. "Has he graduated from an accounting school in a wilderness?"

"In time you will get to know him better." Farid chuckled. "He doesn't mean to be rude, and he is not really as nasty as he seems to be. He merely speaks his mind—and quite loudly. Unfortunately, what is on his mind is not always refined, if you know what I mean."

"And in this firm, I am supposed to put up with the rude behavior of this cultural bore?" I asked. "Evaluating how I work is his business, but what I wear is nobody's business."

"Now, Leila," Farid replied, growing serious. "This is Iran, not California, USA. Here, much of what you have come to see as normal from a Western point of view is incomprehensible. Please go back to Ali's office while I call him." He picked up the phone to dial and then paused. "And, Leila, please do wear longer skirts to work, and let's have this over with."

Ali belonged in a primitive village, not an international accounting firm, I mused on my way back to his office, to find Ali on the phone.

"I understand, Farid," I heard him say. "Yes, sir."

He pointed to the chair in front of his desk. I sat down.

"Yes...Fully understood...The firm's policy...Nothing to do with me...Understood...Bye." He hung up the phone laughing. "What did I say to upset you so much?" Ali asked me. "Why did you have to go to Farid?"

He did not sound offended or hurt. He was still laughing. For what had happened between us, he should have either apologized or asked for an apology. Yet he didn't. Instead, he simply continued from where we had left off.

"As I was saying, I want you to go to General Metals and join our team there. But before going to our client's office, why don't you go home and change into something more appropriate."

"Didn't Farid just order you not to criticize my way of dressing?" I demanded.

"No, actually he didn't. What Farid said to me is that rather than dictating how you should dress, I should have directed you to read for yourself our firm's dress code policy."

"Which is?"

"For men, suits with white shirts and dark ties. For women…" Ali paused. "To be honest, I don't know, I've never read the woman's part. So you go read it."

As I worked for Ali, I got to know him as an arrogant, chauvinistic man who was clearly made insecure by my professional capabilities. Almost every time he criticized my performance, I proved him wrong, but that did not stop him from repeating like a broken record that my having been educated in America did not make me a better accountant than he was. There I had to agree with him. What made me a better accountant than Ali were my superior skills and intelligence. I ignored his attacks as much as I could, but that only made his criticisms increase.

In the meantime, the turmoil in Iran was reaching new heights. The ever-deepening opposition to the Shah had brought about unending widespread demonstrations and rioting. The police and military tried to crack down, but nothing it seemed could smother the blaze of rebellion that was flaring throughout my country. And then the unthinkable happened: in the middle of January 1979, the Shah abdicated the Peacock Throne and departed Iran.

As I came to work on that fateful day, the streets were alive with jubilant pro-fundamentalists laughing and congratulating each other. At the firm, many staff members believed this would be a welcome mat for Khomeini, handing over to him the reins of power. Others believed that Iran would fall under the influence of the Iron Curtain and become communist. And then there were the royalists who were struggling to bring back the Shah.

A few days later, Ali asked me to have tea with him. I didn't see how I could avoid it, and a part of me felt encouraged that maybe he was trying to make peace, so I accepted his invitation. We went to a small coffee shop next to our office, where we sat at a table facing each other. We ordered our tea, and then Ali startled me by asking how old I was.

"Why? You want to marry me?"

"No, I have a wife. But maybe I could put you together with a friend of mine, if you're interested."

"Before we discuss that, let me say that I don't understand why you are not comfortable around me."

"Leila, you're wrong. I'm not uncomfortable around you, but I do think you consider yourself above me." He paused. "Maybe that's why you're not married. Don't you want to have a family of your own and children?"

"I thought you were a communist who believes in equality of men and women in a 'just and equal' society," I said.

"Well, if you'd like to know," he began, "now that the Shah is gone and his dynasty has been thrown into the wastebasket of history, the uprising of the masses is inevitable, and soon we will begin living in a communist utopia..."

And so he began his lecture on the history of communism, but I hardly listened to the provincial fool.

As we left the coffeehouse, Ali said, "We should do this more often. I like these discussions. They are so intellectually stimulating."

Not in your wildest dreams, Ali...

CHAPTER 15

March 25, 1980

The fourth day of Nowrooz. I have become resigned to my fate. I am going to die in this prison.

"On my way here, I passed by Tehran University," Skunk told me this morning. "There was a huge demonstration against the university."

Why would there be a demonstration against the university?

It had to be that the glorious revolution had decided to eat its own children, guaranteeing that the darkness of ignorance and bigotry would win out over the light of reason.

How many of us were left in our prison cells who fondly remember our country as it was?

• • •

As an employee at Jenkins Brothers & Associates, I finished my first assignment at General Metals and returned to the office so Ali could assign me to the next job. That was when I heard that Cyrus had been promoted to senior partner and that all employees were expected to attend the upcoming office gathering to celebrate his advancement.

So far, I had been able to avoid running into Cyrus. Since starting my job, I had spent most of my time at General Metals, after all. What's more, I suspected that the news of the hiring of a junior accountant like me would not rise to the top floor where Cyrus and the rest of senior management resided. But then I realized that I was actually looking forward to seeing him again. It would be my trial by fire to prove to myself that I was over him. And who knew? Maybe we could truly be friends and enjoy each other's company now that he was a married man and all hope of love was gone.

At the party, I took a deep breath, walked up behind Cyrus, and said, "Congratulations!"

He turned and stared at me. God how I'd missed those blue eyes!

"Leila?" he stammered. "Am I dreaming?"

"No, you are not dreaming." I smiled. "You really should step out from that corner office more often. I've have been one of your employees for a while."

I gloated as I caught him staring at my cleavage. Ali be damned, I had chosen one of my most revealing blouses to wear to this party. I wanted Cyrus to see what he was missing.

"Let's sit down and catch up."

"No, Cyrus. I don't think we have anything to say to each other about the past," I said, cool as cucumber and yogurt mixed together, and then I sauntered away, so that Cyrus could check out my ass and see what else he was missing.

"Leila, wait…"

I turned around.

"Please. I have to know why…" He paused and looked around cautiously. "You are right. Not here, but I will definitely want to see you some other time." And then he walked away.

I left the party early and returned to my desk to catch up on work. An hour later, the phone rang. It was Cyrus, summoning me to his office. It was my first time up to the top-floor executive suite. As I stepped out of the elevator, I felt like I had journeyed to another building entirely. Up here on Mount Olympus, instead of the dull gray and white color scheme and endless expanses of metal desks and file cabinets, there were colorful Persian carpets on polished oak floors, antique furniture, and walls lined with paintings by contemporary Iranian artists. My heart began to pound as the receptionist stepped out from behind her desk and escorted me to Cyrus's elegant office. As I stepped inside, she softly shut the door behind me. I couldn't help thinking about how long it had been since I had been alone with this man who had once been the love of my life.

"Sit down, please," Cyrus said as he looked up from some papers strewn across his massive mahogany desk.

Why? I wanted to scream at him. Why did you have to betray my love by fooling around with a married woman—and causing her husband to kill himself?

"I was longing to see you alone, Leila," Cyrus said. "Ali gave me my excuse to do so."

"What about Ali?" I asked, trying to keep calm.

"He's complaining about the way you dress."

"What the hell is it with him?" I blurted out. "Cyrus, forgive me if I'm being presumptuous, but I must tell you he is not the caliber of man I would have thought you'd want as an employee."

"That's the Leila I know." Cyrus laughed.

"Seriously, how in the world was he ever hired?"

"I'll tell you if you promise to keep it to yourself."

I couldn't help myself. "Like I've ever broken a promise to you."

"Excuse me?" His gorgeous blue eyes narrowed as he stared at me.

"I'm sorry," I said. "I don't want to dredge up the past. I'm your employee now, and that's all I am. I understand that. You're married, after all…and anyway, Ali has informed me that he's looking for a suitable husband for me." I chuckled.

"Ali wants to find you a husband?" Cyrus shook his head. "You can take a villager out of his village, but you can't take his village out of him. Do you remember the story I told you many years ago about a schoolyard fight I had?"

All of a sudden it clicked.

"You're kidding me," I exclaimed. "He's *that* Ali? Your tormentor at school who became your friend?"

"The very same."

"But if I remember right, his name was Gholam something. Gholam…"

"Gholam-Ali. Now he just calls himself Ali. Anyway, after high school, he disappeared from my life, and next time I saw him was when I had returned from the States. You see, although I was a prime candidate to become a partner in our New York office, circumstances obliged me to return home and join the Iran office."

Circumstances obliged you because you were caught messing around with someone's wife…"Please tell me about Gholam-Ali or Ali or whatever his name is."

"One morning, about two years ago, as I got out of my car in front of the office, he approached me. I immediately recognized him as Gholam-Ali. We hugged and he told me that he was a graduate of the Tehran University College of Accounting and he was looking for a job.

"I invited him up to my office. As I was reviewing his resume, which, by the way, was certainly satisfactory, I heard him sigh. 'You and I were schoolmates, but look where you are now!'" Cyrus smiled wearily. "Leila. It was clear that the old tensions still existed between us and that my hiring him was a not going to be trouble free."

"So, why have you kept him?" I asked.

"Two reasons. First, this is not America. Here, you don't hire and fire people so easily. Second, he is actually a good accountant, which is why he's a group manager. Now, having confided all this to you, I hope it will help you better understand what sort of a person you are dealing with."

"Believe me, I already understand quite well who I'm dealing with." I sighed. "He is intelligent, but also very conservative and, I think, sexist."

"A fair assessment." Cyrus nodded. "But Ali's prejudices aside, like all other professional firms, we have dress codes, both for men and women. I mean, look at me. My suit is navy blue, my shirt white, and my tie…" He paused, apparently realizing that he didn't remember what color tie he was wearing.

"A nice floral design with dark lavender background."

"Thank you. Now, do you think I enjoy dressing so rigidly? Of course not. So, will you promise me to dress as the firm, and not Ali, requires?"

"Sure, boss." I shrugged, raising my hands in submission. What I thought of the company's dress code was irrelevant I had to admit. If I wanted to continue working here, I had to play by the same rules as everyone else.

"Thank you, Leila," Cyrus said. "Now, on to more pleasant matters. I have so many questions to ask you…"

So do I, I thought.

"And I'm sure you agree with me that here is not the right place to talk about it. So, I'd like to take you to lunch. Let's see…"

I stared at him in disbelief as he thumbed through his calendar.

"How about the day after tomorrow, at one o'clock?"

"No, thanks, boss…"

Cyrus looked up at me. "Listen, Leila. We both need to come clean with one another about what happened to us. So! As one old friend to another, may I have the pleasure of taking you to lunch on Wednesday?"

Damn it. How could I resist those eyes?

CHAPTER 16

March 30, 1980

The sixty-third day of my incarceration.

This morning, Skunk stormed into my cell, yammering so quickly I couldn't understand what he was trying to say. He grabbed me by the shoulders, slammed me against the wall, and cried, "You are the granddaughter of General Omid, the traitorous right hand of that jackal the Shah!"

My first thought was that they had arrested my grandfather.

"You don't have to answer me," Skunk sneered as he let go of me and lit a cigarette. "I'm taking you to a place where they will make you answer." He roughly blindfolded me, saying, "They are waiting for you in the Central Revolutionary Committee."

Skunk led me out of my cell, along hallways; then we were outdoors. I felt the sun on my face and inhaled fresh spring air—what a blessing after my months of captivity in the damp and darkness!

I reminded myself that I was being taken to the Central Revolutionary Committee. Perhaps I would be beaten, or even executed. Well, so be it. For this moment, at least, I had the fresh air and the sun, and if I was about to die, I thanked God for these small blessings.

Skunk pushed me into a vehicle. "You'd better say your *ashad*," he sneered as he sat beside me.

Ashad—the first word of the Muslim death prayer. I felt strangely calm at the thought of escaping from all this, even if it was only to escape to a grave.

"Haji Agha Khalkhali is going to interrogate you," Skunk said.

Now my brief serenity left me and I grew frightened. Khalkhali was infamous. They called him "Khomeini's Angel of Death." He was known for enjoying the torture he inflicted on his victims during interrogations.

After a drive, I was herded into another place where they took off my blindfold. I opened my eyes to find myself sitting on a folding metal chair in front of Khalkhali. I recognized the mullah from his speeches on the television. He was fat and wore a white turban. His oversized eyeglasses with thick lenses magnified his dark eyes, and his beard was long and wispy, like gray tendrils of cotton candy descending from his chin. He was sitting behind a metal desk, with a giant poster of a stern-looking Khomeini hanging on the wall behind him.

"Jendeh pedar sag"—dog father whore—"you who have fornicated with a thousand donkeys…"

This is how he started speaking to me, and on and on he went, his every question laced with profanity as he interrogated me concerning my grandfather's involvement in Operation Ajax. When I told him I had no idea what he was talking about, he shook his head and called to one of the guards holding a baton.

"Give this sister a few knocks to jog her memory."

"Wait, please!" I begged, raising my hands. "Operation Ajax was a CIA plot to overthrow Mossadegh."

"Go on," Khalkhali demanded.

"Your Holiness. This coup happened two years before I was born. What I know, I only know because I have read about it. I swear to Allah that's all I know."

"Listen to me carefully, sister," Khalkhali said. "You know my reputation?"

"Yes, Your Holiness," I whimpered.

He seemed to take pleasure in my obvious terror. "Then don't you think you should be more cooperative?

"Haji Agha," I said. "Ask me anything and I will answer truthfully, but as I said, I was born two years after Mossadegh was overthrown."

"I don't even piss on Mossadegh's grave, that nationalist, donkey-fucked bastard. I'm only looking for those who, Allah forbid, with the help of the Great Satan's CIA, might be dreaming of overthrowing the first government of Allah on the earth. What I want to know is the whereabouts of your grandfather, General Omid!"

So Grandpa has escaped, thank God! I was careful to hide my joy.

"Haji Agha," I said. "Before I was incarcerated, months ago, he lived in his own house. Since I've been imprisoned, I've had no contact with the outside world, so you see, sir, I have no idea where he is at present."

Khalkhali stared at me in frustration. My circumstances as I had explained them were irrefutable: I had no way of knowing where my grandfather, the general, was. I could only hope this psychopath would not choose to torture me for his idle entertainment.

"Listen to me, whore," Khalkhali spat. "Your donkey grandfather CIA agent has run away like the coward he is, but I swear I will find him."

He sat contemplating me. I could hardly breathe. I was so frightened. His next words could easily condemn me to the physical tortures of hell on earth.

"Guards," Khalkhali said calmly. "I'm hungry, and looking at this whore is affecting my appetite. Take her to Brother Zabihi, and give him this"—he handed the guard what seemed to be my file—"and tell Zabihi she is a *mohaareb.*"

Mohaareb. An enemy of Allah. That meant they were going to execute me.

"Farewell, sister," Khalkhali said.

With one of his guards in front and Skunk bringing up the rear, I was escorted from his office.

"Somebody bring me some kabob!" were the last words I heard from Khomeini's Angel of Death.

I was marched down the hall to another office, feeling heartsick. My captors had not bothered to once again blindfold me. I guess they figured, what was the point? I was soon going to be dead.

"Mohaareb. Haji Agha Khalkhali's order!" the guard announced as he handed my file to the mullah in this new office. The guard then told Skunk, "You stay here to help Brother Zabihi. He will tell you what to do."

I watched this mullah, who was evidently named Zabihi, flip through the pages of my file. He was thin, with a reddish-brown beard, and wore a black turban.

Just please kill me as painlessly as possible, I pleaded silently. Please just make it be over with. I began to weep.

Zabihi gazed at me, and then turned to Skunk. "What's your name, brother?"

"Pasdar Zaki, Your Holiness," Skunk cried, standing at attention.

"Why don't you go to *sofreh-khaneh* and get yourself something to eat," Zabihi suggested. Today there's both beef and chicken kabob. I will send for you when I need you."

"Yes, brother." Skunk eyed me as he left the office, his expression a mix of pity and disdain.

The mullah waited until Skunk had shut the door behind him, and then asked, "Are you related to Dr. Aria Omid?"

"Yes. I'm his daughter."

"Allah Akbar!" Zabihi stood and went to the window. "How in the name of Allah can I kill the child of someone who has saved my child's life?" he said with his back to me.

I was breathless. He knew Pedar!

The mullah returned to his desk and sat. "Have you eaten?"

The condemned's final meal, I wondered? I shook my head.

"Brother Ghasem!" he called. The door of an adjacent office opened and another one of these bearded brothers stood in the doorway.

"Go get me some food!" Zabihi ordered.

After this brother rushed to do his bidding, the mullah turned to me. "When my daughter was five years old, your father saved her life…"

He told me what had happened, how his child had suffered a late-night fever, how she was unable to breathe, and how the frantic call to my father—who had come instantly and had administered medicine—had restored her health.

Brother Ghasem, returning with a tray of kabob and rice, interrupted Zabihi's story.

"Anything else, Brother Zabihi?" Ghasem asked.

"No. Leave us."

Once the guard was gone, Zabihi pushed the tray toward me. "Eat peacefully. I will not harm you, but I warn you. Once I've sent you back to your prison, if you say a word to anybody—and I mean anybody, including your father—about having met me, you will be executed. And likely, so will I be killed.

My relief fueled my appetite. Ravenous, I devoured the food as I watched Zabihi tear pages out of my file and stuff the folded sheets into his pockets.

"I am removing everything connecting you to General Omid—and your father—because they would go after him next."

"Thank you, Brother Zabihi," I said, my voice quivering.

I wish I could help you more," he said. "Alas, I don't have the power to give you back your freedom."

"Thank you for sparing my life!"

"Brother Ghasem!" the mullah yelled.

When the assistant once again appeared, Zabihi handed him my folder. "Put this in the dead file and fetch me Brother Zaki from the sofreh-khaneh."

Zabihi and I sat together quietly for a few moments until Skunk returned.

"Pull up a chair and sit next to this sister here," Zabihi instructed my guard. "Now, Brother Zaki. When you were away, Haji Agha Khalkhali came in and said this sister of ours was not related to General Omid, after all. So, take her back to her cell, and in time, she will be tried for whatever she's done in accordance with Islamic justice."

"Of course." Skunk smiled—yes, he smiled—then turned to me. "Let's go, Sister Zahra." He gestured me toward the door.

As he was taking me back to my cell, Skunk was vividly in a celebrative mood. Why not? I thought. After all, he had gotten back his dance partner, or maybe his sex slave.

I was never so grateful to be blindfolded. It meant that I was going to live! And I swear that I think even Skunk was relieved that I was not going to be executed. He seemed to demonstrate a rare gentleness as he led me back to my cell, where he removed my blindfold and left, locking the door behind him.

The adrenalin was still coursing through me over my near-death experience at the hands of my fundamentalist captors. To try to calm myself, I sat cross-legged on my cot and resumed writing my story…

CHAPTER 17

For the two days before my lunch date with Cyrus, I was torn about whether or not to cancel. In the meantime, my parents were nagging me about why I did not call Amir. I was so confused. One thing I knew for sure was that I would never marry the chosen one. On the other hand, the stakes of going out with Cyrus went far beyond the personal. Islamic fervor on the rise—never had I seen so many women suddenly adopting the veil in Tehran—and I was concerned about the physical risk in being seen in public with a man who was not my father, brother, or husband.

When I confided my worries to the woman who had become my best friend in the office, Farnaz, she agreed with me. "Before this revolutionary mess," Farnaz said, "no one cared who had lunch with whom. Now, you don't know whom you can trust, Leila," she cautioned. "Take Cyrus's driver, Nabi. Like so many of these losers, he's become a radical Muslim overnight."

But despite Farnaz's advice, I told her that I had made up my mind to go. On the day of our appointment, Cyrus called to say that he was at a meeting in a client's office and that he would appreciate it if we could have a late lunch at about three-thirty. I spent the next couple of hours reliving memories of my past with Cyrus, beginning with the day I had first seen him lecturing to the day I awoke in that hospital bed to see him sitting next to me...At three-thirty, Cyrus came down from his office in heaven to escort me to lunch. We walked side by side, out of the office and into the backseat of his limo, with Nabi behind the wheel.

"We are going to ChetNick's," Cyrus instructed his driver

"*Baleh ghorban*"—yes, sir. As Nabi glanced at us in his rear-view mirror, I could not help but notice the disapproving look in his dark eyes.

We drove along Persepolis Street and turned north on Roosevelt. Lining the curbs on both sides of the road were masses of demonstrators who threw their fists into the air as they shouted, "Death to the Shah, America, Zionists, Israel—and long live Khomeini."

"What do you think will happen, Agha?" Nabi asked Cyrus.

"I don't know, Nabi. Please keep your eyes on the road."

"I wonder if this is a good idea," I whispered to Cyrus. "I mean—"

"I quite agree with you. We have a major problem at Global Batteries," he said, loudly interrupting me, clearly playacting to appease Nabi. "From what Ali has told me..." Cyrus went on talking nonsense until we arrived at the restaurant.

As we entered ChetNick's I remarked to Cyrus that it looked like a high-end American restaurant in, say, California.

"That's because it's owned by these two American guys, named Chet and Nick," Cyrus explained as we were led to our large corner table.

"Do you still have Chateau Sigalas Rabaud, Jasmin?" Cyrus asked our waiter.

"Yes, sir, we do. Nineteen sixty-nine."

"Bring us a bottle, please."

I waited for an endless few minutes for Cyrus to begin to talk, but when he did, he asked, "So, how's everything?"

Trying hard to hold back my rage and sound calm, I said, "Cyrus, I understand many years have gone by. Things have changed. You are married. I have a future ahead of me. But what I'm curious to know is why you dumped me."

"I didn't dump you!" he exclaimed.

Heads turned in the restaurant in response to his outburst. Some, those who obviously knew Cyrus because of his position, smiled.

"OK," he said, lowering his voice. "Trust me, I don't want to dramatize, but you did hurt me so badly with your anti-Semitic remark that my fury surpassed my feelings for you. It is not the religion, it's the fact that when you have been born, raised and suffered intense discrimination in the cradle of prejudice, when someone you adore addresses you as 'You Jews,' in America of all places for crying out loud, these words cut into your heart. I don't remember where I heard or read this, but prejudice, Leila jaan, begins when you categorize people in groups. The moment you open your mouth and address someone as 'You Muslims' or 'You Jews,' you have revealed your inherent prejudice."

I had completely forgotten how Cyrus could eloquently rationalize his logical convictions.

"I fully understand your rage," I replied. "But I hoped that as an adult, after a while, you would realize how upset I was and that maybe I wasn't thinking straight when I..."

"You are right." He sighed, his head down while he played with his fork. "It took me a very long time to realize this, and once I did, I tried to reach you—first from New York and then from here, but you were gone. Then I called Hamid, my friend and former roommate in Los Angeles, who told me you had moved from your previous address.

"And then, perhaps to take your revenge, you began sleeping with people's wives."

"What are you talking about?" he exclaimed.

"Does the name Piran ring a bell?"

"How do you know about Piran and what has he got to do with you and me?" Cyrus asked, looking confused. "I mean, Piran, may he rest in peace, was married to my cousin…"

My jaw fell open. "Your what?"

"My cousin. Bita is my cousin. Like you and Bijan are cousins."

The waiter returned with our wine and went through the rigmarole of opening it and pouring a bit for Cyrus to taste and approve, which he did.

Once our wine had been poured and the waiter had again retreated, Cyrus asked, "What's Bita got to do with you and me?"

Thank goodness he forgot about my source of information.

"Tell me about the events that led up to her husband's death," I said. "And then I will explain."

"All right. In 1974, about a month after I had moved to New York, Bita, who had just finished high school, was sent by her parents to the city to study. Naturally, her family asked me to look out for her, but it turned out that Bita didn't belong in America. She was terribly homesick for everything Persian: food, culture, and so on. She was weeping all the time, pleading with me to arrange for her return home. Well, to make a long story short, her family arranged for her to be married to Piran, a guy older than her father, who'd made his fortune as a rare carpets dealer. It was not a good marriage, to say the least. The final straw was that it turned out this fellow Piran had become prematurely senile. He began having delusions. For example, he forgot that Bita and I were cousins and accused us of having an affair. Bita filed for divorce and Piran killed himself. That's that."

"I had no idea," I stammered. "I'm sorry."

"Why would you be sorry?" Cyrus asked. Then his blue eyes widened. "Wait a minute. Don't tell me that you had suspected that Bita and I were…Jesus, Leila!"

"I didn't know she was your cousin, Cyrus! Not that I don't believe you, but one wonders why you ran away back to Iran in the middle of this tragedy."

"Because my father had suffered a major stroke, and I had to return within a day. I lost him the day after I arrived in Tehran."

"I'm so sorry, Cyrus," I whispered. "Oh man," I breathed. "I guess I jumped to conclusions, Cyrus. I thought…"

Cyrus interrupted me. "You thought wrong, of course, just like with Professor Rossi four years ago."

"What can I say?" I whispered with my head down. I knew if I looked at him and saw anew all that I had lost, I'd burst into tears.

Cyrus gulped down his wine and reached for the bottle to refill our glasses. "Anyway, my father's death was just the tip of the iceberg. As we sat shiva, my mother confessed her own health problems to me. She had leukemia. I took her from one doctor to another, and before I knew it, two weeks had gone by. I knew I couldn't return to America and leave my mother alone. I called my boss and told him that I was stuck here. He arranged for me to join the Tehran office of our firm as a partner until I was ready to return to the States."

Cyrus asked me if I wanted more wine. I'd already had more than enough. In fact, the wine had loosened my tongue so much that I had the gall to ask, "Why don't you tell me about yourself and your lovely wife?"

"My lovely wife," Cyrus repeated, looking sad. "I'm in no mood to talk about it now. I promise I will tell you some other time."

Then he became silent and I knew I had touched a raw nerve. "My apologies," I said. "OK, let's talk about something else. I suggest politics and I will go first. The way I see it," I continued with the same breath, "with the Shah gone, Khomeini will take his place."

He shrugged.

"Forget it then." I sighed. "We might as well go."

"No, no," Cyrus said. "I'm sorry, Leila. What's done is done. I want you to understand that I am not the same person I used to be. I have learned to tolerate prejudice. In fact, I have a much thicker skin now than when I lived in the States. Being called 'you Jews' or even 'you najes Jew' doesn't bother me anymore. I have learned that an epitaph or even a curse doesn't make you a lesser person than you are. So, we can at least salvage our friendship, yes?"

"I'd like that," I said, feeling heartsick over my lack of trust and just plain stupidity.

"So," Cyrus said briskly, "do you think that as Khomeini proceeds to sit on the Shah's throne, America will sit back and watch this happen? Did not the US president Carter pledge his country's backing for the monarchy?"

"What the US wants is no longer relevant," I said. "We are now witnessing a major cataclysmic event in our political history. Didn't you see the people in the street on our way here? To me, it is clear that among those on the street, at the university, and, of course, the mosques, that the Shah's reign is over."

"First of all, they don't allow Jews in the mosques," Cyrus joked. "Seriously, I think the Shah has seen worse days. He fled Iran once before in 1953 and the CIA helped him back to power. I think the West and especially the Americans are still behind the Shah and you underestimate their power to influence events. I'm almost certain that history will repeat itself and the king will return."

"I don't think so."

"Then we have a bet." Cyrus grinned. "If you turn out to be right, I'll owe you."

CHAPTER 18

The day after my lunch with Cyrus, Ali called me to his office to tell me that he was taking me to my next job, Global Batteries.

"They're new clients and are affiliated with a major American corporation," he said. "Their offices are on Karaj Road, about forty-five minutes away from here. And by the way," he added, looking me over, "I approve of your attire."

"Thank you, sir," I tried to put a sarcastic spin on it, but I think it was lost on him. Taking Cyrus's request to heart that I dress more conservatively, I was wearing a long-sleeved white blouse buttoned up to my neck and a dark blue skirt that swirled about my ankles.

Ali signed out one of the firm's cars and together we drove to the office of the new client. The traffic was unusually heavy and the streets were packed with demonstrators. I asked Ali if he knew what was going on.

"You mean you don't know?" he demanded, staring at me.

"Am I supposed to know?"

"Imam Khomeini is arriving from Paris and people are celebrating," he said markedly disappointed at my ignorance.

"For your benefit, Leila, we will arrive at the client a bit later. It's not often we get the opportunity to see history in the making."

Ali parked the car on Eisenhower Boulevard, and we found a space on the sidewalk among the frenzied crowd. People, determined to enjoy the best possible view of their imam, were perched in the trees and hanging from the lampposts. I had to put my hands over my ears to muffle the incredible roar as the Khomeini's motorcade approached.

"Look, Leila," Ali exclaimed, obviously caught up in the excitement. "There he is!"

I saw Khomeini. He was sitting in the front passenger seat of a Chevy Blazer that was inching along the boulevard. Bearded, armed militiamen were walking along both sides of the vehicle shouting revolutionary slogans that were drowned out by the tumult from the crowd. The Blazer came to a stop directly in front of me and Khomeini's eyes locked with mine. Then he frowned. As Khomeini glared at me, he said something to somebody in the Blazer with him.

"Wear a chador, you indecent woman!" I heard behind me, as I was jostled by a man who had noticed the way Khomeini was scowling. Other men around me began to mutter their disapproval of the way I looked. Frightened, I hurried back to our car and huddled inside.

When Ali came back, he was keyed up. "It's the beginning of a new era," he said as he started the car and we took our place in the clogged traffic.

"Are you telling me that this mullah has become your Lenin?"

"No," he said. "We'll let Khomeini and his gunmen do the dirty work, and before you know it, we communists will take over and establish The People's Republic of Iran."

"Easy as that, huh, Ali?"

He smirked at me. "As a person coming from a rich family, I guess it's hard for you to comprehend the joy of these people who have suffered so much under the rule of the tyrant Shah."

I was still upset by the way I'd been accosted on the sidewalk while watching the motorcade. There I'd been, wearing my most conservative outfit, and I'd still drawn the rough criticism of those men. What was happening to my country?

The traffic was still bad. Ali squirmed in his seat, seemingly uncomfortable with my silence.

"You see that factory on your right? A few years ago, a filthy rich industrialist set up this factory to manufacture underwear and lingerie, but he couldn't make it profitable and he went bust."

I was aching to ask him why another person's financial failure pleased him, but my fear had transformed itself to anger over the way I'd been criticized by those cretins worshipping Khomeini. How was Ali any different from those men? I couldn't get back at them, but I did have a target at hand.

"You're right. Who needs underwear?" I said indifferently.

"What?" Ali turned and looked at me curiously.

"Keep your eyes on the road, please."

"You mean…"

I nodded giving him a narrow smile, implying—falsely, of course—that I didn't wear any underwear.

He sat up straight, reached in his pocket for his cigarettes, and lit one. "You just won't give up, will you?"

"Give up what? You said yourself that you approved of my attire."

"This is the most stupid conversation I have ever had in my life," he fumed.

He was so annoyed, which made me so pleased.

CHAPTER 19

April 9, 1980

Since the Khalkhali interrogation ten days ago, there has been a significant change in Skunk's behavior toward me. I do believe that he was relieved that I was not executed! Of course, he gave himself credit for saving my life.

"You were saved because of this brother," he said patting his chest.

And so I continually express my gratitude to my savior. After all, as long as he is busy talking, I am protected from his advances.

This morning Skunk came in carrying a plastic bag. He sat down on my cot and began taking out containers of *adas-polo,* steamed rice and lentils; dates; and other foods traditionally served at a time of mourning. I noticed his small eyes looked gloomy.

"Anything the matter, Brother Zaki?" I asked.

He nodded despairingly as he zipped down his jacket, showing his bloodstained shirt.

"Who did this to you?" I winced.

"*Baradaram*"—my brother—he moaned

"Your brother?"

"*Monafeghin,* these anti-Allah traitors, killed my brother, Zahir, because he was a pasdar loyal to our Imam."

Now I knew the reason for his injury. It was tradition for a Muslim such as Zaki to cut himself on the occasion of a sibling's death.

Of course, by Monafeghin, Skunk was referring to the Mojahedin.

"I'm so sorry, Brother Zaki. I didn't know you had a brother," I said in a low voice.

"I did have one, but not anymore," he said. "He has left a young wife and three little children. What am I to do?" said Skunk, offering me the container of dates. "Eat and pray for his soul."

"*Enna le-Allah va enna elihe raajoon*"—We are from Allah and to Him we shall return—I recited before I ate the sweet date.

And I couldn't help thinking that here we were, jailer and prisoner, both suffering in the political and cultural maelstrom that had become Iran.

• • •

About a week after I'd started working at Global Batteries, I got a call from Cyrus. "You won our bet," he said. "Khomeini has arrived triumphant. I owe you. What shall be your payment, my dear? How about another lunch, to start?"

"I never accepted the bet, Cyrus, and no. This is not right."

"Lunch...only...please..." he pleaded.

I was sure he could hear me panting on his end of the phone. "OK," I said, ignoring repeated calls from Amir and resumed pressure from my parents to go out with him. "Where and when?"

"Your wish is my command, says your genie," Cyrus replied. "How's this coming Friday?"

Iran, like all Islamic countries, held Friday as a weekend holiday. I had to wonder how and why this man, who was my boss and who had been my boyfriend, but was now married, could contemplate spending that weekend holiday with me.

"Friday, Cyrus? Are you going to mention to your wife that we're having lunch?"

"There's a lot I want to share with you, especially about my marriage," he replied. "Please let's just get together, Leila."

"Will you answer the question, please," I insisted calmly. I was not going to lose my temper, but I was going to keep control of the situation and make it clear to Cyrus that while we had had a relationship in the past, I was not interested in any funny business with married men.

"My marriage has been over for some time," Cyrus said.

"It's over? What do you mean?" I hated how my heart, involuntarily swelling with love, was fluttering like a caged bird.

"Let's have lunch this Friday, and I will tell you everything."

On Friday, I showed up a half hour late at ChetNick's. "I'm so sorry," I said as he stood up and hugged me. "On my way here, I got caught in terrible traffic due to the demonstrations."

I was referring to dueling mobs in support of Bakhtiar, who had been appointed prime minister by the Shah before he escaped Iran, and Bazargan, Khomeini's appointee. Cyrus said that he had heard the news of the demonstrations on the radio and had driven there from the back streets.

"You were well informed, as usual," I said as we sat down.

"And you're as gorgeous as ever." He smiled at me.

I couldn't help being pleased by his compliment. I'd dressed as stylishly as possible for this meeting in a modest black skirt and high-buttoned blazer, taking into account the reality that more and more men on the street were taking it upon themselves to publicly chastise women in Western garb. The women I knew who hadn't acquiesced by wearing the veil were feeling the fear of God whenever they went out in public—no pun intended.

I looked at the cover of the menu in front of me on the table. It read Farhad Kabob House.

"What's going on?" I asked Cyrus, tapping the menu.

He shrugged. "While I was waiting for you, I found out that the Americans who owned this place decided it was time to go. They sold it to this Iranian guy who has turned it into a kabob place. And here comes the new owner."

A short, heavyset, bearded man in a dingy gray suit and green shirt with no tie approached our table. "What can I get you, brother?"

"Excuse me," Cyrus objected. "You ask the lady first, then me."

Before the man had a chance to address me, I said, "Chicken with rice and a ginger ale, please," and handed him the menu.

"I'll have the same," Cyrus said.

As the owner went away, I remarked, "I'm surprised he would even serve us. I mean a man and a woman eating lunch together."

"Before you arrived I said I was meeting my wife," Cyrus explained.

"You wish," I muttered.

"Pardon?"

"Nothing," I presented him with an icy smile. "Cyrus, you were going to tell me about your marriage?"

Before he could reply, our attention was captured by the spectacle of two men grappling with each other just outside the restaurant's windows. I flinched, shrinking back in my chair as they exchanged blows.

"Take it easy," Cyrus said, soothing me. "You're safe here."

"I'm not interested in getting hit in the head with another brick," I said, as several revolutionary guards arrived to hustle away the brawlers.

"Chicken kabob for our brother," the owner announced, sitting one dish in front of Cyrus, "and another one for our sister, and two bottles of Coke."

We'd ordered ginger ales, but never mind. "I hate it when these idiots call me sister," I complained after the man left.

"What is there to like about a religious, autocratic government that has put our country in reverse gear?" Cyrus asked. "I only wish they would disappear."

"As I told you, I believe that they are unfortunately here to stay. Now, tell me about your marriage."

"I've explained to you how I so abruptly returned to Iran due to my father's stroke," Cyrus began. "And how after his death, I learned my mother was ill with cancer. As I escorted her to doctors and the like, it wasn't long before she began getting after me about not being married and presenting her with grandchildren."

I wanted to say something in my own defense, but what? The truth was that for the second time, I'd let my doubts about Cyrus get the better of me, and for the second time,

I had misjudged the situation. How could I blame him for picking up the bits and pieces and carrying on?

Just then, the waiter-owner appeared and asked if everything was OK.

"Any *mey*, brother?" Cyrus asked.

I was shocked to hear Cyrus ask for alcoholic drinks. Then he showed the restaurant proprietor a hundred *toman* note.

The owner looked around to make sure no one was eavesdropping and then whispered, "This will buy only two shots of whiskey."

"That's fine," Cyrus said. "Get us the two."

The owner grabbed the note and disappeared into the kitchen.

"I can't believe this," I said. "Where does he get the booze from?"

"Mainly from the revolutionary guards who rampage major hotels and restaurants, break a few bottles in front of the cameras, and sell the rest to guys like him."

"And they serve it openly?"

"Of course not," Cyrus scoffed. "The booze will come in coffee mugs. You'll see."

I nodded, and then took a deep breath. "So! How did you meet your wife?"

"My aunt introduced me to her," he said. "It was on a bad day for my mother. We were coming back from the oncologist who had given her a poor prognosis: she had less than a year to live. As we returned to my mother's home, there was my aunt waiting for us so as to arrange my blind date with a young woman named Roxie, the daughter of a widowed businessman. I wasn't going to accept this invitation. My heart was set on finding you, Leila, and I told both my aunt and mother as much. My aunt replied, 'You want to go back to America so badly! Why? This country is where you belong!' And then my mother said it would make her happy if I went on the date. Given the circumstances…" he trailed off.

"Of course you would do this trifling thing to please your dying mother," I reassured Cyrus. "I totally understand."

The restaurant proprietor returned with our whiskies in coffee mugs, just as Cyrus had predicted.

"So you went on your blind date with your Roxie, and I guess you hit it off," I offered. "I'm not surprised she scooped you up, Cyrus. You are a catch, you know."

I'd expected him to laugh off my compliment, but it was as if he hadn't even heard it.

"Leila, there was no attraction between Roxie and me."

The same here, I mused as I thought of Amir.

"She is a beautiful woman." Cyrus continued. "Actually, Leila, to be honest with you, I mean…" he paused and took a sip of his whiskey. "I don't know how to put this to you. Here, my sister could take care of our mom in my absence. But she wasn't what kept me in Iran. It was you."

"Me?" I echoed. "I don't understand."

"The thought of being back in America without you was a nightmare," Cyrus replied. "At least here in Iran every sight didn't remind me of you. The months passed, the emotional devastation I was feeling watching my mother fade before my eyes was unbearable. I took comfort in my relationship with Roxie, and, as it grew more serious, and as my time without you grew longer and longer, I felt myself taking root here. A day came when I was at my mother's bedside, helping her to eat, and she said to me, 'I want to see you married before I die.' And I thought to myself, why not? It's not like I'll ever find anyone like Leila again."

The way Cyrus was positioning all this—like I had caused him to marry—angered me. It was as if he was begging for sympathy for a calamity that he had caused himself.

"I understand the pain of losing me, then losing your father, and then dealing with your mother's ailment," I said. "But to allow yourself to be pushed into what was essentially an arranged marriage doesn't make any sense to me."

"You have no right to talk to me that way," he said. "You had taken yourself out of my life, and Roxie said she loved me. I suppose I loved her in a way."

Cyrus must have read the anguish in my eyes because he hurriedly said, "Not the way I loved you, Leila." He shrugged helplessly. "I don't want to play the blame game here. The fact of the matter was that you were gone, Roxie was here, and my mother had expressed her devout wish to see me married in what was to be the last winter of her life. Did I marry Roxie partly due to my mother's wishes? Perhaps. But I won't deny that another part of me longed to be married and settled so as to help me make peace with the fact that you were gone." Cyrus looked at his watch. "Leila, I have to go. I have a meeting."

"I still have to hear how your marriage came apart."

"Another day," Cyrus replied, signaling for the check. "Next Friday, perhaps? Same time, same place?"

"OK. For lunch. But not here. I'm tired of kabob places," I said. "It's hard to get used to the fact that this is no longer the Shah's Tehran."

"Leave it to me," Cyrus said with a wink.

CHAPTER 20

April 15, 1980

Day seventy-five of my incarceration. Due to his brother's sad murder, Skunk has been in a somber mood for the last few days. "How do I know that I'm not the next on their murder list, Sister Zahra?" he asked me this morning.

Better to be his confidant than the target of his animal instincts, I thought. "As you have taught me," I said, waving a bundle of papers I kept handy with some notes of his so-called sermons, "Allah is the protector of all believers. As for your martyr brother, he is resting in paradise with many virgins, drinking heavenly wine. And as for his children, they will be shielded by Allah and protected by you, their loving uncle."

Skunk nodded appreciatively, but he still looked scared that he was on the Mojahedin's hit list.

• • •

The following Friday, Cyrus took me for our lunch date to a little-known, European-style restaurant run out of a converted town house.

"Brigitte, the owner, is French, and her chef is excellent," Cyrus told me. "But what seals the deal is that she still has some good old French wine that she serves to the customers she knows."

"In coffee mugs, of course," I said.

"Nothing's perfect anymore, my dear," Cyrus said.

As we were seated in the restaurant, the owner offered us some of her "special coffee."

"I have a bottle of Monsieur Cyrus's favorite Chateau," she said.

"We must have this, Leila," Cyrus said, and when I nodded, he ordered it.

Brigitte bowed and walked away.

"That woman has a lot of guts," I said under my breath.

"She does, but she is well connected. Her Iranian husband is a graduate of Sorbonne University and a top official in the Atomic Energy Organization who has pledged loyalty to Khomeini."

After the "coffees" and the lunch order—sole with lemon, capers, and almonds, as Cyrus recommended—we talked idly about the CISNU students we knew who were now populating key government posts. We also talked about what was happening in the office. We even talked about the weather.

I raised my cup of wine and said, *"Salamati!"*—to your health—I took a sip, and then asked Cyrus to tell me what had happened to his marriage.

"I married Roxie in late February 1977, six months after I had first met her. I was determined to make it work, but before long, what little spark we had was extinguished. I traveled in my circles and Roxie in hers."

"And you had no children?"

Our food arrived. Cyrus, his brow furrowed, was quiet until our waiter had departed.

"In the beginning we tried, Leila. But it turned out Roxie couldn't have children."

I took a bite of my lunch. It was delicious, but I had no appetite listening to this sad story. I felt so sorry for Cyrus and his wife! For a woman to be barren was difficult enough emotionally. But in Iranian society, for a woman to be unable to have children was publicly shameful and humiliating as well as personally and emotionally devastating.

"I guess you and Roxie have come to this restaurant often," I said, hoping to change the subject. I wanted to hear more about the marriage, but this aspect of it was just too painfully intimate.

"Never," Cyrus said. "Foreign food was not for her. She was quite provincially Iranian, you see. Anyway, my mother died a few months before my first anniversary."

"I'm sorry."

Cyrus smiled and nodded his thanks. "*Raahat shod*"—she went in peace. As for the rest of the story about Roxie and me, it's quite mundane and clichéd. First, we stopped sleeping together; then we stopped talking; and one morning, coming from our separate bedrooms to stare at each other across the breakfast table, we both knew at the same instant that our marriage was over. Our breakup was quite amiable and pleasant, actually." Cyrus ruefully chuckled. "Our divorce was as passionless as all the other phases of our relationship."

CHAPTER 21

April 24, 1980

Day eighty-four on my jail calendar. In the past two weeks, Skunk's mourning over the loss of his brother has faded. This morning, he came into my cell with a triumphant swagger.

"Today, Sister Zahra, Allah gave that stupid President Carter of America the lesson of his life!" Skunk crowed. "The Americans sent helicopters to rescue their hostages in the embassy, but the hand of Allah created a storm in the desert that crushed their helicopters and killed their soldiers."

"A joyous day, indeed, brother," I said, agreeing dutifully.

"Remember His Holiness Khalkhali?"

How could I forget the man who'd sentenced me to death, I thought.

"Allah Akbar!" Skunk continued. "You should have seen His Holiness on the television!"

"What did he say?"

"Sister! Not just what he said but what he did!" Skunk smiled. "His Holiness stuck his bayonet into the burned bodies of those dead Americans around their burned helicopters and proclaimed, 'This is the destiny of all those who dare face up to the government of Allah on the earth!'"

I felt sad over the fact that the Americans had failed to rescue their hostages. I truly wished them their freedom, even if my own freedom was long gone.

"I know you think I'm a bad person, Sister Zahra. But I'm really a good person," Skunk abruptly declared, startling me out of my gloom. Where the hell did that come from?

"I'm sure you are a good person, Brother Zaki," I responded calmly.

"Are you?" Skunk looked at me distrustfully.

"Yes I am. I'm certain you are a very nice person who's truthfully seeking to aid me in my salvation."

He nodded, indicating his pleasure at my compliment, and was about to leave when an idea unprecedented in its audacity struck me. The odds were one in a million it would work, but what did I have to lose? I mustered my courage and said, "Brother, it is because you are so good and kind that I'm sure you will do me this favor."

"What?" he asked as he turned around.

Wasting no time, I quickly wrote my father's phone number on a piece of paper and put it into his hand, then folded his fingers over it, and held his hand firmly in mine as I knelt in front of him.

"I beg of you." I pretended to weep, turning on the tears for his satisfaction. "Please call my father at this number and only tell him that I am alive! You don't need to tell him anything about my whereabouts. Just tell him that I'm in your safe hands. That's all! May the God of Mohammed and Ali and all the sacred prophets and messengers of Allah protect you, your family, and all those who are dear to you!"

I abruptly realized I was truly sobbing, no acting needed, as the enormity of what I was asking, and the possible positive ramifications of establishing contact with my wealthy and powerful father hit home.

"I beg you, Brother Zaki. Please don't say no to me. I promise I will be a good Muslim woman. Please!"

He was staring down at me in distrust, yet extremely satisfied to see me kneeling on the floor and begging him.

"Give me one good reason why I should do this for you?"

"Because it is not my parents' fault that I have ended up here. Like you, they are good Muslims who at least deserve to know that their daughter is alive."

I kissed his hand, which I was still holding tightly. "You are a good person, as you said yourself. You are a man of God. You are the cause of my salvation. Because of your teachings, Allah willing, I will be a better woman."

"You are not answering my question," he raised his voice. "What is in this for me? *Kari ya khari*?"—Are you deaf or are you a donkey?—"What do I get from your father for doing this?"

My goodness, Skunk was asking for money! What an idiot I had been so far. I wanted to punch myself. Why had I not appealed to his sense of greed from the very beginning?

"Whatever you say you want, my father will pay, Brother Zaki. He will be so generous. I swear to you he will!"

He jerked his hand out of mine and thoughtfully stroked his beard. "I will think about it."

• • •

In early May 1979, I was between assignments at the firm. I spent my days at my desk, reading the newspapers concerning what was happening in Iran now that Bakhtiar, the last of the Shah's prime ministers, had fled the country, allowing Khomeini to tighten his grip as the ruler of the newly christened "Islamic Republic of Iran."

In the meantime, to my utter dismay, Amir was still in my life. To keep everyone happy, I had dinner with him a couple of times and continued to regret stringing him along. These two men in my life were worlds apart. How I looked forward to my dates with Cyrus...and how I dreaded getting together with Amir just to keep my parents happy.

Eventually I was assigned to bookkeeping job at Persian Petrochemical Industries in the southern part of the country. I objected to the menial nature of the assignment, arguing that I hadn't become a CPA to spend my days balancing ledgers, but my superiors were adamant.

"Don't try to appeal to Cyrus," said Ali. "First, he knows about this assignment. And second, he left for Europe on a business trip."

I said nothing, stung that Ali knew more about Cyrus's schedule than I did. But what right did I have to be angry? Just because Cyrus was divorced from his wife and I happened to still love him didn't make him once again mine. I flew to the main office of Persian Petrochemical Industries in Abadan, a city in southwestern Iran, feeling uncertain about my future at the firm as well as my relationship with Cyrus. After two weeks of being bored out of my mind doing work that should have been assigned to a junior bookkeeper, I made up my mind that whatever the future held for me in terms of my personal relationship with Cyrus, I was going to resign from the firm.

I called the main office in Tehran every day to check on Cyrus's itinerary. The day I learned he was returning from his travels, I booked my flight and, disregarding my manager's objections, walked out of PPI.

From Tehran airport, I went straight to the office. All through my flight back, I had pledged to myself I would remain calm, but of course, as soon I arrived at the office, my emotions got the better of me. I stormed past Cyrus's secretary on my way into his office.

"Leila!" she admonished me. "You can't just barge in without an appointment!" She followed me in, protesting all the way.

"It's OK," Cyrus said, obviously shocked to see me. "Leila and I have an appointment. I forgot to tell you."

The secretary nodded and closed the door behind her. Cyrus, looking pale, stood facing me. "What are you doing here?" he asked. "I thought they had sent you to PPI?"

"They sent me to PPI? They?" I cried.

"Please lower your voice, will you?" Cyrus motioned me to the chair in front of his desk. "Sit down, please, and I will explain."

"You'd better have a good explanation, or I will resign," I said as I sat down. "Why did you exile me to the South?"

"Really, I don't know what you are talking about, Leila."

"After all this time, I know when you're lying to me," I shot back. "Your eyes betray you. I mean, if I had done something to upset you, why didn't you tell me? Why aren't you telling me now?"

"Leila, you're making too much out of this. The firm has clients throughout this country and—"

"And you send a CPA to do the work of a bookkeeper?" I demanded. "Tell me the truth, please,"

Cyrus shrugged and smiled. "No matter how hard I try, I can't hide anything from you." His eyes were as bright as blue bulbs in a disco. "I will tell you what happened if you promise to be honest with me."

"Honest about what?"

"Do you promise?" Cyrus insisted.

"OK, OK, I promise," I said impatiently. "Now tell me what's going on."

"Very well," Cyrus said. "The day after you'd finished working at Global Batteries, Farid came to my office to tell me that Ali had requested that you be transferred out of his group."

"Why?" I said, surprised. "I admit Ali and I are like oil and water together outside of work matters, but I have always respected his professional capabilities. I also thought he respected me as a professional."

"Leila, Ali accused you of making sexual advances toward him."

"What?" I cried, appalled. "That's ridiculous on so many different levels I don't know where to begin!"

"All I know is what Farid told me," Cyrus said.

"And you believed this nonsense?"

Cyrus looked down at his desk, once again blushing.

"Oh my God," I whispered. "You were jealous..."

I couldn't help it. I started to laugh. A moment later, Cyrus began to laugh as well.

"What can I say?" Cyrus began. "The very thought of my adorable Leila coming onto another man was like a knife in my chest. Are you OK, Leila? You suddenly don't look well."

I lied. "I'm fine. Just tired from my travel."

I wanted to throw myself across his desk and kiss him madly, showing him once and for all that I belonged to him in heart and soul, but I couldn't bring myself to let down my guard. So much had happened between us already. Twice I had doubted his love for me groundlessly; nonetheless, it was how I'd felt at the time. Now I needed Cyrus to somehow irrefutably prove to me that I was the only woman in the world for him. Illogical? Perhaps. But who said a woman's heart was or could be ruled by logic?

"Farid was the one who suggested that we send you to PPI," Cyrus was saying. "I agreed, thinking it would buy me some time to come to terms with the fact that I wasn't the man in your life any longer."

"But you had to be mad to think that Ali and I..." I shook my head, unable to even finish the sentence.

"No, I knew you wouldn't be—couldn't be—involved with Ali," Cyrus said. "However, I did need to deal with the possibility, or maybe the inevitability, that from your point of view, we were now merely friends, nothing more."

"You know what?" I began to scold him. "I'm more disappointed at your bad choice of imaginary lovers for me than your mind-boggling stupidity in punishing me for your neurotic insecurities by sending me to that godforsaken assignment in the South. Ali, for crying out loud? What in your wildest imagination—"

"I have never stopped loving you." Cyrus's eyes, so blazing and blue, cut through me like twin jets of fire.

There! He's said it! Is that enough for you?

No!

I didn't know why it wasn't enough. I only knew that I yearned for more than mere words. I needed him to prove his love. Too bad there weren't still dragons roaming the earth. If there were, I could send forth Cyrus to slay me one, and then maybe I could strip away my emotional armor and surrender my heart.

"I think you are in love with the idea of love, which was so tragically denied to you in your failed marriage," I said. "And maybe you are in love with the Leila you knew. But I'm not convinced you love me—or even really and truly know me—as the woman I've become."

"I see," Cyrus said ruefully. "Not only do I have to climb a mountain to reach you, you deny me the use of a rope. But you agree to give me the time to convince you?"

"Your time is yours to spend how you like," I said evenly, but I couldn't suppress my smile. I did so adore Cyrus. Was it simply the minx in me that was making me play hard to get?

"Just the way you flirt with me is enough to set my heart pounding," Cyrus said thickly.

Yes, of course I was flirting, but I truly needed Cyrus to prove to me beyond a shadow of a doubt that as far as he was concerned, I was the only woman in the world.

"I will tell Farid that I ordered your return from your assignment in the South," Cyrus said. "Now, go home and rest."

CHAPTER 22

May 9, 1980

Two weeks ago I gave Skunk my father's number and begged the guard to contact him, but the moment he came to my cell this morning, I knew something had gone wrong.

"Salam, Brother Zaki," I muttered quivering.

Skunk slammed the door behind him, locked it, and glowered at me.

"Your father is a *kooni*."—a faggot—"Your mother is a whore. So are you!"

"Wait, Brother Zaki. Stop and tell me what has happened."

"This ass-torn kooni who is your father," Skunk said, his voice rising to a shout. "He doesn't believe me. Who does this *madar jendeh*"—mother whore—"think he is?"

"Please calm down, brother," I said to soothe him, careful to keep my distance as much as possible in the tiny cell, in case he lashed out at me physically. "I apologize for any disrespect my father showed you. Just, please, tell me what happened."

"That kooni father of yours must think that his Shah is still around and I am the garbageman I was. Maybe I should take this"—he took his pistol out of its holster, waved it in the air, and hollered—"and use it to wipe him from the face of the earth! I have a mission, you know. I have to be on the watch for the agents of America who want to steal the precious gift of our revolution."

I murmured agreement throughout his tirade, and when he had tired himself out yelling, I said, "I beg you to start from the beginning so I can understand the source of your righteous anger."

My obsequiousness in the face of his fury had its effect, taming him. I could see his expression transition from anger to the exhaustion of a child post tantrum.

"Well," he sighed. "You begged me to call your father and tell him that you are alive. I wasted my precious time and did so. And what is his answer? 'How can I trust you? Anybody can make such a claim.'" Skunk spat on the floor. "That kooni!"

Stupid me. Why had I not anticipated this? Of course Pedar would naturally suspect that Skunk was merely a con artist out to swindle a grieving parent.

"You have every right to be upset, Brother Zaki," I said. "My father should definitely have believed you."

"You can't begin to understand how angry I am, Sister Zahra!"

"Oh, I do. But let Allah settle the score for you, for, as it has been written, *Va en-Allah shadidan azaab,* which means, Allah is severe in punishment."

Skunk, calmer now, shook his head muttering and headed for the door. I knew I had to think fast. That if I could even convince Skunk to try again with my father, this would definitely be the last time, so whatever I came up with had to be irrefutable proof to Pedar that I was alive and that this man had contact with me. My handwritten note wouldn't do, for it could have been dictated under duress. Mentioning a birthmark was also no satisfactory evidence since it was something apparent. Perhaps an event in the past, I thought, and the answer dawned...Trellis, the secret word Pedar and I had coined to describe our relationship, like the vine to the trellis...

No interrogator, no matter how harsh, would think to probe for a secret word between a father and daughter. My father would have to believe that I had surrendered the word voluntarily—that I had instigated this contact through Skunk!

"I hope you feel better now, Brother Zaki," I called as he was unlocking the door to let himself out.

He nodded.

"Can I say something before you leave?"

"In defense of that kooni?" he demanded.

"No. I want to apologize for my father's misunderstanding of your humanitarian and pious mission. It has all been my fault, because," I murmured with my head down, "as you have said many, many times, I am a woman with half the intelligence of a man. I should have thought of this before. You see, brother. I have a code word with my father. Please, please, call him again and just say the word *trellis.* I promise that, hearing this, he will reward you."

Skunk scratched his head. "Fine, give me his telephone number again and write down your stupid code word."

After I had done so and handed him the scrap he snarled at me, showing his tobacco-stained, brown teeth.

"I will call him today. May Allah have mercy on both of you if he tries to cheat me."

For the next few days, I resisted every impulse to ask Skunk if he had called Pedar. Finally, I could not hold back any more.

"What do you think, Sister? Have I called him or not?" Skunk teased with the sadistic satisfaction of someone who had won a game of patience.

"I hope you have, Brother Zaki," I said in a low voice, keeping my fingers crossed.

Two cigarettes and another long lecture later, he seemed to have forgotten my question. Then, as he was about to leave, he surprised me.

"All right. Today is Friday, Allah's day, the day to make even a miserable, sinful woman like you happy. So, I might call him."

Skunk walked out.

The click of the key as he locked the door of my cell set forth wave after wave of despair in my soul.

CHAPTER 23

It was the last days of May 1979. Khomeini had tightened his grip on Iran, but turmoil still reigned as the self-ruling gangs of revolutionary guards—the country's street trash before the revolution—reveled in their newfound authority and power.

Now that I was back in Tehran and once again working at the main offices of Jenkins Brothers & Associates, I was extraordinarily busy. Filling the vacuum as American companies abandoned the country were European and Japanese corporations. These new enterprises all required CPAs to audit their accounts, and Jenkins Brothers & Associates was still the largest such firm in Iran. Accordingly, Cyrus assigned me to a new client, an Iranian-Japanese joint venture.

What's more, in doing so, he promoted me to a managerial position equivalent to the one that Ali held. At last, I was free of this narrow-minded male chauvinist's managerial clutches!

I worked hard to get a grasp of my new client's business, and the days flew by, only to be interrupted by my parents' pressure for me to marry Amir.

"The poor man has been waiting for you for such a long time, he likes you a lot and you keep him in the air," Pedar complained.

"They are both family and friends," Madar chimed in. "You've told me so many times that you like him. His parents have offered to come for khastegari—to ask for your hand in marriage to their son. Why are you procrastinating, Leila?"

After the time that my father had taken to come to the States to put me together with Amir, and after a long—no matter how boring—relationship with this nice man, I found it so hard to tell my parents that I still loved Cyrus. I kept on procrastinating.

One afternoon, Cyrus called me.

"Dinner this Friday night?" he asked.

"Yes, that would be nice," I replied coolly, playing Little Miss Hard-to-Get.

On Friday, at about five o'clock, Cyrus called me to say that every restaurant he could think of was either closed or not coed.

"You mean even husbands and wives are not allowed to eat at the same table anymore?" I asked.

"Unless they show their marriage certificate," Cyrus grumbled. "I suppose we could dash out and get one."

"Such a romantic marriage proposal, how could I say no?" I paused. "How about this: No! And as to the restaurant situation, mark my words, this is just the tip of the iceberg. Things are going to get much worse. Don't I wish we were in America!" I sighed.

"Well, it's a long flight." He laughed. "Marriage would be so much quicker."

"So, I guess I'll see you in the office tomorrow."

"Wait a minute. Why don't you come over?" Cyrus suggested.

"Bad idea," I replied. "What if we were seen and reported to these revolutionary committees that have popped up all over the place? And, quite honestly, I don't want to give you any wrong ideas. We are colleagues and friends." I elaborately fibbed, as if I were not aware of the romantic tension between us. "Please understand this."

"Understood," he said instantly, clearly as adept at lying as I was. "And don't worry about people seeing you. My house is in a remote area and far apart from my neighbors. Please come," he begged.

"You'll never change, will you?" I said, my tone coquettish.

"Only because I know you don't want me to."

"The same naughty boy you have always been."

I thought it over. I really did want to see him. Perhaps I was overreacting to the potential risk of a clandestine visit.

"OK. Give me the address and I'll be there in an hour or so."

I began going through my closet, trying to decide what to wear to my rendezvous with Cyrus. It was a challenge, given that I was limited to sackcloth by the new Iranian government's ordinances on female attire…

From his exile in Iraq, Khomeini had declared that his mission was to overthrow the Shah and replace him with a democratically elected government. After that, he had said, he would go to his small house in Qom—a city considered as the Iranian Vatican—and live a sequestered life. However, soon after overthrowing the Shah, Khomeini took charge and his cohorts released a set of religious proclamations—including one that stipulated men and women must dress according to Islamic codes. This caused uproar among the Ayatollah's secular women followers who had naively considered him the Gandhi of Iran. Khomeini defended his proclamations—and his misleading earlier comments about the secular nature of the government he'd been advocating—by citing what is known under Shiite laws as *taghieh,* meaning "dissimulation." According to taghieh, you can conceal your convictions and even lie under oath to serve a religious cause.

Meanwhile, under the theory that if you put a frog in cool water and gradually increase the temperature, he won't know he's boiling until it's too late, the Islamic dress code laws had been incrementally imposed upon the female Iranian population. First was prescribed the *roosari,* the hijab-like scarf, to cover the hair. At this point, many women poured into the streets, shouting "First roosari, then *toosari*"—the latter meaning "contempt." They were beaten and disbursed by the revolutionary guards, and that was that for women's resistance. Next, the dress code was heightened. By May 1979, the road had been paved for the next increment: the imposition of baggy outfits along with the headscarves.

And so, as I prepared to leave for Cyrus's house, I wore what had now become a mandatory dress code for women: a headscarf that covered your hair, half of your forehead, your ears and your face, except for your eyes, nose, mouth and chin; a baggy manteau, a tunic overall; and walking shoes—no open-toed shoes or high heels allowed. I glanced in despair at all my lovely dresses that I could no longer wear… in public, at least.

The idea, when it came, made me laugh out loud.

I was going to be a bit late getting to Cyrus, I thought, as I quickly undressed.

Cyrus greeted me at the door of his house wearing a navy blue shirt and black cotton slacks. He was freshly shaved, and his long, damp hair was combed back.

"I know I look like a walking bolt of fabric, but are you not going to invite me in?" I asked, feeling unredeemable in my veiled drabness.

"Ah, Leila," Cyrus sighed. "Until they decree that you must wear a blindfold, no amount of clothing can hide your mesmerizing eyes."

My heart quivered as I took pleasure in how I still held allure for him, even in my shapeless garb.

If you like my eyes, just wait, I gleefully thought.

Cyrus led me through his house to the large back patio with a great view of the city. On the patio table, there was a pair of candelabras with jasmine candles, a bottle of white wine in an ice-filled bucket with two crystal glasses, and a tray of cheeses, crackers, and pistachios.

"I thought we would sit out and have some fresh air, if it is OK with you," he said.

"Sure, and I hope you don't mind if I get a little more comfortable."

I pulled the scarf off my head, shaking loose my thick, dark, shoulder-length hair. Next I peeled off my baggy Islamic drag. Underneath I was wearing a tight blouse unbuttoned to reveal some cleavage and a miniskirt that clung to my hips.

"God, you are so gorgeous," Cyrus marveled.

"Like Khomeini, I subscribe to taghieh law," I said. "I, too, shall in public conceal my convictions and even lie under oath to serve a religious cause, which, in my case, is the religious cause to look like a woman and not like a walking pup tent."

I settled into a comfortable chair on the patio, one that I carefully chose to give Cyrus the best view of my legs. "So, this is your house."

"It is," he answered as he opened the bottle of wine and immediately rested its neck on one of the glasses so that I wouldn't notice his trembling hand. It felt nice indeed to be here with my Cyrus.

He handed me a wine glass, raised his own, and toasted, "Besalamati!"

"To your health," I echoed in English as we touched glasses and drank.

"And to the great times we had together," Cyrus added.

I nodded, pretending to misunderstand what he was getting at and said, "Indeed, I'm here to thank you for the way you've mentored my career."

"Five years and one-hundred forty days," Cyrus said.

"Are you drunk already?" I giggled.

"No, Leila jaan. I'm thinking of January 10, 1974—the day I first saw you—until today. And the chances for happiness that have slipped out of our hands."

His beautiful blue eyes were shiny in the lambent candlelight.

"Oh, Cyrus," I whispered, and my own eyes began to fill as he moved his chair close to mine and took my hand. I didn't resist or pull away. I simply couldn't.

He leaned close and began to kiss me. I threw my arms around him and returned his passion. Suddenly remembering Amir, I pulled back.

"I have to share something with you," I said.

"Can't it wait?" he asked, his eyes so intoxicated.

"No, Cyrus. You have to listen to this."

I told him all about my relationship with Amir that had begun after we had separated and how I was obligated to marry him.

"So, you want to marry him?" Cyrus asked alarmed.

"No."

"Then why don't you tell him?"

"He's such a nice man."

"So you do want to marry him?"

"No I don't!"

"Do you have anyone else in mind?"

Of course I do, you, you idiot! I wanted to scream at him. "Never mind," I sighed as I stood and leaned against the banister on the side of his patio.

That was when he said, "When can I come for khastegari?"

In late May 1979, Cyrus came for dinner to our house, in a navy blue suit, a beige shirt, and a turquoise tie, carrying a dozen roses.

I knew that if Madar had her own way, she would scream at me for choosing Cyrus over Amir—who had promptly found himself another fiancée once I'd informed him that we were through—but Pedar's support shielded me. And now that Cyrus had come to ask for my hand, they had both more or less come around to the idea. I think they were relieved that I was at least prepared to marry somebody.

Actually, Cyrus and my father hit it off immediately, talking politics and what they thought was going to happen to Iran under the rule of mullahs. My mother called me to the kitchen and asked me to help her with basically nothing. "Just lay the dining table," she ordered, and as I got busy, I suddenly realized that she wanted to show off my domestic abilities to Cyrus.

Then, as I was done and about to join Cyrus and my dad, she called again. "Take in the tea." As required by this ancient tradition, the bride-to-be served tea at her khastegari to the prospective groom who, seeing his bride for the first time, would accept or reject her. This was so pathetic that I was not going to do it. Then, on the other hand, it was so hilarious that I thought, why not? It was something for Cyrus and me to laugh about later. I entered with the tray full of teacups, swaggering and throwing my eyebrows up and down as Cyrus tried not to laugh.

After dinner, my mother and Cyrus talked about their ghetto, Jewbareh. They knew a lot of Jewbarites. They drew family trees on the back of paper napkins and kept on discussing them until they found out that somewhere in their linage, many generations ago, they had been relatives. "Can you believe that?" Madar cried.

Then Cyrus stood up and addressed my parents. "As you know, Leila and I have known each other for a long time…"

The bells were ringing and beyond that, all I could hear was Cyrus's beautiful voice until I saw him take a small box out of his pocket. "If I may," he said as he opened the box and took out a golden ring, "I want to ask for the hand of your daughter in marriage."

My mother ululated, signaling her approval, once again according to the tradition. Pedar shook Cyrus's hand and congratulated him. Cyrus put the ring on my hand and we embraced.

Then the reality check followed. My family, and especially my grandfather, the general, hid their Jewish roots.

"So," my father said as he held my hand. "Unless Cyrus wants to convert to Islam, which I suspect none of us want, while you live in Iran you can't be married. God willing you will marry in America. Until then, you must not wear this ring and as far as your mother and I are concerned, you are married."

Cyrus and I agreed. He had already broached the subject of transferring to our firm's New York office, but because of the political situation in Iran, he'd been asked to stay until things settled.

"May I make a suggestion?" my mother pleaded to Cyrus.

"But of course." Cyrus smiled.

"You see, in Judaism, the process of getting married occurs in two stages: *erusim,* which means betrothal and *nisuin,* the marriage ceremony. Since erusim is a religious ceremony in its own right, more binding than an engagement, and once it occurs the woman is considered the wife of the man, why don't we—"

"Excellent idea," Cyrus cried. "I'll be here tomorrow with my rabbi."

Madar ululated again.

Nevertheless, at long last, Cyrus and I were engaged, or as Madar wished, erusimed!

CHAPTER 24

May 15, 1980

One hundred and five days since my incarceration into this black and grimy pit.

It is springtime. I imagine the blossoms garnishing the trees I cannot see flourishing in the world beyond the bars of my cell. I think of my childhood; of being surrounded by my loving family; of how our house cats, during their spring mating, filled the night with their passionate voices; of how our gardens were lush with flowers—roses, Persian jasmines, orchids, daisies, lilies, and so many more…

This morning, as I was writing this, I heard the key turning the lock. I quickly gathered my papers and tucked them underneath my mattress. By the time Skunk came through the door, I was studying the Koran had given me.

"*Befarmaeed*"—come in, please—Skunk said to someone behind him. He led in a man with a sack over his head, carrying a small suitcase.

"Sister Zahra. I have a surprise for you," Skunk said as he lifted the sack off the man's head.

"Pedar!" I screamed as I threw myself in my father's arms, sobbing. I had to be dreaming. This could not be real.

And then I thought—My father in my cell? My God! Has he also been arrested?

I whispered in English, "What are you doing here? Are you a prisoner?"

"No, don't worry. He's been paid. I'm only here as a visitor."

We embraced again, neither of us able to stop crying.

"Your daughter, Sister Zahra, she is learning a lot here," Skunk lectured.

"Who the hell is Zahra," Pedar whispered, again in English.

"Just thank him."

"Thank you, Brother Zaki. I appreciate your kindness. May Allah bless you," my father said, barraging Skunk with the customary Persian compliments.

"I have done what my religion requires," Skunk said pompously, as if he had treated me like a sibling or no bribe money had changed hands. "I leave you now to visit with your daughter, as we arranged."

He went out, locking the door behind him.

Sitting side by side on the cot, for a while, we did not exchange a word—hugs and tears only. Then Pedar spoke, and as was his way, his demeanor was that not of a man sitting with his daughter in a jail, but as though we were sitting in a five-star hotel lobby, sipping aperitifs.

"We have a lot to discuss in a short amount of time, Leila," he said.

"I know I must stink. I'm sorry."

"Don't you dare say that! You are and will always be my jasmine," he said. "But does this Brother Zaki ever stink!" He waved his hand in front of his nose, shook his head, and smiled.

"That's why I call him Skunk."

"Good choice." He laughed.

"Tell me, how is our family?" I begged.

My father filled me in on how they'd all made it to the United States, all except for him, because he was resolute not to leave until he knew my fate.

"Leila, I'm so frightened to ask, but are these fanatical brutes treating you honorably?"

I wasn't going to lie to him. Never had I hidden anything from my parents. Nonetheless, there were things I didn't have to share, like my brush with death in front of Khalkhali at the Central Revolutionary Committee or Skunk's now-and-again attempts to have his way with me. "It is a difficult situation, Father. But so far I have not been physically violated."

He turned his face away, trying to hide his tears, then reached for the small suitcase and opened it. "I thought you might need these." He sniffed.

I might only have brief moments with my father, and I was damned if I was going to ruin our reunion with my lamentations. So, I giggled joyously as he demonstrated the goodies he had brought me: a dress conforming to Islamic propriety, of course; clean underwear; a few soft towels; a bottle of rubbing alcohol; and some dried fruits and nuts.

"By the way, how much did he charge you for this visit?" I asked.

"A thousand dollars—green American dollars, of course—for four hours only," my father replied. "When I asked if I could bring you these few items, his price went up another five hundred. But let's not waste time talking about matters of no consequence, Leila jaan. We must come up with a workable plan to rescue you from this dungeon."

"It won't be easy, Father." I sighed.

"Believe me, we both know it. We have torn our hair out trying to find you, but it remained for my resourceful daughter to find us. You were so clever to offer your guard a bribe to reach out to us."

"Wait," I said. "Who do you mean by 'us'?"

"Why Cyrus, of course. And your cousin, Bijan."

"So Cyrus is still here?" I asked, my heart pounding. I had not let myself dare to think that he…

"Is he still here?" My father chuckled incredulously at my naïvety. "My dear girl, your Cyrus is so much in love with you that he would never leave Iran without you. Bijan also has refused to leave until we knew your situation. Now that we three have found you—or you've found us—we will work on getting you out of here."

"So why don't you negotiate a ransom with Skunk to release me?"

"He's like a powder keg when he talks to me," Pedar replied. "There is an elaborate ruse he goes through with himself concerning how he's allowing me contact with you because he's religiously devout, and not just greedy. I'm afraid of what he might do to you if, in trying to negotiate your release, I say the wrong thing and inadvertently reveal something that might upset him. All I know is that he just wants money."

"No one is a better negotiator than Cyrus," I said. "Let him deal with Skunk. Trust me, he is very good at this sort of thing."

"All right, then, I will," my father assured me.

Pedar told me about what was going on in the outside world, especially in Iran and as for Madar and my brothers, he said that he was in regular contact with them in the States and...

"Hush," I put my finger to his lips. Over time, in this cell with nothing to look at, my sense of hearing had grown sharper. I could hear Skunk shuffling down the corridor.

"Skunk's back," I whispered. A moment later, we both heard the sound of the key in the lock.

Pedar looked at his watch and whispered, "The bastard is very punctual."

"Ya, Allah," Skunk said as he came in.

"My daughter was just telling me what a kind and caring brother you are to her," father gushed.

"*Va ateya-Allah va rasool lalakom tarahomoon*—And obey Allah and his messenger—Mohammad—so that you may obtain mercy," I interjected, reciting and translating a passage from the Koran.

"This daughter of yours knows much of Kalam-Allah," Skunk said. "You should be very proud of her."

"I'm sure she has learned a lot of it from you, brother," said my father meekly. Then he turned to me. "My daughter, as you said earlier, Brother Zaki, will be given mercy for being so kind to you. I admire him and love him as my own son."

"Time to go," Skunk said indifferently.

Alone again in my cell, I felt so happy to have seen my father! Yet, having seen him, my heart felt freshly broken over my grim situation now that he was gone. But there was one other thing to rejoice over. My Cyrus had not abandoned me.

I had longed to devise a test that might gauge the depth of his love for me. As the saying goes, be careful what you wish for…you may get it.

What was it that Cyrus has once said to me? "You make me climb a mountain to reach you, and you won't even throw me a rope…"

Now I could only hope Cyrus could surmount this vast peak that fate had put in the way of our happiness together.

• • •

After Cyrus and I got engaged, we resumed our relationship where we had left it in the States so many years ago, except that this time around, in the Islamic Republic of Iran, we were involved in a seriously romantic relationship. We were also well aware that our intimate relationship, a love affair between a Jew and an unmarried supposedly Muslim woman, if it became public, would be viewed as sinful and unlawful adultery. If caught, a man, if a Muslim, of course, would receive whatever lashes the judging mullah prescribed; whereas, for a Jew adulterer and the woman, the punishment was incontrovertible: stoning to death!

Yet despite the mortal risk, during that summer of revolutionary fervor, while the roving packs of revolutionary guards prowled looking for sinners to prey upon, the flames of passion flared ever hotter between Cyrus and me.

At the office, Ali brooded over my promotion to his level. I knew from third parties that he was going around complaining that my promotion was the result of Cyrus's infatuation with America and those who had been to that country over local talent. What's more, Ali was telling all who would listen that given the current politics of Iran, it was inappropriate for a woman to be at management level. I shuddered to think about the ramifications if Ali were ever to find out about my love affair with Cyrus! However, fortunately for me, during that month of August 1979, a "people's revolution" was in the works. There were widespread waves of unrest among the unemployed due to the number of closed factories and businesses, a side effect of the revolution since so much investment capital and entrepreneurial talent had fled the country.

Thus, Ali was distracted from his campaign of innuendos against me because he was determined to strike while the iron was hot and was busy advancing his socialist doctrine. By leveraging the widespread fear of layoffs throughout the country, Ali was able to unite almost all of the employees against the partners.

Besides the communists who Ali led, he also had the support of the majority who were—or had considered it expedient to become—Muslim fundamentalists. By now, an Islamic dress code for men had also been fully imposed. Men could no longer wear ties—these leashes to the Great Satan—and even short-sleeved shirts were prohibited. Shaving was now also considered undesirable, but was tolerated.

Ali, who had enthusiastically complied with the Islamic dress code requirements every step of the way, had gone one step further and switched to wearing a camouflage military-type uniform. In his mind's eye, he probably thought he looked like Omar Sharif portraying Che Guevara.

One sultry day in late August, my cousin Bijan called to invite me to dinner. “It’s been awhile since we’ve spent some time together,” he reminded me. “Don’t you miss my cooking?”

Perhaps because he never had a wife to prepare meals for him, Bijan, now in his fifties, was an excellent cook of Persian food. The next evening, my beloved cousin and I were sitting on the balcony of his apartment in Niavaran—a hillside town north of Tehran—having dinner. It was only after our meal, as Bijan’s tone turned serious, that I realized there was more to his invitation than our having dinner together. As was his way, he went directly to the point.

“Cyrus’s driver, Nabi, is spreading a lot of gossip about you and Cyrus,” he said calmly. “He is saying you and Cyrus are in an affair—is that true?”

I felt myself blushing with embarrassment, but I saw no way to deny it—or even why I should to my beloved cousin. “Yes, we are in love, Bijan. What I haven’t shared with you is that Cyrus has officially asked my parents for my hand in marriage to him.”

I opened my collar and showed him the engagement ring Cyrus had given me, now on a gold chain hanging from my neck.

“Congratulations.” He jumped and hugged me. “But why no one told me…Never mind. Your personal life is none of my business, but your welfare is. I think it’s wonderful that you and Cyrus love each other and are engaged, and I wish all the best for you. Having said that, there is a much bigger issue we have to take care of. These are dangerous times, Leila, and Nabi has a big mouth.”

“Are Cyrus and I in danger?”

"Who knows, with these fundamentalist madmen." Bijan shrugged. "I know from a contact I have in the government that for some reason Cyrus has been added to the regime's list of individuals who are not allowed to leave the country."

"What is it that you are trying to tell me, dear cousin?"

"What I've already told my friend, Cyrus," he said. "You should stay a safe distance from each other until, God willing, the social and political situation changes and you can get together any way you choose. In the meantime, at work, play along with whatever political nonsense is going on to avoid attracting attention to yourself and to allay suspicion that you are obsessed with Western ways."

"Easier said than done, Bijan," I replied, and bit my lip as I thought about how galling it would be to attend Ali's propaganda meetings and pretend to buy into his bullshit.

"Do it for Cyrus's sake, then," Bijan lectured me. "How you and he behave apart and together for the immediate future may well have an impact—or even decide—if the two of you will ultimately be together happily ever after."

"Do you think I can at least have contact with Cyrus in the office?" I implored.

"Oh indeed! In fact you must see him in the office, often, but briefly and publicly," Bijan explained. "In this way you will hopefully erase speculation and gossip concerning your affair. But it must appear to be strictly business between you from here on in."

I sighed.

"An additional word of caution," Bijan went on. "My contact tells me that phones are being tapped. So don't presume your telephone conversations with Cyrus will be private."

"Ah, it's so heartbreaking," I said.

"Cheer up, my dear," Bijan said. "This too shall pass. For now, once in a while, you and Cyrus are most welcome to have dinner with me, here." He playfully wagged his finger. "But just dinner, please, and with me present."

I jumped out of my chair to embrace my adorable cousin and thank him, even as my heart ached over the fact that I had to keep my distance from Cyrus.

How many times must our love be thwarted!

CHAPTER 25

May 30, 1980

Day 120 of my incarceration. Two weeks have gone by since my father came to see me.

"I have been counting every single day since you were so kind to bring my father here," I tell Skunk, but he ignores me.

"Have you called him again?" I plead, but he won't answer.

"Does he want to see me another time?"

Skunk remains silent.

"Do you want me to write him a note on your behalf?"

Skunk turns away.

I am mystified by his behavior. If it is true what my father surmised—that, concerning me, Skunk had found the goose that lays the golden eggs—why was he not more anxious to profit from it?

The uncertainty of my situation torments me, but at least I can put pen to paper and savor past freedoms...

• • •

At the firm, I remained angry with Ali for the way he'd been badmouthing me and for his demeaning attitude toward women. I decided to teach him a lesson. Through my friendship with some of the women at work, I arranged to be introduced to Ali's wife, Neda. Eventually she and I became friends. Often we would go shopping together, wearing our baggy dresses and headscarves as we frequented the shops lining the alleys of Tehran to avoid getting caught up in the eternal demonstrations against the West that clogged the main thoroughfares.

Once Neda became comfortable with me, she asked me why her husband and I didn't get along at work.

"It is mainly my fault," I said, trying to sound as sincere as I could. "I was trying to live in Iran with American values and customs, and that upset Ali. It's taken me awhile to un-Americanize myself. I hope Ali understands that."

Soon Ali asked me to visit him in his office. "I want you to know that I'm pleased you and my wife have become friendly," he began, eyeing me warily. "Neda also tells me that you have again embraced your homeland's traditions."

"Yes. I've learned that as a fish, you need to live in water, not on dry land," I said, amused at my own absurd analogy.

"Are you telling me that you no longer feel compelled to defend the inherent injustice of capitalism?" he asked suspiciously.

"Ali, did I ever tell you that I was a member of CISNU in America?"

"No!" he said, leaning back in his chair and looking astonished.

"Well. You are a member of People's Martyrs Organization, and you have access to the list of CISNU members, so look me up."

"Why didn't you tell me before?" Ali asked, and then shook his head. "Never mind. Here's the real question. Are you with us or with them?" He pointed to the ceiling, so I supposed he was trying to indicate the partners up in their executive suite.

"Of course I'm with you, if you'll stop talking about me behind my back," I countered.

Ali blushed. "I promise."

On September 10, 1979, Ali, representing the employees, demanded of management that the firm should fire us all, pay each of us a huge amount of severance pay, and then rehire us. The partners laughed in his face, and so Ali declared a sit-in strike. The employees gathered in our downstairs common room and refused to work. The arrangement was that the men would remain twenty-four hours a day, but women could go home at night.

In the meantime, anti-American demonstrators had taken to gathering in front of the American embassy, which was just down the block from us on Persepolis Street. Even with our windows closed, we could hear the roaring crowds as they taunted the grim-looking American soldiers who stood guard at the gates of the embassy compound. To keep our striking co-workers motivated, Ali and his disciples encouraged groups to periodically walk down the street and join the demonstrators for a few choruses of "Death to America!"

Meanwhile, my parents were seriously concerned about the safety of our family. My mother, a Jew, and my father, the son of General Omid, wanted to depart Iran for the United States. Through his many Muslim fundamentalist patients who now held powerful positions in the new regime, Pedar had obtained counterfeit passports with fake names for all of us, including his parents and even Cyrus. My grandfather had prevailed upon Peter Novak, his old CIA associate, to procure US visas for us.

"Before things get worse," my parents pleaded to me, "let's leave."

"I can't go without Cyrus," I told them.

And they wouldn't leave without me.

CHAPTER 26

June 1, 1980

Day 123. This afternoon, Skunk came in with two plates of lamb kabob.

"Salam, Sister Zahra," he greeted me. He was in a festive mood. He sat on the floor of my cell and invited me to join him. Then he put a huge handful of rice and kabob in his mouth, and immediately another one.

"You rich people," he snorted, spewing the half-chewed contents of his mouth into the air. "Your brother has sent you this."

"My brother?" I said incredulously, knowing quite well that both my brothers were in the States.

"Yes," he declared. "How come your brother has blue eyes? Your mother must have given it to..." He laughed so forcefully that the food caught in his throat and he began choking.

Blue eyes? These two words had stunned me. Cyrus, I thought, as Skunk coughed up a gob of chewed meat, spat it into a corner of my cell for the roaches and mice to feast on, and resumed eating and bragging.

"Yes, clearly your mother has been giving it to a blue-eyed Satan!" He began laughing again. "So, you didn't tell me why your brother's eyes are blue?"

"Well, there are many people with blue eyes in this country."

"And they're all bastards," he replied and continued to shovel food into his mouth. "Sit down and eat what your bastard brother with his blasphemous, non-Islamic, Zionist, Zoroastrian, Persian name has sent you. Cyrus! I mean."

I could hardly contain my excitement over the turn of events. If Cyrus was in touch with Skunk, the negotiations for my release must be proceeding!

"I mean, what's wrong with beautiful Muslim names?" Skunk's voice brought me harshly back to my miserable reality. "Names like Ghasem, Abdullah, Ghanbar-Ali?"

"So, Brother Zaki, when is my brother coming to see me? I mean, I miss him so much!"

"I miss him so much," he mimicked me. "Like your father, he is a kooni. He's a bastard and you are so lucky I brought you the food he sent you. I should have taken it to my children. And don't look at me like that! I might bring him if he listens to me, but he haggles with me over every condition of the deal like a mother-whore Jew!"

• • •

On November 4, 1979, I was sitting with many of the other strikers in the firm's common room downstairs when we heard an uproar coming from the street that was unusual in its intensity even for these tumultuous times. We all dashed out and saw a mass of protestors led by a cadre of students carrying banners with anti-American slogans. Curious, we tagged along on the sidewalk as the demonstration wended its way toward the American embassy.

What we next witnessed blew our minds.

As the first line of demonstrators approached the embassy gates, the small cadre of armed American soldiers fell back from their positions. More men from the demonstration, dressed in Muslim garb or baggy camouflage military fatigues, climbed atop the embassy walls, where they proceeded to wave placards with posters of Ayatollah Khomeini and revolutionary sayings: "*Marg bar Emrika,*"—death to America.

A short, thin young man with bushy black hair and a wiry beard, wearing faded jeans and a grimy, olive-green military jacket, straddled the wall and began shouting, "*Allah Akbar, Khomeini Rahbar*"—Allah is Great, Khomeini is the Leader! The multitudes below echoed his chants and a group of my striking co-workers joined the now frantic crowd, screaming, "*Marg Bar Sahyoonist-ha,*"—death to the Zionists.

Then, in response to the exhortations of the hairy little gnome in military drag who had been shouting slogans from atop of the wall, the gates to the embassy were pushed open, and the demonstrators surged inside the compound. There came an earsplitting roar of triumph from the crowd. I caught a glimpse of an American soldier being stripped of his rifle, blindfolded, and led toward the embassy building. Then all I could see were more and more demonstrators trying to wedge their way through the compound's narrow gates.

By myself, I made my way back to the firm. In the common room, the TV was already blaring the news that the American embassy personnel had been taken hostage.

"They say they have sixty Americans," Ali said excitedly as soon as he noticed me in the room. In his army surplus green cargo pants and tunic, and laced-up military boots, he looked like an extra-large version of the bearded pipsqueak I'd seen shouting to the crowds from atop the embassy wall.

"This is bad, Ali." I stood with the others, riveted by the broadcast scenes I had just witnessed with my own eyes. "Do you think the United States of America is going to sit back and watch a gang of hoodlums take over its embassy? I think these clowns are playing with the lion's tail."

"Nonsense," Ali replied scornfully. "We have every right. The Americans have held Iran hostage since their devil CIA put the Shah back on the throne in 1953."

"Something like this would not happen without encouragement and direct orders coming from the highest levels of the Revolutionary Council," I said.

"There, we agree, Leila," Ali said. "If you want to know my opinion, I think this is Khomeini putting Prime Minister Bazargan in his place for suggesting that relations with the US could be normalized."

"The hardliners now certainly seem to have the upper hand," I said.

"Speaking of the upper hand, Leila, you returned just in time." Ali said.

"Just in time for what?" I asked absently.

On the television, the little hairy man in the military jacket I had seen instigating the crowd to invade the embassy was being shown leading a parade of blindfolded hostages past the cameras.

"That fellow's name is Mahmoud Ahmadinejad," Ali said offhandedly. "He's a student organizer for the Revolutionary Committee. They say he's destined for big things."

"He reminds me of Napoleon," I said. "Short and crazy."

Ali shrugged. "Anyway, what's happened at the embassy has given us members of the firm's Revolutionary Committee, a great idea." His followers gathering around us nodded their approval. "We are going to take the partners hostage!" Ali said excitedly.

"What?" I stammered. "Do you think that's the best course of action?"

"We do," Ali said firmly, scrutinizing me. "Would you like to come with us?"

Undoubtedly, he was putting me to test.

"Sure! Now that I've gotten over my surprise, I think it's a great idea!" I said, trying to lose the shiver in my voice.

"Let's go then," Ali shouted. "To the elevator!"

I sheepishly trailed our fearless revolutionary leader, along with a half dozen of his committee members.

"Brothers and sisters," Ali began when we were in the elevator. "Leave all the talking to me!"

I could see the adrenalin surging through him.

There was no longer a secretary outside Cyrus's door to stop unannounced visitors. We all barged into Cyrus's office, where he and his partners—Farid, Ramin, and Niku—were standing by the window watching the crowd downstairs.

"Brothers!" Ali called as Cyrus and his partners turned around. "We are all witnessing the first blossoms of our glorious revolution, the seeds of which our great Ayatollah has planted for us."

Ali strode forward confidently to confront the partners, declaring, "It is only the beginning of what will be a long road to our ultimate victory. As you must by now know, the revolutionary masses have taken over America's spy nest and are enslaving the imperialist, Zionist mentors of their agent, the Shah."

Were both Cyrus and Ali remembering their long ago schoolyard fight, I wondered, as Ali, his little speech over and done with, insolently sprawled onto the leather sofa against the wall.

"Sit down, all of you!" Ali commanded the partners. They ignored him.

"And you, brothers and sisters," Ali turned his attention to us. "You sit there." He pointed to the circular table in the corner, and we dutifully took our places as Ali lit a cigarette and swung his boots up onto the coffee table in front of the sofa.

"Look, Cyrus," Ali said in a calmer tone, exhaling cigarette smoke. "I know that what's going on at the embassy and our confronting you like this must be frightening. Please sit down and let's talk."

Cyrus hesitated a moment, and then shrugged. He settled into his desk chair and motioned to his partners to find seats.

Ali took a square of yellow lined paper from his pocket, unfolded it, and began reading. "On behalf of the staff members, I have an announcement to make. We, the elected members of the Revolutionary Committee of the firm—of which I am the spokesman—inspired by the glorious turn of events at the American embassy, have devised a solution to settle the stalled compensation negotiations between management and workers. On behalf of the Revolutionary Committee,

I invite all of you to stay in the office until we have settled our terms."

"You mean until the end of today?" Farid asked naïvely.

"If we come up with the final version of our proposal and you approve it before five, there's no reason why you shouldn't be able to go home tonight," Ali replied.

"And if not?" Ramin ventured to say.

"As I said, you will stay here for as long as it takes for you to agree to compensation terms that meet our satisfaction."

Niku said, "I still don't understand why we should—"

"Don't you get it, Niku?" Cyrus said. "We're hostages. Just like those poor souls at the embassy."

"Exactly!" Ali said, sounding relieved that Cyrus had used the *h*-word that he himself hadn't had the courage to articulate. "If we are not done with our negotiations by this evening, you may sleep on your very comfortable sofas in your offices." He tapped the couch he was sitting on and then stood. "And by the way, for your security, your offices will be guarded by us."

Ali dropped his cigarette to the carpet and ground it out with the heel of his boot. "Let's go," he told us, and we followed him out of Cyrus's office.

At the elevator, the others were piling in when I put my hand on Ali's elbow to hold him back and whispered that I needed to speak with him in private.

"You go on down," he ordered the others. "Leila and I will join you shortly."

"What is it?" Ali asked as the elevator door closed on the others.

"Was it really necessary to ruin his carpet with your cigarette butt?" I couldn't help scolding.

"I know you like Cyrus and you care for him," Ali replied, blushing at my reprimand. "Quite honestly, I like him also, but our movement is going through critical times. Speaking of which, I don't think you should have contact with Cyrus any longer. After all, both you and he are from America."

"Thanks for giving me free American citizenship, Ali."

"All I care about is the success of our revolutionary mission," he insisted. "Cyrus and his partners will be held hostage, and as the leader and the head of the Revolutionary Committee of the firm, from now on, I will be the only one who negotiates with them."

"May I speak frankly?"

"When do you not?" Ali chuckled.

"Since you are in charge, I will obey your orders."

"Thank you," Ali said, sounding relieved.

"However, there is one thing you are forgetting," I admonished. "As a result of this lengthy strike of yours, the firm is generating no revenue. Cyrus and the partners are the only ones who know how to go about collecting the few fees that are still owed to us."

"You don't seem to understand, Leila," Ali said in exasperation. "The Revolutionary Committee is in charge now, not Cyrus!"

"You don't have to shout, Ali. All I'm saying is that beyond you negotiating with Cyrus, someone has to audit the firm's books. If you know better than Cyrus how to manage our accounts receivable, perhaps you would like to be in charge of that, as well."

I could see Ali pondering the notion that no revenue flowing into the firm would mean he would not receive his own salary. "All right, Leila, you may confer with Cyrus about account receivables, but nothing else!"

I sensed that I had our local ayatollah on the ropes. "No one tells me what to talk about! You want to be the boss? Fine. I hereby submit my resignation. Good-bye," I murmured coolly as I pressed the elevator button.

"Please forgive me, Leila," Ali said quickly. "I respect you, and so does everyone else in the firm."

"And you are scared that if I left, you would not be able to gain access to the partners' closely held books the way I will be able to, thanks to my long friendship with Cyrus," I said.

"All right. Perhaps that is so."

"My threat to walk out is not a bluff, Ali. I want your word not to interfere—"

"You have my word." Ali held up his hands in surrender.

"That I will have unsupervised access to Cyrus?"

"Yes!"

Ali looked at me with a forced smile. "You always seem to prevail in our discussions, Leila. But someday, the tables will turn."

CHAPTER 27

Yesterday, Skunk brought the food Cyrus had paid for and ate it in front of me. I didn't care; I have no appetite except for sweet freedom. I also yearn to know if Cyrus will arrange to visit me.

I could simply ask Skunk, of course, but I am determined to deny him the pleasure of torturing me by withholding the information. It would have to be enough for me simply to know Cyrus was now actively involved in my dismal situation. I have faith in his negotiation skills.

• • •

At the end of the business day on which Ali had taken Cyrus and the other partners hostage and had confined them to their offices, he called a meeting for all employees in the common room. There he gave a progress report detailing the plans of his Revolutionary Committee.

"We will keep the partners here until they give in to our demands!" he proclaimed. "We salute our comrades who took American spies hostage today, and we will follow their example!"

Of course, I was worried about Cyrus. Before this meeting, a few of the others and I had taken dinner upstairs to our hostages. We carried trays of shish kabob into Cyrus's office and set them down on the round table in the corner. "Courtesy of the Revolutionary Committee," said the man holding a tray. "For breakfast, we will serve you boiled eggs with fresh bread and tea. Anything else you need?"

"Thank you all. This is better than a five-star hotel." Cyrus said, taking a few coins out of his pocket and scattered them across the rug, where I couldn't help looking at the ugly burn hole from Ali's cigarette. If the others understood Cyrus's disdain, they didn't show it. As for me, I wanted to cry over the madhouse the world had become. "Ali has told me that Leila shall be my liaison to the firm's accounting department," Cyrus said.

"That's correct," one of my committee "comrades" replied.

"Then I ask that Leila remain behind for a few words," Cyrus said.

After the other committee members filed out, Niku, one of the partners, said accusingly, "Leila, Cyrus has told us of your education in the United States. How can you stand with Ali and his fanatics?"

"You must know," I told Niku, "I hate this mess more than you do. I'm with Ali only in the hope that I can somehow turn the situation around in your favor."

"And we never thought otherwise," Cyrus interrupted, looking disapprovingly at Niku. "Now we have to come up with a plan of action."

"What plan of action?" Ramin asked, nervously cracking his knuckles. "The firm's business has gone down the drain because our employees have been on strike for so many weeks. Now, they are holding us hostage and you talk about coming up with a plan of action?"

"I can't think right now." Niku headed for the door. "I'm going to my own office to call my family and tell them I'm not coming home tonight."

Farid and Ramin muttered their intentions to do the same, and Cyrus and I were alone.

After Cyrus had secured the door of his office, we embraced and hugged for a long time until I warned, "We have to be careful." And Cyrus agreed, dismayed.

"Your partners are scared and confused, this I understand," I told Cyrus after we sat on the sofa, facing each other. "But must they act like idiots?"

"Calling them 'idiots' is inappropriate, Leila," Cyrus said evenly. "You must understand the unprecedented nature of this experience for them. They are well-educated Muslim technocrats who have never been in a minority and have never been looked upon as outsiders within their own country, whereas we are Persian Jews and so can bring a certain perspective to unfolding events. Over the course of the twenty-five centuries of our history in this land, we have the advantage of knowing that we have suffered and survived much worse catastrophic situations."

"And what the hell are you going to do to leverage this historical perspective?" I demanded, my voice rising.

As was his way of handling me, the more agitated I got, the calmer Cyrus became. "I have my work cut out for me, my dear," he said. "As the senior partner of the firm, I have the responsibility to resolve the situation."

After Cyrus and I had briefly discussed a few accounts receivable matters, I returned downstairs and went to the women's bathrooms. Alone at last, and overwhelmed by the events of the day, I began to weep uncontrollably. After I was all cried out, I remembered that Ali had set the rule that male employees had to stay, but women could go home, except that I had no desire to be alone in my family's guesthouse tonight. And as much as I loved Pedar and Madar, I could not comfortably discuss the situation at the firm and my feelings about Cyrus, although he was my fiancé.

Back at my desk, I remembered that my cousin Bijan had made it clear to Ali that he had no intention of being a part of this circus and that he was not going to stay at the office during the strike and hostage taking. Ali had conceded, considering Bijan was the most senior employee of the firm.

I called Bijan. I guess my tears were still in my throat, because as soon as he heard my voice, he became concerned.

"What's the problem, Leila?" he asked.

"I'm sorry to call at the spur of the moment, but may I come see you? There have been developments here at the firm and I need your advice."

"Of course," Bijan said. "Call home and tell your mom and dad that you are staying at my place tonight," my loving cousin offered. "I will cook us a delicious dinner."

Within a half hour of Ali ending his meeting in the firm's common room, I was in Bijan's kitchen, watching him prepare a dish of chicken and rice for us while I confessed my misery, especially, how it broke my heart to see Cyrus incarcerated in his office by Ali, of all people!

"Why Ali, especially?" Bijan asked, looking up from his cutting board, where he was mincing shallots.

"Have I never told you the story?" I began and then quickly filled him in on Cyrus's experiences with Ali in high school and their schoolyard confrontations.

"Fascinating," Bijan said after I was done. "We can only wait to see how the entwined fates of these two men ultimately play out."

"The love-hate relationship between the two is far more passionate and potentially violent than I think you understand, Bijan," I said. "We live in dangerous times. I fear Ali's repressed envy and anger toward Cyrus could erupt with tragic results."

"I know Cyrus, and I'm sure he has the ability to act rationally in the face of Ali's mixed emotions," Bijan said, taking the heavenly smelling casserole from the oven. "And remember, he is not alone."

"He has me." I nodded adamantly.

"And he has me," Bijan, said. "And let's have dinner!" he added lightheartedly as he set the steaming casserole dish on a trivet on the dining table.

CHAPTER 28

June 8, 1980

Day 130 of my incarceration, but it was a joyous day, nonetheless, because today Skunk led another man with a sack over his head into my cell.

It was Cyrus.

"*Baradar jaan man*,"—my dear brother—I whispered as Skunk pulled the burlap from Cyrus's head. My beloved's blue eyes narrowed in the weak sunlight penetrating the small window of my cell as he looked at me. I knew how terrible I looked. I prayed Cyrus would not abandon me due to the hag I'd become in prison. My mind raced through memories of Cyrus and me as students strolling across the UCLA campus during lazy fall afternoons...walking barefoot in the sand along Santa Monica beach on hot summer days...and toasting each other in swank Beverly Hills cafés. I remembered the many holidays we spent in the forests of Carmel, the glorious Grand Canyon sunrises and Pacific Ocean sunsets we'd witnessed and, then, the way he had proposed to me at my parents' house.

But to me, on this eighth day in the month of June, in the year 1980, to be together with Cyrus again—even in this horrid cell—was…Oh God, what's the right word? Delicious? Yes, so delicious that I could taste its sweetness on my tongue.

"Your brother is here to see you in my presence," Skunk announced.

"What?" I could not stifle my disappointment.

Cyrus held up his hand. "*Khahar jaan*,"—sister, dear—"Brother Zaki is quite right. This is what we have agreed," he said in a neutral tone. "I'm here to reassure you that this brother and I are working on—"

The shout of another female prisoner interrupted us.

Skunk sighed. "I have so much responsibility here," he said self-importantly. "I will quickly return."

He went out, and the moment the door locked, I threw myself in Cyrus's arms and kissed him.

"Careful," he whispered.

"To hell with him." I wept as I felt him trembling against me.

He pushed me back gently. "Leila, very quickly, your dad and I are negotiating with this mule. He is tough, but conquerable. So far, you have done a great job putting us together. So, keep on staying on his good side and remain strong. He wants a lot of money, but that is not the problem. My concern is that—"

"Hush!" I hear Skunk taking his keys from his pocket.

"I don't hear anything," Cyrus began.

The cell door swung open.

"Sister Zahra is a *khanom*"—a lady—"as compared to those two down the hall," Skunk grumbled as he came in.

"Thanks, Brother Zaki," Cyrus said, quickly recovering his smooth composure. "She is indeed an Allah-fearing, observant Muslim woman. There's been a big misunderstanding here. We are in touch with the Revolutionary Prosecutor's Bureau, trying to resolve her case."

I knew Cyrus was bluffing to scare Skunk into expediting the deal to release me.

"But your sister's case is under the Central Revolutionary Committee, not that bureau you mentioned," Skunk shot back like a seasoned negotiator.

My heart sank a little. Skunk was right. There were too many self-governing bodies in the new regime that didn't answer to each other. Cyrus had overplayed his hand.

"Your meeting is over," Skunk said crossly, angry at Cyrus's negotiating ploy.

"But, Brother Zaki—"

"I said it is over!"

Skunk put the sack back over Cyrus's head, grabbed him by the elbow, led him out, and locked the door on me.

• • •

The morning of the day after we had taken Cyrus and his partners hostage, I left Bijan's house for the office. When I arrived at the firm, I found the street in front of the building and all the way down to the American embassy packed with demonstrators. A great number of the firm's employees were among them, shouting themselves hoarse with an unbearably loud and monotonous litany of anti-American slogans. I put my hands over my ears against the din and made my way inside. To avoid Ali, instead of going to my own office, I went to a smaller common room on the third floor and was happy to find my office friend, Farnaz, there. She was busy reading her newspaper.

"Leila, you won't believe this," she called out as I was about to sit down. "My goodness, Cyrus and his partners are in hot water."

"What is it?" I asked as I went and stood behind her, looking at the paper. "What? Prime Minister Bazargan has resigned?"

"Yes he has, but I'm talking about this." She tapped her finger on the picture of a frowning man in a camouflage revolutionary outfit. The photo's caption read, "Brother Hassan Assad, Deputy Revolutionary Prosecutor."

"Do you remember this guy?" Farnaz asked.

"Am I supposed to know him?"

"This is Hassan the Pockmarked," she replied and giggled. "At least, that was our nickname for him behind his back. He used to work here, but Niku fired him. Boy, he's going to grill those poor bastards upstairs."

"Tell me everything you know about him, please?"

"Now that I think about it," Farnaz mused, "Hassan was fired before you joined the firm. Even then, he was an Islamic fundamentalist, so our rather secular partners couldn't stand him—Niku especially had a grudge against him. I think it was a year ago while Cyrus was away that Niku fired Hassan."

"Why would Niku wait for Cyrus to be away?" I asked.

"Because, it has always been Cyrus's policy not to fire anyone unless he absolutely has to," Farnaz said affectionately. "I actually seem to remember that when Cyrus got back, he reached out to Hassan and asked him to come back, but Hassan refused the offer."

"You know, when things go wrong and one feels slighted by another," I said, "you hope for the opportunity to get even, but it never comes."

"Except for Hassan," Farnaz said, picking up my line of thought. "For him, the chance to get even has come in spades!"

CHAPTER 29

For the next few weeks, every time I visited the firm's executive suite, ostensibly to deal with accounts receivable issues, my heart went out to Cyrus and his partners due to their ever-deteriorating living conditions.

Since they had been taken hostage, they'd had neither a shower nor a change of clothing. Meanwhile, Ali, as the sole representative of the strikers, was holding regular meetings with the partners—during which he wouldn't budge from his outrageous demand of $20 million to be distributed to the employees as a good-faith token from the partners that they endorsed the Khomeini revolution.

"There has to be a way for me to help end this mess," I said to my cousin Bijan during one of our many dinners together. "Perhaps I can leverage Ali's naïvety."

"My dear cousin," Bijan said. "Those Americans trapped in their embassy are held by a bunch of morons equal to Ali in their naïvety. And yet, Carter, the president of the United States of America, one of the two superpowers of the world, is not able to resolve this crisis. What makes you think that you can set Cyrus free?"

A few days later, one afternoon, I went up to the third floor's common room, where I found Samir lounging, smoking a cigarette.

"Salam," I greeted him.

"Aleike Salam," he responded glumly. He took a long drag on his cigarette and exhaled the smoke out of his nose.

"Everything all right?"

He shook his head despondently. "No, things are terrible."

Samir was in his early twenties. He was a calm, shy man who came from a religious family. Cyrus had told me that he had hired Samir out of pity. If Cyrus had not given Samir a part-time job, the young man would have had to drop out of college to support his elderly and infirm parents.

"Is it because of what happened between you and Cyrus?" I asked solicitously, and Samir nodded.

Ali had appointed Samir—apparently against his will—as Cyrus's guard during the evenings. In the first week of Cyrus and the other partners being held hostage, Samir and Cyrus had clashed...

"It was two o'clock in the morning, and I was unable to sleep," Cyrus had recounted to me during one of our private meetings to go over the firm's ledgers. "I decided to go to the bathroom. I stepped out of my office into the hallway. I heard somebody yell, 'Halt!' I turned and saw Samir pointing a pistol at me. For a few seconds that felt like an eternity, I stood shocked and immobilized, looking into the barrel of that gun. 'Samir,' I said calmly as I raised my arms in surrender, 'I'm just going to the bathroom.'

"'Bathroom?' Samir's eyes widened. Maybe he thought I was trying to escape. Who knows, Leila. I continued talking to him, trying to calm him. 'Samir jaan,' I said, my throat dry. 'It's me, Cyrus! I won't run away. I-want-to go-to the-bathroom,' I stressed each word, as you would to a young child.

"'*Estagfor-Allah*'—May God forgive me—Samir gasped. The gun slipped from his fingers and, I swear to God, I almost peed in my pants at that moment thinking it was going to go off by accident when it hit the floor, but it didn't. 'I apologize,' Samir said. He rushed toward me and embraced me, and then he started to cry.

"By now, Leila, my fear had turned to rage," Cyrus had told me. "'What have I done to you to deserve this?' I demanded of Samir. I pushed him away and he ran to the elevators. The poor jerk left his gun lying where he'd dropped it.

"I know he didn't mean to threaten me," Cyrus had said. "But the fact remains that just one twitch of his finger and he would have shot me. He would have been sorry, but I would have been dead."

"What happened next?" I'd demanded, enthralled.

"Well," Cyrus had said, looking embarrassed, "What happened next is it was my turn to do something dumb, but in my defense, I must say I was just so angry and charged with adrenalin, I wasn't thinking clearly."

"Go on," I'd urged.

"I heard the elevator doors opening," Cyrus had continued. "So I picked up Samir's pistol. When Ali and Samir came charging around the corner, this time they were looking down the barrel of a gun."

"My God, Cyrus!" I'd scolded him, appalled. "You all could have killed each other!"

He'd shrugged. "Fortunately, neither was armed. 'Cyrus, I owe you my life,' Samir said. 'Again I apologize for my stupidity.' But I wasn't even paying attention to him. My eyes were locked with Ali's. I walked toward him, and then handed him the gun. I said, 'Just like old times in our schoolyard, isn't it, old friend? But this time there is no Headmaster TabaTabai to protect me or to punish you. Only us, two men.'

"Ali just took the gun and walked away."

Cyrus's story now played through my mind as I sat with Samir in the common room, watching him glumly chain smoke.

"Do you have any idea where this thing is going, Samir?" I asked. "I mean the strike and taking the partners hostage?"

"You are a Muslim?" he asked, avoiding my question.

"Yes, of course," I said as I adjusted my scarf.

"It's been written: 'Those who have bought the life of this world at the price of the Hereafter, their torment shall not be lightened nor shall they be helped.'"

"Samir, I don't understand your point."

"My point is that I never should have stood guard over Cyrus—not after all he has done for me and my family. He has been kind and compassionate, and I repay him by threatening to shoot him." Samir hung his head in shame. "I can't get over my sinful stupidity. Go read it for yourself."

The Koran…I thought. Could that sacred book be my bludgeon to facture Ali's hold over the firm and free Cyrus and the other hostages?

"It's in the Koran, Sureh Albaghareh," Samir continued to mutter as he lit a fresh cigarette off the smoldering butt of his last. "Read for yourself."

"I will, Samir. I will," I said as my plan took shape.

CHAPTER 30

That night, after my fateful conversation with the regretful Samir, I contemplated a way out of the firm's hostage crisis...a way to save the man I loved.

In so many ways, including our own mini hostage crisis, the situation at the firm was a microcosm of what was happening in Iran. Both the firm and the country were in chaos, with no reliable source of authority one could appeal to but a bunch of impetuous and self-righteous hoodlums drunk with power.

On the other hand, there was a certain hierarchy to the gang rule. At the top of the pyramid was Khomeini. Beneath him were his cohorts and various numbingly similar-sounding revolutionary committees, and beneath them, the roaming gangs of revolutionary guards. At the very bottom were those men who, through their circumstances and charisma, had managed to gather a handful of their own adherents. These were like Ali, who had become the leader of the strikers and hostage takers at the firm. However, Ali was a communist, while the revolution that had appeared to hand him power, was Islamic.

From my earlier exchange with Samir, it had come to me that the majority of my co-workers were observant Muslims, and yet, like Samir, these devout Muslims had unthinkingly pledged their allegiance to a leader who put secular socialist theory above religion. Bottom line, I thought Ali would be easy to topple from power. All that was required was to find an observant Muslim contender to challenge him. I ran through all of my colleagues in my mind, but none measured up to Ali.

None except myself.

I would become the spokesperson for my observant Muslim co-workers, who vastly outnumbered the few communists, and thus steal from Ali his leadership role. I would use my new power to free Cyrus, and then the two of us could escape to America.

The next morning, I began preparing to stage my coup.

Fortunately, nobody but Cyrus knew of my Jewish ancestry, so like so many Iranian women who, in the fervor of the revolution, had regained their faith and become observant Muslims, I could do the same. But to confront Ali, I had to be more than merely knowledgeable about Islam—I had to be an expert!

My mastering the Koran would take time, but that was OK. I knew the key to establishing my credibility would be to move gradually. Nobody would buy my overnight conversion, but if I enhanced my Muslim credentials in a step-by-step basis, it would be like gradually changing one's hair color—no one could ever put a finger on the day the transformation was complete.

I started by revamping my wardrobe with the most conservative Muslim female attire. If anybody questioned me on it, I would simply say I was following the prescriptions of the ruling regime. A bit more difficult than changing my clothes would be gaining religious knowledge. I started by contacting a pious Muslim friend of my mother who had a wealth of religious books. Like all devout individuals, she was more than happy to extend her hand of welcome to one of true faith.

My mother's friend tutored me and I learned quickly, especially that Persian and Arabic alphabet are almost the same and many words share the same root in both languages. I focused on memorizing many verses of the Koran in both in Arabic and Farsi, because nothing impresses others more than the ability to rattle off verse by memory. Even if the verse isn't particularly relevant, you score a lot of points just by being able to put it out there in front of others. In addition to the classic religious texts, I studied the new literature released by the government. I also made myself familiar with the many rules set forth by the various mullahs, many of whom were going nuts issuing endless proclamations now that they finally had the country's attention.

Within two months, I was well on my way to talking Muslim rings around anyone, with the possible exception of Khomeini, himself—even if gossip had it that unlike his charisma, Khomeini's knowledge of the Koran was poor. What's more, I had established a pattern of dress, in which I had gradually assumed the attire of the most observant of Muslim women—black scarves; wider, baggy black pants; black oversized shirts; black boots; and a couple of black chador overalls, just for good measure. And, as I'd thought, the fact that I had gone slowly to revamp my wardrobe, gradually covering more of myself with layers of dark, had allowed me to make my transformation without my co-workers noticing.

It was only on the day when, in addition to my long and baggy dress and pants, I wore the double scarf—one covering all my hair down to the middle of my forehead and another over that, that my mother challenged me.

"In the name sanity, what on earth has gotten into you?" she asked me as I was on my way to work. "I mean being careful is one thing, but this? And two chadors?"

"Things are getting so tough; it's better to be on the safe side."

"Safe is one thing," she clucked. "But to go around like Khomeini's wife?"

Madar knew me well enough to guess that I had something else on my mind. But try as hard as she might, she couldn't pry it out of me.

In the office, my friend Farnaz looked at me in my fundamentalist drag as though she were seeing me for the first time. "I realize you have become very religious," she began. "But this seems a little extreme."

"As the proverb has it, 'embrace or lose face,'" I replied. "I'm embracing the new regime and I'm determined to be a good Muslim."

Farnaz just nodded. I could tell she was impressed. I gave her my most serene and beatific smile.

"*Ya Imam Zaman*!" Samir exclaimed, in the name of the Holy Hidden Imam, as he passed by me. "Congratulations, Sister Leila!"

Bingo, I though triumphantly. Samir was the first of Ali's lieutenants I wanted to recruit.

"Thanks to the teachings of our supreme leader, I have studied the Koran very closely and learned so much," I told him.

"That is good, sister," Samir said.

"And it is my duty to dress properly, for it is written in Sureh Noor, '*Va ghol lel-momenat...*'" I recited the chapter in Arabic, followed by its Persian translation, "'And tell the believing women to lower their gaze from looking at forbidden things, and protect their private parts and not to show off their adornment except only that which is apparent.'"

If I'd wanted to really show off, I could have told Samir that the passage I had just recited had been interpreted in the seventeenth century by Ayatollah Allameh Majlesi to mean specific parts of a woman's body—like the eyes or the hands—had to be exposed for practicality's sake. But I didn't want to lay it on too thick all at once. The secret to winning over the Muslim men would be to demonstrate my knowledge without humiliating them with their own ignorance. It wouldn't do for them to think that I thought any woman could be a man's equal.

"Samir, as my respected colleague," I went on like little Ms. Mullah, "I want you to know how excited I am to have found my own salvation."

"Oh, sister, I am so proud of you," Samir gushed. "I wish the rest of the women in this office were as Allah fearing as you have become."

The hook was in his mouth. Now to set it firmly.

"You know, Samir? This didn't happen to me out of nowhere. I am so grateful to you, because it was after I heard your words of wisdom in the common room awhile back that this revelation overtook my soul."

I couldn't recall exactly what Samir had said to me, and I suspected he couldn't either—but being a man of Allah, he would merely assume that whatever he'd said had been worth its weight in gold.

"Of course, Sister Leila," Samir said. "It is a man's duty to guide women. Just let me know how I can be of help, and I will be at your service."

Oh, you'll be of service, my boy, you may be assured of that.

"We should all be at Allah's service," I said. "Go, you man of faith. And we shall talk about this more."

So far, I had kept my plan from my cousin Bijan, because I knew that out of concern for me, he would do his utmost to stop me. But it was time to tell him. That afternoon I telephoned him from my office. After I'd filled him in, he was, of course, alarmed for my safety.

"By God, Leila! Think, woman!" he warned me. "This is a lions' den that you are stepping into."

"I know what I'm doing and you can't convince me otherwise," I said, adding that I didn't want my parents or Cyrus to know of my plan.

"Very well," Bijan said. "But, Leila?"

"Yes?"

"Remember what I told you about telephones being tapped."

"Oh my God, I forgot!"

"I guess you don't know everything, after all, eh?" Bijan scolded mildly. "Next time you have something as incendiary as this to tell me, save it until you can do so in person."

As I hung up the phone, I saw Ali in his military costume through my office doorway. It occurred to me that he and I were both playing dress-up, but that my costume was going to trump his. Ali, passing by, glanced in at me behind my desk and stopped short. "I'll be damned! Has the sun arisen from the west this morning?" he exclaimed.

"Excuse me?" I asked. The expression on his face was a wonderful combination of surprise, disbelief, shock—and most of all, confusion.

I stood up from my desk and pushed past him as he blocked my doorway. I knew full well that he was totally thrown off balance by the new me.

"Wait, wait," I heard him coming up behind me. "Since when—"

"Since when, what?" I demanded as I wheeled around to confront him. "Since when have I found my religious roots, Brother Ali? Is that what you are trying to ask me?"

"I know you, Leila," he began. "Who are you trying to kid?" He was doing his utmost to sound confident, but his voice betrayed his uncertainty.

"I pray for you, brother," I said loudly, hoping to attract an audience for this performance. "I pray for the day that you come back to the bosom of your religion; be born again and find your salvation from your secular preoccupation with communism. I pray for your deliverance and the emancipation that it will bring you."

To my delight, a dozen co-workers had gathered around us. That was when Ali made his first big mistake.

"You and your deliverance and emancipation bullshit!" he groaned contemptuously.

"Did everybody hear that?" I asked for the benefit of our audience. "Let this be the last time you insult Islam, Brother Ali. I'm saying this in front of all these sisters and brothers. If I hear you offend our sacred religion once again, I will report you to the local Islamic Revolutionary Committee." I walked away.

"Will you run this by me once again?" he called.

I ignored him and waited for him to make his second big mistake, which he obligingly did by coming up behind me and grabbing my arm to stop me.

"Are you telling me that of all the people in the world, you have become—" he began, but I drowned him out with my own outraged reply.

"Let—go—of—my—arm!" I growled, stressing each word. "How dare you touch a woman who is not *mahram* to you? I'm neither your sister nor your wife!"

He pulled his hand back as if electrocuted. It was struggle for me not to laugh aloud.

"And don't you dare question my religious values!" I continued, intent on leveraging my advantage in front of the growing crowd. "It is hard for an atheist to understand divine values."

The look of intimidation in Ali's eyes was gratifying.

"I have no idea what's wrong with this brother," I told to the crowd as Ali, his tail firmly tucked between his legs, hurriedly retreated.

CHAPTER 31

A cat keeps its balance on the edge of a narrow wall with its whiskers, says an old Persian proverb. Trim its whiskers and it will fall.

I had begun to trim Ali's whiskers, but I knew I still had a lot of cutting left. To become the leader of the Islamic radicals who made up the majority of the firm's workforce, I had to neutralize their innate sexism and set forever to rest any doubts they might have had that my transformation from liberal "daughter of Satan" to observant Muslim woman was genuine.

I began inching my way to power by winning over the firm's female employees. I championed on their behalf the assertion that it was demeaning for us to stand behind the men during our daily prayers held in the downstairs common room.

"There's not such a requirement in the Koran, although there is clear reference that we should pray separately," I argued at the end of every prayer session.

Soon we women had our own separate prayer room.

And all the while, I continued to cultivate Samir, stroking his ego until he was convinced that I viewed him as my spiritual "big brother." He had never had a woman who looked up to him. Frankly, I wasn't sure he'd ever had a woman at all. By batting my eyelashes at him while I stroked his masculine ego, it didn't take long to twist him around my little finger.

One day, I commented to Samir about how the employees were frustrated with the months of fruitless striking, especially given that the firm's financial resources had dried up, leading to a suspension of salaries for everyone.

"What do you think we should do, sister?" Samir asked.

"I am a woman and know little of these things, brother. But as great a man as Brother Ali is, perhaps we might take another look at the road he is leading us down. What do you think, Brother Samir?"

"Maybe you are right, sister," Samir said thoughtfully.

Having fanned the flames between the Islamic fundamentalists and the communists, I staged another challenge against Ali. The communist organization he belonged to, the People's Martyr Guerillas or some such nonsense, was providing food and other basic necessities for us sit-in strikers.

Intent on putting a stop to our relying on Ali for the essentials of life, I led Samir and several other fundamentalists to a local mosque, where I described the situation to the mullah in charge and pleaded with him to take the place of the secular atheists in supporting us good Muslims. The mullah agreed to send us food and other supplies daily and gave us a generous financial contribution while urging us to come back and ask for more money if we needed it. That was really the turning point in my quest. Now, quite literally, instead of eating from Ali's hand, the striking employees were eating from mine.

I further solidified the Islamic radicals and became their undisputed leader by having a few of them demand that the communists begin to attend our daily prayers. They actually intimidated some of Ali's core followers into doing so. I knew in just a matter of time, Ali would be forced into the confrontation I was hoping for. Sensing the threat I had become, he was already behaving in an irrationally rude and disdainful manner toward me.

Finally, in early January 1980, he launched his long-expected counterattack. He called for a general meeting, which he began by leading the crowd in a few cliché revolutionary slogans. Next, he enumerated the steps he had taken to pressure the firm's partners to give in to his demands. He finished his boring speech by telling everyone to be patient and that they could count on him getting the $20 million "from those leaches upstairs." Then he made a great show of looking directly at me and said, "Religiously observant or nonobservant, we all have the same goal—the victory of our revolution. To attain that, we must remain united."

I raised my hand to get his permission to speak. "With all due respect, Brother Ali," I began, "the entire country has arisen in the name of Allah and our religious values. This is a divine movement led by our supreme leader, His Holiness Imam Khomeini. You either are an Islamic revolutionary or you are no revolutionary."

I turned to the crowd and loudly asked, "Am I right?"

Except for Ali and his very few friends, everyone else cried, "Allah Akbar! Sister Leila is right!"

I turned to Ali and waited expectantly.

As if on cue, he jumped out of his chair shouting, "We must remain united! That filthy Jew upstairs and his partners are few, but united. We, on the other hand, are many but divided, thanks to Leila." Ali pointed at me, demanding, "Why don't you admit that you are taking their side?"

Of course I don't like the idea of taking people hostage, I was tempted to scream back at him. "Correct me if I'm wrong, Brother Ali," I said instead. "I have been with this firm for just over a year and hardly know the partners. The only contact I have had with Cyrus has been at your behest, as the liaison between your committee and the partners concerning financial matters at the firm. But isn't it true that you and Cyrus are childhood friends?"

I heard the rest of the employees murmuring to one another in response to my letting that bombshell drop.

"That has nothing to do with our revolution," Ali began, looking worried.

I didn't let him build up a head of steam. "The fact is, Brother Ali, your own deeds belie your words. You also want to dictate your atheist terms to us believers, and this brings us to the next subject."

"There's no next subject," Ali said disdainfully.

I ignored him, knowing I had him on the ropes, feeling the adrenaline rush as I pounded home my attack. "Brother Ali, as it has been written in the Koran, Book of Emran, '*Va shaaverahom fel amr,*' which means, 'consult people in affairs relating to them.' I suggest that from now on, no one makes a decision on behalf of the strikers unless it has been ratified at our general meeting. If I may, I call for a vote." Not waiting for his permission, I went on, "All those in favor of my suggestion, please raise your hands."

To my deep satisfaction, the sea of hands attested to the fact that I now had the support of the majority. On the heels of this successful vote, I proposed to change the name of our committee to the Islamic Revolutionary Committee, which was also approved by the majority vote as Ali and his dwindling number of followers looked at him, shocked.

Next, I threw my knockout punch. I suggested dismantling the "existing committee that was handpicked by Brother Ali," so as to elect the members of our new Islamic Revolutionary Committee democratically "as required by Islamic laws."

We moved quickly through the procedure, and when it was finished, there were twelve people elected: me and eight of my followers, including my now most devoted advocate, Samir, and Ali along with only two of his supporters. What's more, the committee immediately elected me as its chairperson.

And so, by wielding Islamic garb and garble as my weapons, I had defeated Ali, who now fidgeted in his chair, looking pale and dumbfounded. Now that I had this tin pot chauvinist where I wanted him, I needed to keep him close so I could keep my eye on him.

"For all the hard work that Brother Ali has done so far," I said, "I move that he should be elected as the committee's vice-chair in charge of negotiations with the partners—reporting directly to me."

Naturally, Samir nearly swallowed his tongue rushing to be the one to second my motion, and so it passed with eleven votes.

Ali looked like he didn't know what had hit him. His machismo was shriveling before my eyes. I decided I had publicly spanked him enough for today.

"Shall we reconvene three days from now?" I called out.

"Allah Akbar," the crowd cried.

That same day, while visiting Cyrus in his office, I realized that I couldn't keep what I was doing from him any longer. Of course, Cyrus had been surprised to see me in my increasingly conservative Islamic attire, but I had managed to mollify his curiosity by claiming that I was simply trying to avoid being confronted on the street by fundamentalist zealots. Now I came clean with Cyrus, explaining how I had convinced everyone that I had become a devout Muslim and how I had successfully staged my coup against Ali.

Cyrus was both amused and worried as I told him everything. He had let his beard grow long and wild over the three months of his captivity. He had also lost a great deal of weight, making his marvelous blue eyes look even larger above his pronounced cheekbones.

"Don't underestimate Ali," he said. "You have outsmarted him, true, but if you push him too far, humiliate him too much, he may lose control and do you physical harm. I don't believe he's inherently an evil person, but he is an impulsive one who often acts first and thinks later."

"You let me worry about Ali," I said confidently. "Better you should be thinking about how you're going to make it up to me when I get you out of here."

"Oh, I have a number of ideas in mind," Cyrus said, his blue eyes sparkling.

I wanted to tell Cyrus how much I loved him. But I needed him to say it first. Only that would release my own words of adoration. And so I said nothing, trying my utmost to let my own upturned dark eyes communicate the depths of my passion.

Three days later, we had our next staff meeting—which I called to order as the new chairperson. I started things off by asking Ali to report on the status of his negotiations with the firm's partners. He took a deep drag on his cigarette. "Unfortunately, there is not very much to report. Cyrus seems more stubborn than ever. Sister, during your business discussions, did you tell him that you are now in charge?"

"If I'm not wrong, Brother Ali," I replied, ignoring his question, "you have all along promised us that you would get us $20 million. So, what do you suggest we should do now?"

"We will stop treating them like royalty," he growled.

"We will?" I cut him short. "Who's 'we,' Brother Ali? I thought we decided that any future decisions should be subject to a majority vote. The echoes of these words are still in the air and yet again you attempt to make a unilateral decision on behalf of all of us?"

The assemblage murmured its agreement.

Ali said, "All right then, let's take a vote and have it over with."

"So, Brother Ali has moved that we should take a vote on instituting harsher treatment of our hostages, but before that"—I turned to him and continued—"I wonder if you heard the news, Brother Ali?"

"What news," he said impatiently.

"Just this morning, Imam Khomeini decreed that our revolution has reached complete victory and that all hostages in all factories and offices throughout the country must be released immediately," I said. "Of course, the Ayatollah, in his supreme wisdom, has provided us the means of resolving our own hostage stalemate. He somehow has divined that our situation here has dragged on for so long that the circumstances have changed to our disadvantage."

"Then why haven't your American friends at the embassy been released?" Ali hollered.

"Brother Ali," I said, shaking my head. "Why must you be so childish? Had you read the newspapers today, or at least listened to the radio, you would know for yourself that our Imam has declared the Americans not ordinary hostages but spies."

I paused for Ali's response, but could see by the poleaxed look in his eyes that one wouldn't be coming anytime soon.

"His Holiness has issued this fatwa not only out of the goodness of his blessed heart," I said loudly for the benefit of my rapt audience at the back of the room, "but also according to the holy commands of our prophet, who says, '*en-Allah ya'merakom bel-adl val-ehsaan*,' that is, 'Allah orders you to be just and beneficent.'"

"But we have treated our hostages justly," Ali stammered.

I had successfully played catch and release with my obliging Ali-fish before. Now I wanted to see if he would indeed swallow my hook again.

"Brother Ali, please tell us what you think we have gained so far by our hostage taking?"

The hook was dangling.

"So, you are suggesting that we should set those leeches free?" Ali replied, heartily gulping the hook down his throat.

"No, I'm not suggesting," I replied meekly. "It is not my place to suggest when our Imam's fatwa to release all ordinary hostages is the law of the land."

"No!" Ali sputtered. "I say we take a vote!"

"Brother, I say to you once again that it is not our place to take a vote on His Holiness's blessed decrees."

"Is everybody listening to this?" Ali roared. "After all our struggles, she wants us to let them go!"

"What's your suggestion, Brother Ali?" I asked calmly.

"I…I think…"

"I recommend that we do as the Great Ayatollah Khomeini says and let the partners go home," I declared gently. "We can still continue our strike and thus maintain our leverage in the negotiations."

"Allah Akbar," almost everyone cried.

"Is there anything else you want us to vote on?" Ali said sarcastically as he stood up to leave.

"No," I said seriously. "I think we have had a very meaningful meeting. In closing, I move that, in order not to waste everyone's time, from now on, Brother Ali and I will discuss the details of strike issues, present them for consideration to the Islamic Revolutionary Committee, and then put them to a vote at the general staff meetings."

This was also approved. In front of the crowd, I suggested to Ali that he and I should have our first meeting in my office immediately.

A few minutes later, I was behind my desk and Ali was sitting across from me.

"My dear Sister Leila," he said, his voice trembling with suppressed rage and dripping with obvious sarcasm. "Since you are the initiator of this stupid meeting and you are apparently so concerned with the commands of your Allah and Ayatollah, why don't you tell me what's on your mind?"

"Listen, Ali," I said firmly. "Let's cut to the chase. You represent the minority. I represent the majority. That's all there is to it. Can you get that through your head?"

"Wait a minute, Leila."

"No! You wait a minute and listen to me carefully, Ali. I appreciate that you are an atheist."

He was quick to react. "And you are a pious Muslim sister, I suppose."

"As the Good Book says, '*al-molko yabqi ma-alkofr va la-yabqi ma-alzolm,*' which means 'a country survives blasphemy, but not oppression.' As you noticed in the meeting, we tolerate you as an atheist, but we cannot give in to your oppressive ways."

"Cut the act!" Ali said. "There's nobody else around. Tell me honestly. When did the promiscuous girl who herself told me she doesn't wear underwear, and who has likely slept with half the world, become such a saint?" He was clearly trembling with rage. "Oh, I could easily crush you."

My fury threatened to get the better of me, never mind that I was the one who'd months ago taunted him with that phony underwear story.

"How would you like me to taint you once and for all as the whore you are!" Ali threatened.

"Listen to me carefully, Ali. If you should ever dream of actually doing such a thing, remember this: all I need to say is that you are spreading rumors about me because you made sexual advances to me, which I rejected. Who do you think they will believe, you or me? And never mind our colleagues! What do you think your wife would think if she heard a thing like that?"

Ali was beside himself as he realized the truth of what I was telling him. "Calm down, Leila. I never said I was going to do any such thing."

"All right, brother." I was content to let the matter die, knowing my point had been made. "Let's talk business, shall we?"

"Fine, fine," Ali said, surrendering. "Just please don't call me 'brother,' OK?"

"Here's all you have to remember. I have the influence to allow you to be on the committee, and I can have you voted off the committee if I want. From here on in, think of me as your boss. Tomorrow, you and I will go to Cyrus's office and will inform him that he and his partners are being released, do you understand?"

"I understand," Ali said, suddenly disconcertingly calm.

"You may go."

I watched him leave my office, wondering why it was that despite my victory, I was trembling so.

CHAPTER 32

It is June 15, 1980, a week after Cyrus's hasty visit and day 137 of my imprisonment.

Skunk is mute about the world outside my cell and especially his negotiations, if any, with my father or Cyrus. He is mute and I am mostly emotionally numb, except when I'm not…when I plummet and soar between the shadowed valley of my depression and the sunlit peak of my confidence that somewhere out there, Pedar and Cyrus are going to save me.

And I write…

• • •

On January 5, 1980, Ali and I went to Cyrus's office to tell him that he and his partners were going to be released. He tried to look surprised to see us, and he and I locked eyes for a second, but I quickly looked away, fearful of having Ali suspect anything was going on between us.

"Brother Cyrus," I began, "we, the members of the Islamic Revolutionary Committee, have reached a point in our discussions where we need to make a final decision about the state of our negotiations with the firm's partners. Since we are not certain that we will be able to come up with our final offer within the next few days, we have decided to allow you and your partners to return to your homes. We will finalize our demands, offer them to you, and if you don't submit to our claim, we will continue our strike until we reach a just conclusion to our negotiations."

Saying this, I turned around and left. Ali followed me. "I'm going home," he said as we waited for the elevator.

"That's fine," I replied, choosing to infer that he was asking my permission. "Go and get some rest."

I wasn't back at my office ten minutes when the phone rang; it was my cousin Bijan, saying, "Why don't you join me for dinner, this evening? It'll be just the three of us," he added meaningfully.

"Three?" I began and then laughed as it dawned on me what Bijan was hinting at. The third individual at dinner would be Cyrus, of course. The man was barely free of his hostage ordeal and he wanted to see me!

"I will come around for you at seven," Bijan said.

True to his word, Bijan came for me at my parents' home at seven and we drove to Cyrus's house. When we arrived, Cyrus greeted us. His beard was gone, and he looked radiantly healthy, although his clothes looked a bit large since he'd lost so much weight.

Before I knew it, I was in his arms and he was squeezing me so hard that both my scarves fell off my head. I was shaking.

"You smell great, Cyrus," I said under my breath.

"You mean I don't stink," he chuckled, and then he hugged Bijan, thanking my cousin for providing cover for this visit and for being a chaperone for propriety's sake.

Cyrus led us out to his patio, where he served us tea. Bijan averted his eyes as I took off my despised scarves and baggy clothing to reveal the slim black cocktail dress I wore underneath. Cyrus again thanked me for what I had done to release him, but expressed his deep concerns about the risk I was taking, endangering my own safety because of him.

"Ali is an unpredictable snake," he said. "Add to that the chaotic political situation we live in. It is a dangerous game you have undertaken, Leila."

The appropriate answer would have been: I will always gladly risk my life for you, my beloved. But for now, my actions will have to speak louder than my words. Although, by asking me to marry him in front of my parents and giving me an engagement ring, which turned out to be his mother's and which I had to hide under the circumstances, Cyrus had proved to me that I meant as much to him as he did to me.

"Don't worry about me," I said. "As I have told you before, I know what I am doing." Anxious to change the subject, I added, "Why don't you tell us how it feels to be home after such a long, unpleasant experience?"

"It's hard to explain," Cyrus began. "I mean, opening your office window to get some fresh air is one thing, but inhaling it out in the open, out of confinement is an entirely different experience. As I returned home to bathe and wear clean clothes, I remembered what Saadi wrote, seven centuries ago: 'Only he who has experienced calamity appreciates the great value of well-being.' The simple pleasure of personal freedom is like paradise after long confinement."

I could hardly listen because my heart and soul were in such turmoil. The princess had rescued the prince by slaying the dragon named Ali. But when, oh when, would the prince be hers forever?

After dinner, we talked about our future strategy. Cyrus asked if from now on, he could be involved rather than merely informed after the fact concerning my schemes.

"Of course," I said, "and here is where you can play a pivotal role. Did you know that Hassan Assad—the man you hired and your partner Niku fired while you were on a business trip somewhere—has become deputy chief revolutionary prosecutor?"

"You're kidding me," Cyrus cried. "Why didn't you tell me sooner, Leila?"

"Because you had enough on your mind," I said. "Hassan has been given the task of auditing all companies nationalized by Khomeini's regime, but it's clear that he does not have the slightest idea how to go about doing it."

"I don't understand what you're getting at," Cyrus said.

"Don't you see? Hassan and our firm, Jenkins Brothers & Associates, are each other's ideal redeemers. As the chairperson for the Islamic committee at the firm, I will arrange a meeting with Hassan."

Cyrus looked panicked. "Am I hearing you right? The girl known for her open blouses and miniskirts, accompanied by the Jew partner of the Big Satan firm that fired Hassan, is going to meet with him now that he is deputy revolutionary prosecutor of the Islamic Republic? Forget it."

"What has happened to your self-confidence, Mr. Great-Negotiator?" I teased Cyrus. "All you have to do is convince Hassan that he needs our skilled auditors' help and that we can give him that. We've got over five hundred such talented employees sitting in our office doing nothing."

"I get it, now," Cyrus said slowly as my idea took hold in his brain. "In effect, we help Hassan by giving him access to the pool of our employees, and he can use his clout to help us end the strike crisis at the firm."

"Exactly," I said triumphantly.

"I'm in, Ms. Strategist!" He laughed, and then added to Bijan, "Isn't this gorgeous fiancée of mine brilliant?"

"Hopefully not too brilliant for her own good," my cousin said, eyeing me worriedly.

"OK, Leila," Cyrus said. "Reach out to Hassan."

"Do you want to take this up with your partners, first?" I asked.

"In time I will let them know," Cyrus said.

CHAPTER 33

June 25, 1980

Day 147 of my incarceration.

"Are you a Jew?" Skunk yelled at me this morning.

I swear my heart stopped beating at that moment.

"Answer me!"

"Where did you hear such a thing?" I stuttered. "Of course I'm not!"

"You must be," he said, pacing the cell. "That blue-eyed bastard." He shook his head as he sat on the cot and stared at me in fury.

Skunk must have found out about Cyrus, I thought, as I leaned against the wall, struggling to think clearly so I could plot my next move. So far, for almost five months, I had dodged all his faltering physical advances and most of his punishments. But now I was doomed. I had to know how he had found about Cyrus's religion.

"Excuse me, Brother Zaki. I wonder what makes you think that my brother—"

"He is a bastard, that's what he is! *Jewed-bazi!* That's what your brother does all the time!"

Jewed-bazi! This derogatory expression meant acting like a stingy Jew—not actually being a Jew. Dared I hope that Skunk had not actually discovered Cyrus's secret, but was merely being derogatory?

"It is payback time," Skunk went on. "In his sermon last night, our mullah said, 'It is your religious duty and holy obligation to take back the money these rich bloodsuckers have stolen from us, pay the *khoms*—the one-fifth Islamic tax—to the mosque fund, and take the rest for yourself.' Every revolutionary is doing this, but no matter how hard I try to deal with your kooni brother, he reneges."

So! Skunk had merely been disparaging Cyrus. I was relieved, but also puzzled. Why were Cyrus and Pedar stalling negotiations with Skunk?

"Can I make a suggestion, Brother Zaki?"

"I mean, if he doesn't care if his sister rots to death..." Skunk rambled on, ignoring me.

"What I think," I said when he had finished grumbling, "is that my brother doesn't know you as well as I do. Please forgive him, because there's a simple solution to this problem." I sat down next to Skunk on the cot. "Please bring my brother here and leave us alone to talk. I promise I will convince him to close the deal with you."

"That blue-eyed son of a whore!" Skunk shrieked as he stormed out, locking the door of my cell behind him.

• • •

The day after we'd released the partners, I telephoned Hassan, introduced myself as the head of the firm's Islamic Revolutionary Committee, and requested an audience.

"You are joking, of course," Hassan said. "I thought your leader was that atheist, communist Ali! Wait a minute. Aren't you the American CPA girl who—"

"Yes, Brother Hassan, and now I am a *mohajabeh*"—a hijab-observant—"sister who heads the firm's Islamic committee. What's more, I am calling you because as a devout Muslim, it is my duty to serve our glorious revolution in any way I can. You see, Jenkins Brothers & Associates is in a position to assist you in your important work."

After expressing his pleasure with Ali's discharge and his replacement by an "observant sister," Hassan promised he would call me back, and so I waited anxiously to hear from him. I knew that time was not on my side. Ali was taking every opportunity to try to undermine my authority with the committee and the firm's staff. I found myself locked in a constant tussle for the upper hand with him. For all Ali's faults, he was not a quitter. I had entered into my scheme merely to win Cyrus's freedom and now I was looking for an exit strategy. But Ali was a true ideologue who was in this fight for the long haul.

I was also becoming more and more frightened of being exposed as a fraud beneath the hijab. On the street, posters everywhere carried the chauvinist writings of Bani Sadr, a leader of the revolution, declaring that a woman's hair emitted seductive rays that targeted innocent men's sexual organs, luring them to commit sinful acts. Then there were those notorious women called the Decency Guards, who patrolled the streets and arrested other women for not complying with "Islamic decency laws." If they caught you with your scarves pushed back even half an inch, exposing your hairline, you were in big trouble. I knew Ali had never really bought into my religious conversion. I could feel his eyes on me all the time, watching and waiting for me to slip up in my Islamic impersonation just once, so he could nail me.

My parents were still after me to leave the country with them, but that was out of the question. I would not desert Cyrus, who was still on the regime's travel blacklist. And finally, despite all my fears of being exposed as a fraud, I took pride in the fact that I, a woman, had become the leader of the committee. I knew the other women at the firm looked up to me. Just as I knew that if Ali brought me down, my degradation would stain them, as well.

There was only one way out of this mess. That was to see it through. I had to end the strike.

A week after I'd telephoned Hassan, he called me back with the good news that he would grant me an appointment at his office. Surprisingly, before I had a chance to suggest it, he told me to bring along Cyrus, saying, "I like that Jew boy better than all his Muslim partners. I will see you both tomorrow at two o'clock. I will send some guards to pick you up."

That afternoon, Cyrus and I met in his office, rehearsing our presentation to encourage the Islamic Revolutionary Prosecutor's Bureau take over Jenkins Brothers & Associates.

CHAPTER 34

On January 11, 1980, at one thirty, I was staring out my office window, awaiting the arrival of Hassan's men to pick up Cyrus and me. If I craned my neck, I could see the beginnings of the American embassy compound and the permanent circus that had taken root there since the taking of the embassy hostages.

It was a damp, raw day, with a light snow falling on the street vendors who'd set up stalls on the sidewalk. Beneath placards that read "Death to America" and "Death to Israel," they sold sandwiches, broiled beetroot, hot tea, and knickknacks to the people who came and gathered in front of the embassy, stretching their necks to look inside, perhaps hoping to catch a glimpse of the Great Satan himself. Although I couldn't see them from my office window, I knew that revolutionary guards had also clustered around the embassy's chained gates. Directly beneath my window was a group of our employees looking cold and bored as they smoked and chatted.

The snow tapered off and for a moment the clouds parted and I saw a bit of the Alborz mountain range to the north of Tehran. In my excited and nervous state about the upcoming meeting with Hassan, I decided to take the parting clouds as a good omen for a bright future. I was thrilled with the idea of brokering some sort of a deal with Hassan. At the same time, I was terrified. Since coming to power, the Revolutionary Prosecutor's office where Hassan worked had made a notorious reputation for itself by sending scores of anti-regime activists to their deaths.

In the absence of Khomeini, who had moved to the holy city of Qom in December 1980, the street confrontations between the communists, Islamic fundamentalists, and Mojahedin had escalated. Determined to smother all but his own fundamentalist Islamic movement and ensure that his candidate, Bani Sadr, was elected president, Khomeini had returned to the city, ostensibly to see doctors to treat his weak heart. The word on the street, however, was that the ayatollah had really returned to personally direct the lethal war against the communists and the Mojahedin—the two factions who had helped him gain power, but now he no longer needed them. As Khomeini's crusade escalated, there was little doubt that both movements would be decimated.

I was pulled from my reveries by the arrival of a confiscated American military van parked in front of our office. Three uniformed revolutionary guards exited the vehicle. I rushed downstairs and joined the crowd of my idle co-workers who had gathered at the entrance of the office. The three pasdars—husky and formidably sullen, a picture of Khomeini pinned to their jackets, and squat, black, oily looking automatic weapons slung over their shoulders—entered and the biggest of them cried, "Who is Sister Leila?"

I raised my hand as everyone looked at me in awe.

"And who is Brother Cyrus?" the big guard shouted.

"He is upstairs," Ali said, elbowing his way to the front of the crowd. "May I ask—"

"The two of them have been summoned by Brother Hassan Assad to the Revolutionary Prosecutor's Bureau," the biggest guard said.

"Brothers," Ali called out, "did you know Cyrus is a Jew, a spy of Israel?"

I held my breath as Ali pointed at me. "That he and this sister—"

"Shut your mouth," ordered the big guard, brushing Ali aside like a fly. Somebody bring me the Jew!"

"I'll get him," Samir yelled, hurrying toward the elevator. The three pasdars followed him.

"What the hell is happening here?" Ali asked me.

"I have no idea. Perhaps they want to question Cyrus in my presence," I said. "I think you should ask them."

And so Ali made the mistake of following my advice when Samir and the guards returned with Cyrus.

"Brothers," Ali said. "Before you leave, can I check this with Brother Hassan?"

"You can call anyone you want," the big one replied. "But I have no intention to stand here and waste my time on mouse shits like you."

And with that, the lead guard told Cyrus and me to follow them to the van. Surrounded by these three brothers as they escorted us out to the street, I had time to notice on closer inspection that they were armed, ironically, with Israeli-made Uzi submachine guns left from the Shah's era.

I knew a little something about guns—at least those that were in the Shah's armory—thanks to my grandfather, General Omid. When I was a teenager, the general and I would spend many early mornings at our desert compound out on the dunes while it was still cool, where he would tutor me in the use of his personal weaponry. I got quite good at blasting bottles and cans.

One of the pasdars got behind the wheel and the big one sat next to him. Cyrus and the third guard took the second row of seats and I sat in the last. Looking out of the windows as we rattled along the streets, I was again struck by how my beloved Tehran, this once lively and beautiful metropolis, had morphed into a city of ghosts—unsightly and gloomy. The avenues we passed were strewn with a gray mix of snow and garbage. Walls everywhere were layered with a peeling, lurid collage of Khomeini posters, revolutionary graffiti, and wind-tattered banners proclaiming "Bani Sadr for President."

We passed open-bed military trucks filled with young men with scrawny beards. They wore camouflage uniforms, had cigarettes dangling from their lips, and now and again would fire their guns into the air like bored children idly fidgeting with their toys—regardless that their stray bullets falling back to earth had killed many innocent pedestrians since the start of the revolution.

We arrived at the Revolutionary Prosecutor's Bureau complex of buildings. I knew it well, for I had often as a little girl accompanied my grandfather, General Omid, here when it had been the headquarters for the Shah's joint chiefs of staff. The checkpoint at the entrance gate was swarming with people. As the van idled, and the driver rolled down his window and snarled orders for the crowd to make way, I saw a woman at the sentry post sobbing and begging.

"Please, brother," she pleaded to the stony-faced guard. "Let me inside to inquire about my missing son!"

"Do you see all these people out there with you, sister?" the guard demanded. "Every one of them has someone missing."

"I know, brother," the woman moaned. "But—"

"Listen to me, sister," the guard said. "Has your son worked for SAVAK—the Shah's secret police?"

"No, brother. He is only sixteen."

"At school, has he been a Boy Scout?"

"What is a Boy Scout?" pleaded the desperate mother, sounding absolutely bewildered.

"This American thing, you know? They take the boys camping and they make them sleep together, make faggots out of them."

"No, brother. I swear my son is a good boy. He is an observant Muslim who has fought for the revolution. Last year he went out to demonstrate against the Shah and he never came back."

"Last year?" the guard said. "That was when the Shah was killing everyone. That's the answer. Congratulations, sister, on your son's martyrdom. Now, go home and celebrate this blessing instead of wailing like this."

Someone in the crowd shouted, "Is this Islamic justice?" Others took up the protest. Immediately, the three pasdars in our truck jumped out and took up positions around the sentry post. They pointed their machine guns at the crowd.

"You damned enemies of Allah," the big one roared. "Either you get lost or I will send you to hell!"

He fired a burst from his Uzi into the air. Instantly, the crowd disbursed, all except the brave mother who had come to plead for help in locating her teenage son. But the big guard who had fired his gun kicked her—the sickening thud of his boot into her belly was somehow more disturbing and frightening than the sound of his machine gun a few moments before. The woman, jackknifed by the kick, fell to the ground and, weeping, scuttled away like a crab.

In front of me in the van, Cyrus sat silent, his head down. I wiped my tears with the corner of my scarf as the acrid stench of spent gunpowder drifted from the guard's smoking gun. Truly, the madmen were running the asylum.

Now that the entrance was clear, the three pasdars returned to drive us through the gate. Eventually we parked and the guards escorted us across the vast, front courtyard, where a statue of the Shah on horseback lay toppled next to its marble base. We entered the tall building through a doorway above which was a banner torn from a bed sheet that read Revolutionary Prosecutor's Headquarters in dripped red paint.

Cyrus and I were led through a maze of lengthy, cold corridors. In all the offices we passed by there were metal desks and chairs in place of the expensive furniture I remembered from the Shah's days. The official word was that furniture here and in other government buildings had been burned, but the gossip on the street had it that the revolutionary guards had looted the furnishings. Eventually we got to Hassan's large, rectangular office at the end of the corridor.

"That's Hassan," Cyrus said under his breath, gesturing with his chin toward a small man wearing a dark suit and a black shirt seated behind a large metal desk at the far end of the room. Even at this distance. I could see that Hassan's thick beard could not cover the pockmarks all over his face. Around his desk and lining the walls of Hassan's office were many chairs, all occupied.

So far, Hassan had not noticed us, but when the big guard announced our arrival, Hassan the Pockmarked, now the deputy revolutionary prosecutor of the Islamic Republic of Iran, sprang out of his chair and came forward. He embraced Cyrus and uttered the catchphrase that had become an integral part of post-revolution greetings.

"Congratulations on the victory of our revolution!" Hassan cried.

"Congratulations on the victory of our revolution," Cyrus echoed.

Don't let your guard down, even for an instant, I warned myself as Hassan turned his attention to me. I knew that unlike most business negotiations, in this one, Cyrus and I might not just lose some money or some power.

We very well might lose our lives.

"Allah Akbar!" Hassan exclaimed to me as he continued to embrace Cyrus. "Congratulations, sister, on being mohajabeh."

"Thank you, and many congratulations to you on your new position, Brother Hassan," I replied, stretching my hand to shake his, but I snatched it back quickly, pretending I had meant only to check my head scarves, as I realized he would never touch a *na-mahram*—religiously impermissible—woman.

Hassan returned to his desk and invited us to sit down. "I hear Sister Leila has taken over the Islamic Revolutionary Committee of the firm from that communist guy…"

"Ali," Cyrus reminded him.

"Yes, Ali, I remember him quite well from when I was your employee, Cyrus." Hassan was grinning. I could see how much he was enjoying this opportunity to rub in the reversal of fortunes between himself and Cyrus. "I'm glad Sister Leila got rid of Ali as leader of your revolutionary committee," Hassan said. "So, what brings you here, Brother Cyrus?"

"Well," Cyrus said. "First, I wanted to say how pleased my partners and I were to hear of your position—"

"Donkey's ass! Since when have I become a pleasure to your partners? You fired me, remember? That pussy partner of yours, Niki"— he seemed to be referring to Niku—"who threatened us revolutionaries with his connections in the Shah's SAVAK, may both names be erased. Where is Niki these days? Is that faggot pleased that I am the deputy to His Holiness, the chief revolutionary prosecutor? That should make his balls rise to his throat."

"But to forgive is the golden rule of Islam," I said, trying to both change the subject and take part in the conversation.

"Sister Leila," Hassan said evenly. "Do you know that I was fired from this American Zionist firm?"

"But I'm sure you remember, that, at the time, I—" Cyrus stammered.

"At the time you what, Brother Cyrus?" Hassan asked.

"I just want to respectfully remind you," Cyrus said meekly, "that you were fired when I was abroad. When I came back, I did send for you, didn't I?"

"How could you possibly have expected me to step foot in your office after the disrespect that was shown to me?" Hassan took a deep breath. "However, yes, you did send for me, and you did offer me back my job, and I thank you for that."

"No thanks are necessary, brother," Cyrus replied.

"Now, now"—Hassan wagged his finger—"A good deed is a good deed and should be repaid. My debt of gratitude to you is why I asked you, a Jew, and not any of those quasi-Muslim sons-of-Satan partners of yours to come here with Sister Leila."

"Thank you, brother," Cyrus said.

I could only imagine how he was controlling himself not to react to Hassan's Jew remark.

"Let me tell you something, Sister Leila," Hassan said. "Although Cyrus is not a Muslim, he has the soul and the heart of a Muslim, and that is why I proudly call him a brother."

I pulled my courage together. "The reason we wanted to see you, Brother Hassan, is that I think we can be of help to you."

"And you can be of help to us," Cyrus said immediately.

"You see, Sister Leila?" Hassan said, looking at Cyrus admiringly. "As I said, there's so much one can learn from the Jews. You want to help us, but this Jew brother immediately makes your favor into a transaction. Tell me the truth, Cyrus. Are you really impressed with the victory of our revolution?"

"Who isn't?" Cyrus replied rhetorically. "Indeed, it has been a glorious revolution."

"Listen to him, Sister Leila? He answers so beautifully. Every word chosen with precision, like a poet. This is why his people own the world." Hassan chuckled. "A Jew happy with the Islamic Revolution! Now we have seen everything. However, I shall prove to you yet that there is benevolence inherent in Islam. Cyrus, you fired me, but here I am embracing you."

"Thank you a thousand times, Brother Hassan."

"Islam recognizes and respects the followers of all religions that are the People of the Book," Hassan continued, "that is, Jews, Christians, and Zoroastrians. Of course, these religions are not up to the level of Islam, but they are acceptable."

"You are right, Brother Hassan," I interjected. "As I said, Islam teaches love, compassion, and forgiveness."

"Unless, of course, the Jews in question are the blood-sucking Israeli Zionists squatting in Palestine," Hassan added.

"Of course," Cyrus quickly pretended to agree. "So, what exactly are your important duties here, Brother Hassan?" he asked in an effort to get back to our main agenda.

"My boss," Hassan answered, "His Holiness, the Chief Revolutionary Prosecutor, has delegated me to audit and evaluate all abandoned industries and to recommend whether or not they should be nationalized."

Obviously, this was a task over and above Hassan's knowledge and abilities. It demanded top expertise in management and technology, as well as accounting, all of which, thanks to the revolution, were scarce in Iran.

"And who do you have to do all this for you?" Cyrus asked.

Hassan leaned back in his chair. He lit a cigarette and eyed Cyrus with amusement, squinting against the smoke.

"You are so clever, Cyrus, even among the Jews, you must be one of the canniest ones. I see what you're getting at, all right. Perhaps I could use a few people from your office to help me."

"Not a few I'm afraid," I said. "To properly address this major task you will need Cyrus, his partners, and all the rest of our staff."

"All of you?" Hassan pondered, thoughtfully stroking his rough beard.

I persisted. "Think about it. Think of so many devastated industries you have inherited."

"Brother Hassan, we are offering you our expertise," Cyrus said bluntly. "We are proposing that our firm become a part of the Revolutionary Prosecutor's Bureau."

"Allah knows how clever you Jews are!" Hassan laughed, slapping his thigh. "Do you think I don't understand what you are up to?"

"Of course you do." Cyrus shrugged. "You are a brilliant man, and I can't hide anything from you. But consider the facts. You haven't even begun your arduous task, and already you are so busy. You are welcome to take as few of our employees as you want, but I promise you, it won't work that way. As Sister Leila suggested, you will need all of us—from partners to the most junior employees—if you want to accomplish your revolutionary mission successfully."

"And what do you get out of it, Cyrus?" Hassan asked, back to stroking his beard.

"Frankly speaking, brother, this is a barter," Cyrus explained. "Your commandeering the firm will resolve the strike mess we are in. In exchange, we will get your department running in top shape, impress your superiors, and position you to take on even more important and lofty revolutionary goals."

I was astonished by Cyrus's bluntness. I waited anxiously for Hassan's harsh response. But Cyrus's negotiation instincts were as sharp as always.

"As a benevolent person," Hassan said, "I do want to help you." He rubbed his eyes. "God knows how tired I am. I haven't slept for so many nights; I can hardly think anymore."

He lit another cigarette. "Honestly, Cyrus, this is a decision that I can't make on my own. I need the approval of His Holiness, the Chief Prosecutor of Islamic Republic."

"I understand," Cyrus said. "If His Holiness needs any clarification, I would be honored to respond."

"You best let me do the talking with the likes of His Holiness, Jew boy," Hassan remarked wryly. "I will try to get his approval. The two of you come back first thing tomorrow morning and I will give you His Holiness's answer."

Hassan's guards drove us back to the firm. I was in my office when Ali stuck his head through the door, curious to know what had gone on with Hassan. I told him that it was none of his business, and that enraged him.

"I'm going to call a general meeting of the staff members to impeach you," he spat.

"Go ahead, Ali," I said. "Do me a favor and call the meeting for tomorrow, say about eleven o'clock?

"What?" Ali stammered. "You're ordering me?"

"Thank you," I said in dismissal. "Please shut my door on your way out."

CHAPTER 35

The next day, January 12, 1980, at eleven o'clock, I attended the general meeting Ali had called in the common room downstairs.

"Sister Leila will now give a report on the meeting she and Cyrus had with Brother Hassan Assad, yesterday," Ali announced.

"First of all," I began, "I would like to encourage everyone to vote for Mr. Bani Sadr—our Imam's chosen candidate—in the upcoming presidential elections on January twenty-fifth."

"Allah Akbar!" came the answering shout. It's always good to open with a crowd-pleaser.

"In answer to Brother Ali's question, all of you may not know that Brother Hassan was once an employee of this firm. So, it was on the behalf of all of you that I paid my respects to our former employee and congratulated him on his new appointment. During the call, he invited me to his office. I had no idea that he had invited Cyrus also."

"That's all?" Ali interrupted skeptically. "You were in the Revolutionary Prosecutor's Bureau, you had Cyrus with you, and you didn't hand him over to the authorities?"

"Actually, when Brother Hassan's men took Cyrus along, I thought that was what he had in mind," I replied. "But it turned out that he respects Cyrus. Anyway, again, on everyone's behalf, I wished him well and, out of courtesy, asked if we could be of any help to him in his accounting duties on behalf of our glorious revolution. He thanked me and said that he wants to see Cyrus and me this afternoon. He is sending his pasdars for us once again, so please everyone, let's make sure this time not to make such an event out of it."

"Allah Akbar!" cried my co-workers.

I looked at Ali. "Any further questions, Brother?" I asked casually.

Ali, glaring at me, left the meeting.

Thankfully, my colleagues heeded my request and pretended like nothing was happening when the revolutionary guards arrived to pick up Cyrus and me. The ride to the headquarters building and our entry through the gates was this time similarly uneventful. And when we were finally in front of Hassan, he had good news.

"You don't know how lucky you are," Hassan said by way of greeting. "I spoke with His Holiness concerning your proposition. Initially, he disagreed, reasoning that, with the position that Imam Khomeini has taken against America, it would be inappropriate to associate ourselves with the Iranian branch of an American firm. But after I assured him that you are no longer affiliated with the Great Satan, he came around."

"Thank you, Brother Hassan," I said. "We really appreciate that."

"And you, Cyrus? Are you happy now?" he asked and lit a cigarette.

"I'm happy," Cyrus responded. "I'm sure our affiliation will take a big load off your shoulders. However, before we can begin to serve you, there is the small matter of the strike at the firm."

"Right." Hassan nodded. "This is so ridiculous! Sister, you cannot end this strike foolishness?"

"I've tried, brother, but the workers are very invested in the strike idea."

"It's a long story," Cyrus said, coming to my defense. "But Sister Leila has made every effort to resolve the situation."

"If Sister Leila is in charge, what is the problem?" Hassan asked.

"You said you remembered Ali from the office?" Cyrus asked, by way of reply.

"That communist, atheist piece of garbage?" Hassan exclaimed. "What a bully he was to me! He's the holdup?"

Both Cyrus and I nodded. "He's the chief instigator and advocate for the strike," Cyrus added.

Hassan picked up his phone and began dialing the number of our firm. "I'm going to call him now, but I'm telling you two, after today, I don't want to speak with him again. And I don't want him to have anything to do with our work together, that son-of-a-thousand-dogs communist!"

Then Hassan spoke into the telephone.

"Yes. This is Brother Hassan Assad from the Revolutionary Prosecutor's Bureau. Let me speak with Ali." He covered the mouthpiece and said, "I'm going to enjoy this," and then he let out a burp of laughter. "Hello, who's this? Salam, Brother Ali! This is Brother Hassan Assad. Yes…Congratulations on the victory of our revolution…Thanks to you... Yes…Thanks to those who gave their precious lives…Yes, of course…"

Hassan winked at us.

"Now listen to me, brother. I understand you are still conducting a strike at the firm. Ah, in order to negotiate a settlement for your co-workers? Aha...I see...Well, you have negotiated enough." He yelled into the phone. "Enough! It's over! Do you understand?"

I could faintly hear Ali acquiescing to Hassan's commands. I just wished I could see the apoplectic look on his face as he realized his dreams of ransom were up in smoke.

"Now," Hassan continued, "I instruct you to call a general meeting of all our brothers and sisters there at the firm, and to repeat to them, word by word, what I am going to tell you. I will say it slowly so that you can write. Do you have paper and pen handy? Good, now write this: 'As the Deputy Revolutionary Prosecutor, I, Hassan Assad, instruct each and all of you, partners and employees alike, to follow the orders of Brother Cyrus and Sister Leila. Got that? Good!"

Hassan slammed down the phone without even saying good-bye to Ali. He turned to us and said—his voice suddenly calm again, "Petty revolutionaries like Ali make me sick. Anyway. As of now, Brother Cyrus, the strike is over, and if anyone says different, just let me know."

"So where do we go from here?" I asked.

Hassan stretched and yawned. "I'm tired for today. I'll come see you at your—I mean our firm—tomorrow morning."

Next morning, I was standing behind the glass entrance door of our office, waiting for Hassan to arrive. His van rolled to a stop in front of our door and his pasdars jumped out to stand at attention and salute him as he exited his vehicle.

"Salam, Sister Leila," Hassan said as I welcomed him.

I accompanied him to my office and called Cyrus to join us, thinking that this was the third day in a row I was seeing Hassan, and he was still wearing the same black suit and shirt as on day one.

"All right, let's get down to business," Hassan said as Cyrus came into my office. "Assemble your partners and employees so I can address them."

A few minutes later, everyone was in the common room. Hassan made his grand entrance. He looked out at the crowd. "In the name of Imam Khomeini, the savior of our oppressed people, whose words are as precious as pure diamonds, may Allah keep him safe, alive and healthy until the emergence of our Messiah, Mehdi the Hidden Imam, and as the deputy to His Holiness, the chief revolutionary prosecutor, I start this meeting."

"Allah Akbar!"

He took a piece of paper out of his pocket and began reading. "His Holiness the Chief Revolutionary Prosecutor and I have discussed the situation of this firm, Jenkins Brothers & Associates, which we are renaming Allah Brothers & Associates."

"Allah Akbar!" everyone in the room shouted as I heard Cyrus, who was sitting next to me mutter under his breath, "Now we are partners and associates with Allah!"

"These are the terms His Holiness has decreed," Hassan continued. "One: Allah Brothers & Associates shall be under the control of its Islamic Revolutionary Committee, which will report directly to me through Sister Leila."

"Allah Akbar!"

"Two: The members of the staff shall from now on be equal to the partners."

"Allah Akbar!"

"Three: Allah Brothers & Associates will act as consultants to the Revolutionary Prosecutor's Bureau."

"Allah Akbar!"

"Four: The president of the firm, who will be elected by the staff members, should be an observant Shiite Muslim man." Saying this, Hassan glowered at the partners. "No proponents of the Shah—Death to Shah!"

"Allah Akbar!"

"And no atheists," Hassan added, staring at Ali. "That's it! Any comments?"

I quickly raised my hand and said, "Whatever Brother Hassan decides is acceptable to the Islamic Revolutionary Committee."

"All right," Hassan went on. "Who do you brothers and sisters suggest as the president of the firm?"

Farnaz raised her hand. "I nominate Leila."

"Oh no," I whispered to myself.

Thankfully, Hassan came to my rescue, saying that while he admired my leadership, "a man" must be the firm's president, not a woman.

"I suggest Brother Samir," I offered.

"Allah Akbar!" cried everyone but Ali, who was distinctly shocked.

And poor Samir looked absolutely stricken with fear.

To everyone's Allah Akbar, Hassan officially named Samir president of Allah Brothers & Associates.

CHAPTER 36

From that point on, Cyrus and I held daily meetings in his office with Samir and Hassan—neither of whom understood the depth of the financial quagmire our firm had fallen into. In addition to the many clients who owed us fees and had no means to pay, we had acquired a giant of a client who used our services for free. This meant that we did not have enough income to pay our five hundred plus employees who, instigated by Ali, were pushing for salaries owed to them. And that was exactly where we needed Hassan.

"You are financial advisers, find a solution!" he said when I told him about our situation.

"The solution is simple, Brother Hassan," I answered. "We have to trim our costs and receive income."

Frowning, Hassan pretended like he hadn't heard me, and I kicked myself for not being smart enough to realize he would react badly to the notion of taking advice from a woman.

Hassan turned to Cyrus. "What do you think?"

Cyrus, in an obvious effort to get poor, frightened Samir involved in the conversation and help validate him as acting president of the firm, said, "Wasn't it yesterday that you asked to speak to me about this, Brother Samir?"

"Um, uh—yes, of course," Samir stuttered.

"Yes, Sister Leila, Samir, and I talked about this," Cyrus continued, smoothly lying. "We conferred and came to the conclusion that the only recourse was for your bureau, Hassan, to pay our core people their salary, while we begin to discharge nonessential employees."

"Makes sense," Hassan nodded. "I want Brother Samir to consult with Sister Leila and Brother Cyrus and fire all the extras." And as if the shock was not enough for poor Samir, he added, "And remember: no compensation, no past due salaries! We don't have that sort of money."

"Did you hear that?" I asked Cyrus after Hassan and Samir had left. "He said 'we,' which means he now sees himself as part of the firm. Our plan has succeeded beyond our expectations. The strike is history, money will start coming in, and we now have a mandate to rid ourselves of the deadweight and troublemakers.

"So, why don't we celebrate it tonight?" Cyrus murmured, moving close to me.

"No, no, and *no*!" I wagged my finger at him like a mother admonishing a naughty child. "Be sensible, please. We must not risk everything by being vulnerable to gossip and rumor in these critical times."

"But—"

"No!" I said, and quickly left his office before he had a chance to melt my resolve.

I returned to my own office and called Samir, who was totally shocked and appalled by the turn of events.

"How can I fire people?" Samir moaned. "I would rather fire myself."

I tried to soothe him. "Relax. All you have to do is call a staff meeting and pass the buck, telling everyone that you have orders from the revolutionary prosecutor to implement staff reductions."

"They'll hate me," Samir protested.

"Nonsense," I said. "Just lay it on thick how if it were up to you, nobody would be fired, but you have your orders from Hassan, and they must be followed."

"You really think it will be all right?" Samir asked.

"I do," I said firmly. "Now, if you want my advice, you should start from the bottom. First dismiss the drivers, because we have taken away the partners' cars and their drivers are virtually unemployed."

I took grim satisfaction that Cyrus's driver Nabi—who Bijan had accused of spreading gossip about Cyrus and me—would be among those first to go.

"Next you target the Mojahedin and the communists," I added.

"You mean Ali?" Samir whispered in disbelief.

Exactly, I thought triumphantly.

"You need to follow Brother Hassan's orders," I reminded Samir and hung up.

Soon there was a frenzy of firing. After that gossip-mongering Nabi had been discharged, he interrupted a meeting I was having with Cyrus in his office to beg for mercy.

"I am so sorry for the way I behaved," he said, seemingly referring to having spied on Cyrus and me, and spreading rumors about our affair. "I'm a stupid son of a mule," Nabi continued pleading to Cyrus. "You have always been so kind to me and my family."

"I'm sorry," Cyrus said. "I can't help you. Brother Hassan is running things here now."

In less than a week, Samir had lowered the boom on almost all the deadbeats and troublemakers, and our workforce had been winnowed down to less than a hundred handpicked employees.

The only one left to get rid of was Ali.

In the meantime, Cyrus and I prodded Samir to push Hassan to hash out the details on his promise to pay us for our services and to give us new clients.

"I know where all these suggestions that Samir relays to me come from," Hassan told Cyrus and me. "What was I thinking to have allowed a Jew and a woman to advise this lap dog Samir I have put in charge of Allah Brothers & Associates?"

"Cyrus had nothing to do with this, Brother Hassan," I reassured him. "You are an accountant yourself. How do you expect us to survive? As the old saying has it, 'With no yeast, the dough turns into unleavened bread.'"

"Why doesn't this Jew friend of ours have his renegade American partners find us some new clients," Hassan demanded, glaring at us. "And wire back the money they embezzled from us, as well!"

"I hope you're not serious," Cyrus said with a chuckle. "The Americans and their influence and money are gone. Forget about them. On the other hand—"

"On the other hand, what?" Hassan demanded.

"On the other hand, there is plenty of oil money in this country," Cyrus said. "And the Revolutionary Prosecutor's Bureau has a sizable budget. I'm sure you will be able to find the funding to keep our firm alive and your department going."

Hassan laughed. "All right, Rabbi Cyrus! How much?"

"Why don't you ask Sister Leila?" Cyrus said, just as we'd rehearsed. "She is the one who has access to our financial records."

"Well," I said, playing my part, "to keep us going…Let me see. How about we receive our regular fees for the work we do for your bureau—minus a thirty percent discount due to the holy nature of the work we are undertaking together?"

"In addition, you make it mandatory that all the financially viable corporations you are supervising use our accounting services," Cyrus added.

I held my breath as I waited for Hassan's reaction. A decree that using our services was mandatory for virtually every viable company left in Iran was the prize we were after all along.

"Listen to this canny Jew," Hassan said wryly. He lit a cigarette. "Did I ever tell you that my father's best friend was a Jew? 'Always learn from these people,' he used to say—may he rest in eternal peace in paradise with Mohammad and his descendants."

"So, as advised by your late father of blessed memory, I take it you will listen to Cyrus?" I asked. "You will accept our fee proposal and mandate that all companies under your supervision use our services?"

Hassan nodded. "We have a deal."

On his way out, Hassan called over his shoulder, "I think I saw Ali here. Did I not tell you to get rid of all the communists?"

CHAPTER 37

And then came the horrid night of January 28, 1980.

The news was full of outraged reports about the half dozen American diplomats who had been off the grounds of the American embassy when it had been seized. For the past three months, they'd found refuge in the nearby Canadian and Swiss embassies, and today they'd been able to flee the country using Canadian passports. The streets were filled with angry, chanting demonstrators and revolutionary guards firing their weapons into the air in their impotent fury over this handful of Americans who had escaped the regime's clutches.

Cyrus and I held a late-afternoon meeting with Hassan and Samir. When it was over, the three of them left for the day and I returned to my office to catch up on paperwork. The hours flew, as I was engrossed in my work. Before I knew it, it was seven o'clock. I was the only one in the building, or so I thought.

I picked up my handbag to leave when Ali suddenly appeared blocking the doorway.

"I was just leaving," I said.

"You'll leave when I say you can," Ali replied, leaning against the doorjamb so that I couldn't get past him.

"Get out of my way," I ordered.

"Go on," Ali said. "Pretend that you don't know."

"I don't know what you're talking about."

"After getting rid of most of the firm's employees," Ali ranted, "that puppet of yours Samir has finally found the balls to fire me!"

"He did?" I tried to feign surprise and sympathy. "I'm sorry, but I hope you understand that Samir gets his instructions from the Islamic Revolutionary Prosecutor's Bureau, not me."

"I don't buy that," Ali said. "You and that bastard Cyrus have been the cause of all this. Now listen to me. You—"

"No. You listen to me!" I cried. "Samir has fired more than four hundred of your co-workers—the suppressed masses, according to you—and what have you done? Nothing! Your attitude has been 'As long as I have my job, to hell with the others.'"

"That's not true," Ali sputtered. "What was I supposed to do?"

"Ali, look, it doesn't matter," I said, reversing tack. "What you don't seem to understand is that I might very well be the next on Samir's list."

"You don't have to worry," Ali said. " Because for as long as you and that Jew cocksucker of yours sleep with each other, and ride donkeys like Hassan and Samir, you are not going to be touched."

That was when I lost it. All my sense of superiority and the pride I took in my knowledge I could manipulate Ali went out the window as I responded to his insult with raw fury.

"You atheist, communist bastard!" I snarled. "I've warned you once that if you open your mouth and spread such un-Islamic filth about Brother Cyrus and me, I swear I will tell Hassan—and your wife—that you have propositioned me."

"You are such a goddamned hypocrite," Ali growled.

He was continuing to block me from leaving my office. For the first time, I began to feel a nervous about the fact I was alone with him in the building. Still, I figured my best defense was a strong offense.

"Listen carefully," I said. "I believe in religious laws which are absolute. You, my friend, need to remember that we live in the Islamic Republic of Iran, not the People's Republic of Iran as you so devoutly wished."

"And you, Leila," Ali countered, stepping into my office and shutting the door behind him. "You need to remember that you were and still are the slut who wears no underwear underneath her miniskirts." He laughed. "I bet right now you're not wearing any underwear beneath your hijab!"

And so, once again the teasing, flirting games I had made up to tantalize and unnerve Ali were coming back to haunt me.

"Another of your false accusations," I responded quickly to cover my confusion and guilt. "To the path of the righteous I invite all, including atheist liars like you."

"How you used to flaunt your tits at me," Ali said. "How you used to sit in your chair in your miniskirt, showing me your thighs…"

As he spoke, he kept closing the distance between us, always careful to place himself in my path if I were to try to bolt from my office.

"Listen, Ali," I said. "If you don't shut up, you will regret it."

"Oh, really? Well, I won't shut up. Or maybe I will, if you show me your tits again!"

He reached out, grabbed me with both arms, and flung me onto the top of my desk. I screamed as he tore open the zipper of my jacket and pulled my scarves from my head. His eyes were filled with hate and desire as he used one hand to pin me to the desk and the other to fumble with his belt.

"Yes, I bet you're still not wearing underwear," he panted. "Let's see if I win my bet!"

I balled my hands into fists and swung wildly. I connected with the side of his head but he shook off the blows like they were flies. I screamed again and again—screamed until my throat was hoarse.

"You've screwed me enough, Sister Leila," he laughed. "It's time I screwed you."

The next thing I knew pasdars—stinking of cigarette smoke, sweat, and gun oil, the leather slings of their automatic weapons creaking—were pulling Ali off me.

"Thank God! Thank you!" I began.

"Silence, whore!" one of the guards shouted.

They were averting their eyes from me—from my hair unveiled, I abruptly realized.

"She took off her veil, brothers!" Ali was howling. "She seduced me with her wanton ways!"

And to my utter astonishment, they left Ali alone.

And arrested me.

CHAPTER 38

I barely had time to grab my scarves as the guards dragged me from my office and out of the building to the sidewalk. A throng of curious bystanders was clustered by the entrance. I guessed one or some of them had heard my screams and called the guards.

These people now began to curse me. "Cover up!" one of them shouted. And others, men and women, took up the chorus. I hurriedly wrapped my scarves around my head as best I could as the guards hustled me into a parked car. They drove me to the same Revolutionary Prosecutor's Bureau complex where Cyrus and I had on two occasions met with Hassan. But now I was arriving under quite different circumstances, I knew. I wondered if I should mention Hassan, claim that I was under his department's protection, but I was too frightened to speak. I was marched into a different building in the complex, taken to a windowless room with nothing in it but a table and three chairs, told to wait, and left there. I sat, trembling, weeping aloud, my mind spinning with awful thoughts of doom. I knew my situation quite well.

Ironically, in this insane, violent, repressed, and angry fundamentalist society, if nothing had happened between

Ali and me, I could have made good on my potent threat to bring about his character assassination among his colleagues and wife through innuendo and gossip, but now that the authorities were involved, the advantage had shifted to Ali. In this new Iran, in a matter of rape or attempted rape, the burden of doubt was always on the woman—on me—to prove that I had not been the witchy seductress luring a good Muslim man to sin.

The door opened and a short, stout mullah with an ivory beard stepped in, followed by a pasdar.

"Stand up for Hazrat Agha!" the guard shouted, poking me with the barrel of his rifle. I did as I was told, murmuring, "Allah Akbar."

Another man entered the room. To my surprise, he was the same, young, small hairy fellow dressed in military drag who had led the takeover of the American embassy. He had some sort of ledger tucked under his arm. Ali had told me his name, but for the life of me, I couldn't recall it.

"Sit down, sister," this little bearded fellow said as he took a seat next to the mullah, and the guard took his place behind me by the door. "My name is Brother Mahmoud Ahmadinejad, and I will be recording the notes of this proceeding."

The mullah cleared his throat and began, his voice weak and infirm. "*Besm Allah Al-Rahman Al-Rahim*"—in the name of Allah, the Beneficent and the Merciful—"What's your name?"

"Leila, Hazrat Agha," I answered.

The mullah shook his head. Beneath his white turban, and above his bushy yellow Santa Claus beard, his red-rimmed, gimlet eyes flared with disgust and disdain.

"From now on your name is Zahra," the mullah said. "Forget Leila as if you were never born. Understand?"

"I do, Agha," I said, meekly. I hadn't thought it was possible to be more frightened than I'd been just a few moments ago, but things truly can always be worse. By wiping me of my identity and giving me a new name—it would be extraordinarily difficult for my family or Cyrus to discover my whereabouts or fate. I knew I was on the verge of officially disappearing, just like the son of that poor woman whom the pasdar had kicked in the belly on my first visit to this complex to meet with Hassan.

"Sister Zahra," the mullah went on. "For the sin that you have committed, you will be tried and punished according to the laws of Islam." He glanced at Ahmadinejad. "Word for word, you write what I ask and what this sister replies in confessions to her sins."

"What sins, Haji Agha?" I whimpered.

"You talk only when I tell you," the mullah admonished.

I nodded obediently.

"As a religious judge, I require detailed knowledge of the circumstances surrounding your shameful sin. If you tell the truth, I have the authority to reduce your sentence. Do you understand, Sister Zahra?"

"Yes."

"Now, tell me how deeply did he enter you?"

"What?" I blurted out, so astonished by the question that for a moment I forgot to be afraid.

"Why the depth?" the mullah said rhetorically. "Because this is a measure for determining your punishment. If under half an inch, it means that you are still a virgin and the punishment is lighter. But if he has entered you more than that, then there is probable cause that he has deflowered you."

Flabbergasted at this old man's sick mind, I begged, "I swear to Allah, I have not done what you say with anyone, Hazrat Agha."

The mullah held up his finger in reprimand. "I recite from the Koran, Sureh Alnesa, which is the portion relating to women. Listen carefully to chapter four, verse fifteen: 'Those who commit adultery among your women, you must have four witnesses against them, from among you. If they do bear witness, then you shall keep such women in their homes until they die or until Allah creates an exit for them.'"

Ahmadinejad stopped writing and flipped through the pages of his ledger. "The report filed by the pasdars states that three guards and the man you seduced saw you with your hair uncovered and your legs spread wide on your desk, beckoning to them. That is the four witnesses required."

"But I was not naked, and I was being held down!" I protested. "And how can the man who assaulted me also be a witness against me?"

Ahmadinejad only shook his head in what seemed like pity at my question, as if I were an imbecile who could not be expected to understand the obvious. His dismissive attitude made me so angry I tried to go on the offensive.

"It's all lies! Our office is run by Brother Hassan Assad, the deputy revolutionary prosecutor, who had the communist Ali fired. Ali then attacked me because he blamed me for his losing his job. He beat me. He beat an observant Muslim woman, for Allah's sake!"

"I have instructed my brothers to search your office for traces of virgin's blood," said the mullah in his whispery voice, as if he had not heard a word I had said. "Now, let's turn to more important issues. Where did the adulterer ejaculate, inside or outside you? He has confessed that he has tried not to inject his seed inside you, but you clung to him, bit his tongue, and kept him inside you."

I knew then I was doomed, but at least I could take this opportunity to set the record straight—that is, if this little gnome Ahmadinejad was even writing what I was really saying, as opposed to what he and the mullah wanted to have reflected in the official transcript.

"I was fully dressed when they arrested me. I was screaming for help when I was attacked. Why would I scream and draw the attention of the pasdars if I didn't want to be rescued?"

"Did he sodomize you also?" the old mullah intoned. "And if so..."

His lecherous interrogation went on and on, endlessly obsessed with virginity, vaginal bleeding, penetration, and ejaculation. Finally, I simply refused to answer any more of his disgusting questions, realizing my cooperation or lack of it would have no bearing on the grim outcome of these farcical proceedings.

"Let it be written," the mullah finally ordered his court secretary Ahmadinejad, "that after my admonitions, the adulteress withdrew her previous testimony, her claims of innocence, and confessed to her sinful act."

I began to cry.

"Farewell, sister," Ahmadinejad said, snapping shut his ledger, the crack echoing against the bare walls of the interrogation room, as sharp as a pistol's report.

The pasdar led me to a garage. I was handed over to the revolutionary guard who was to become my jailer, who I would come to nickname Skunk.

Skunk blindfolded me, led me to a vehicle, and brought me to this cell, where, for almost five months I have languished, taking whatever respite and escape from my troubles I could by writing this memoir.

CHAPTER 39

June 28, 1980

Three days ago, I asked Skunk to let me talk to Cyrus. Lo and behold, the two of them walked in this morning.

"Here you are, Sister Zahra," he said as he took the sack off Cyrus's head. "You'd better talk some sense into him."

"What do you mean, Brother Zaki?" I tried not to stare at Cyrus. I was so frightened Skunk would catch on that he was something other than my sibling.

"Come on, brother." Cyrus chuckled as he put down a canvas tote bag he had brought with him. "I thought we were friends."

"Maybe we're friends," Skunk warily said. "But I think this *zaifeh*"—weakling woman—"sister of yours is much wiser than you are." He glanced at his watch. "It is eleven o'clock now. As agreed, I will be back at five."

"Make it nine, and I will donate five hundred more in cash to your mosque," Cyrus said. He pulled that amount off a roll of bills and pressed the money into Skunk's palm. Skunk left, grumbling.

The moment I heard the door lock behind us, I threw myself in Cyrus's arms. The feel of him both strengthened me and dissolved my stoicism. I began to sob.

"We are almost there, Leila jaan," Cyrus murmured tenderly. "Please remain strong," he whispered in my ear.

I felt the warmth of his tears on my cheeks. Then he pushed me back gently. "Let me take a good look at you."

"Look and see filth, pain, and gloom," I said as I swiped at my own tears with the cuff of my grimy gown. "I'm so tired," I sighed as I collapsed on my cot.

Cyrus came and sat next to me. I apologized for my stench and he said he wouldn't exchange my scent for the aroma of the best French perfumes. His ridiculous compliment made me feel unaccountably better. After all this time enduring this living hell, I so needed to be complimented by Cyrus, to feel adored even though I stunk.

But there was no time to waste. I asked what was happening concerning the negotiations with Skunk over my release. Cyrus, holding my hand, told me that Skunk had initially asked for ten thousand US dollars, and Cyrus and my father had quickly agreed to the sum, but perhaps they had been a little too quick. Skunk, evidently shrewdly guessing their desperation to close a deal, had reneged, hiking the requested ransom.

"So"—I sighed—"what's his latest asking price?"

"Fifty thousand, but money is no problem."

"What do you mean money is no problem? I know for sure that my father cannot afford that. What does my cousin Bijan suggest?"

"Bijan has escaped Iran. He asked me to send his love and concern for you and to explain to you that he had an opportunity to go to France, ostensibly for a cultural exchange mission, and he grabbed it. He has no intention of returning. He will make his way to Los Angeles. There is an organization in France that will help him on his journey."

So Bijan was gone. I had one less person in Iran to care if I lived or died in this miserable hellhole.

"Skunk will never settle on a final sum to release me," I brooded.

"Calm down, dear," Cyrus said. "We will come up with whatever it takes. You correctly see the problem we face, however. Brother Zaki gets greedier by the moment. I know that as soon as we agree pay fifty thousand, he will quickly raise his price."

"So what will we do?"

"We'll think of some tactic to get him to settle on a firm price," Cyrus assured me. "Your father and I simply need to be as clever as you were to get...What do you call him?

"Skunk," I said.

"Right," Cyrus chuckled. "We simply need to be as clever as you were when you got Skunk to contact your father, in the first place. I was so proud of you! Your father and I did everything we could think of to find you, to no avail. I pushed Hassan to find out something so much that he finally swore on his father's grave that the records were sealed and that he had no authority to pursue the matter. And then, you outsmarted everyone by enticing your smelly guard to contact your father."

"Talking about Hassan, what is happening in the office?" I asked.

"Well," Cyrus sighed. "If you remember, you and I were supposed to visit Hassan the day after you were arrested."

"You were arrested." His words reverberated in my head like a gong. Ever since my imprisonment, I had fretted over what Cyrus might have heard or thought concerning the truth about what I had been accused of.

Cyrus interrupted my thoughts. "Are you listening to me, Leila?"

"I don't know how put it to you. I mean, I hope you don't think that Ali and I..." I broke down, weeping in my emotional stew of anger, fear, exhaustion, and shame.

Cyrus held me by my arms and tenderly shook me to my senses. "Don't be ridiculous, Leila. Assault is Ali's middle name. As young boys, he repeatedly beat me in our schoolyard, remember? I have no doubt that's what happened to you at your office."

"I'm so relieved you believe me," I said, hugging him. "I almost don't care that Ali is getting off scot-free."

"Well, if it's any consolation to you, Ali has been stripped of his accounting credentials and reduced to selling sandwiches from a street cart in front of the embassy," Cyrus said. "He has made some serious enemies with all his talk of communism. They were waiting for a chance to bring him down a peg or two. What's more, he is now a social outcast as well. In the eyes of the fanatical devout, he is tainted goods due to being seduced by a 'witch' into betraying his wife," Cyrus winked at me.

I imagined Ali, so arrogant and haughty, so proud of his accounting education and his resulting status, facing his future as no more than a peddler. And for the rest of his days to be viewed by all who know him as an adulterer who brought shame on himself, his wife, and his children. It was not as much revenge as I was hoping for, but it would do.

"Anyway," Cyrus said, interrupting my grim reverie, "we have more important issues to confront than Ali. Let's concentrate on how to deal with Skunk, because we badly need your input. By now, I would imagine that you know better than anyone what makes him tick."

"What can I say, Cyrus?" I turned away to hide my tears. "He's sly like an animal, but just as stupid. And yet, I think his very stupidity is working against us. Like a dog that's been given a piece of meat, which it has devoured, Skunk thinks that if he just keeps barking, more meat will come."

"I agree." Cyrus frowned. "It seems that you have become Skunk's goose that lays golden eggs. The more we give in to his demands, the more he thinks he can get."

"How much did he charge you for today's visit?"

"Who cares? If he would release you for a hundred thousand or two hundred thousand dollars, I have the money and I would pay him. As I said, it's not the money—"

"I know, Cyrus jaan." I ran my fingers through his hair. "Just tell me how much did he charge for this visit?"

"Your strength is beyond me," Cyrus said. "Three thousand dollars."

"So, negotiation with Skunk is not impossible," I thought out loud. "Cyrus, keep in mind that avarice is only one of Skunk's sins. He also has wild dreams of gaining power and authority."

"Go on."

"What if we mixed into the negotiations the potential for Skunk to realize his social ambitions along with a cash offer? I'm thinking about Hassan. Tell Skunk that the deputy revolutionary prosecutor is a friend of yours. Offer to ask Hassan to promote Skunk to a higher rank, and at the same time, offer him a sum you think appropriate if he will release me."

"I'm afraid Skunk may feel threatened, which will jeopardize your situation," Cyrus said hesitantly.

"For all the months that I have been here, I have got to know this man well. I know what I'm saying, Cyrus. Don't worry. I am willing to take the risk."

"OK then, let's celebrate my brilliant girl's courage and intelligence." Cyrus took a thermos from his tote bag and poured hot coffee into two mugs. "To the memory of our days in your Los Angeles kitchen."

As he handed me a steaming mug, I thought back to Sunday mornings with Cyrus in my apartment near the UCLA campus. Now here we were sipping coffee in the depths of hell...

"Don't cry, Leila," Cyrus said tenderly. "Instead, let's toast to the day we are back in America!"

Half laughing, half crying, I wiped away my tears and sipped my coffee, fervently longing for better days to come.

"Now, let's get back to our strategy to gain your release," Cyrus said. "I'm concerned about handing the ransom over to Skunk and then being able only to keep our fingers crossed that he will uphold his part of the deal. I'm thinking of stipulating payment must be COD—cash on delivery of this most precious commodity," he said and kissed me on my cheek.

"Then, as you said, he will suspect that you might want to trick him." I sighed. "I'm so confused; I don't know what to do. I really don't!"

"Aaraam, Leila. Be calm, please. I know it is easy for me to say, but you have to remain strong. That's the key to our success."

"I have an idea, Cyrus," I said. "Let's double the offer and see how he reacts."

"As I said, I have no problem with the amount." Cyrus shrugged. "But on what terms?"

"Well, let's begin negotiating with him and see where it goes."

Cyrus embraced me, put his nose on the back of my neck, and inhaled deeply. "My genius," he said exhaling.

"Don't…I stink." I pulled myself out of his arms.

"Listen, khanom jaan." He drew me close. "In that emergency room of the UCLA Hospital, you stank worse, but it didn't stop me from falling in love with you. As far as I am concerned, forever you will be my jasmine."

"Huh, my Persian poet." I chuckled, kissing his eyes.

Then I froze. "Skunk's coming."

"He can't be; it's too early," Cyrus said, glancing at his watch.

We heard the key in the lock and then the door swung open.

"Here I am," Skunk said, stepping into the cell.

"It's not even two o'clock, Brother Zaki!" Cyrus cried.

Skunk shrugged. "I have too much to do today. Let's go, Brother Cyrus!"

"But I have already paid…Never mind, brother," Cyrus waved his hand, as if being swindled by Skunk was a small matter not worth discussing. "Now that you are here, my sister and I want to talk to you."

Skunk knotted his eyebrows. "Talk to me about what?"

"About her freedom," Cyrus said.

He filled in Skunk about his friend, Hassan, in the Revolutionary Prosecutor's Bureau, promising to get "our

Brother Zaki" transferred so he could be a proud Revolutionary Guard instead of a jail keeper.

"Plus one hundred thousand American dollars!" I interjected.

Skunk looked awed. "Tell me more, Sister Zahra."

"My father is willing to pay you one hundred thousand dollars to set me free. Now, think of what you can do with so much money, brother!"

"Do you own a house?" Cyrus chimed in.

Skunk shook his head.

"How about a car?" Cyrus asked.

"They have given me an old truck to use," Skunk said.

"Are you telling me that for all the sacrifice that you have done for the victory of our revolution, they haven't even given you car?" Cyrus said, his voice dripping with disgust. "It's unconscionable!"

"It's what?" Skunk asked sharply.

"He means it's unfair, brother," I said.

"Never mind," Cyrus interjected. "Brother Zaki, I'm talking about a brand-new car, with leather seats. You could sit behind the wheel and drive your family to the bazaar and buy them lots of whatever they want with plenty more money in your pocket."

"How wonderful it would be, brother," I said. "Just think of it! You could even build a mosque in your own name. Masjed Al-Zaki!"

Skunk looked dumbfounded as in his mind's eye new vistas of prosperity and potential unfurled.

"All right," Cyrus went on. "Let's shake hands on turning your dreams into reality."

Skunk stretched out a shaky hand, which Cyrus grabbed and shook firmly.

I could see Cyrus was stuck on what to say next.

"So," I cut in, "you will call my father and set a date and a place. He will bring the money, you will take me there, and the exchange will take place."

"Deal?" Cyrus was still clutching Skunk's hand. "Tell me that we have closed the deal, Brother Zaki."

"No," Skunk said. "You pay me first; then I will bring her."

"I think Brother Zaki is right," I said, as I saw Cyrus's eyes widen.

Now Skunk looked confused.

I went on. "It's been written, *Khir al-omoor fi osataha,* which means 'In every matter, medium is ideal.' So, let's meet half-way. We pay Brother Zaki half in advance and the balance on my release."

"Allah Akbar," Skunk said. "I will call your father tomorrow and tell him where and when. We will meet at a place of my choice, where he will give me fifty thousand dollars—half the agreed amount."

"Allah Akbar," Cyrus proclaimed fervently.

"Meanwhile"—Skunk looked at Cyrus—"You will procure from your deputy prosecutor friend my written orders to report to him at the bureau to become one of his guards."

"Absolutely," Cyrus vowed.

Skunk nodded. "When I have half the money and possession of my orders, I will fetch Sister Zahra, take her to an agreed upon spot, release her to you, and receive the rest of the money."

I had to give Skunk credit for thinking so quickly how to cover all the contingencies of the deal. Now was the time to make the deal binding on him, so he couldn't come back later with outrageous demands for millions of dollars and, perhaps, to be made Khomeini's personal bodyguard.

"Look, Brother Zaki," I said. "We all put our trust in Allah. So, to make you feel comfortable, the three of us here will put our right hands on Kalam Allah." I retrieved the Koran. "*Tabarek Allah!*"—Blessed be Allah, I intoned as the three of us put our hands on the holy book. "Surely, that which we have all promised will verily come to pass, lest we risk the punishment of Allah."

Then Skunk put the sack over Cyrus's head and led him out.

"You are in good hands, sister," Cyrus said as he was leaving, his voice muffled by the sack. "The benevolent hands of Brother Zaki who will soon bring you back to us."

Skunk closed the door behind him and locked it. Before the carry of his voice was far diminished, I heard Cyrus regaling Skunk with all the benefits and privileges that came with being a guard at the Prosecutor's Bureau.

CHAPTER 40

Sunday, June 29, 1980

Skunk is playing cagey, again.

I asked him if he had talked to my father; he shrugged.

"Please, Brother Zaki," I begged.

He was silent. I pleaded and pleaded, but he ignored me, and I plummeted from yesterday's ecstatic high over the prospect of regaining my freedom.

"Didn't we reach an agreement yesterday, Brother Zaki?" I shrieked, holding his arm as he opened the door to leave my cell. "Yesterday we all swore on the Koran!"

That got him to open his mouth. "Yes, we did swear and now what does that kooni father and brother of yours think? That they can trick me to release you without paying me the full amount they have offered?"

"But we had a deal, brother. We put our hand on the Koran and swore to be honest!"

"Then why don't they trust me?" he shouted. "I know what they are up to! With all these false promises, they want to follow me here, find you, kill me, and rescue their beloved daughter and sister."

"Why are you so suspicious of my father and brother? They will pay you. I promise. And why would they want to, Allah forbid, kill you if you are so kindly freeing me?"

Again, he cursed my father and Cyrus, called them faggots. "You will do this," he ordered, going to my cot, where he took a piece of paper and one of the pens he had given me. "Write what I say exactly. I want to show it to those koonis."

I sat on the floor and took his dictation.

"Write that you are locked behind three doors," he began, showing me his key ring. "This one"—he showed me one of the keys—"locks the doors of all cells here. This second one opens the metal door at the end of the corridor. And this third one locks the door to the main entrance of the house. They have to know that you are sealed off from the outside world."

As nervous as I was, I was thrilled to receive so much information.

"Thank you for sharing this with me, brother," I said calmly.

"I'm not sharing anything with you. Did you write everything I told you?"

"Yes, brother."

"Give it to me. I want your daddy, that child of a thousand whores, and your blue-eyed bastard brother to know that your life is in my hands, so that they cannot think of any stupid ideas."

Skunk left.

In our lives, there are times that we don't give up hope, but we simply surrender to circumstances. We become so worn down by our problems that something breaks inside of us and we become calm, even serene, as we wait to see what life has next in store for us. That's how I felt for the next few hours as I lay on my cot, staring at the cracked, cobwebbed ceiling, and thought about the one-in-a-million chance that I would be born to go through such misery. I thought of faraway planets and alternative universes…realities where Skunk was a good man…where I was the jailer and he was the prisoner…where Leila was married to Cyrus and had many children in the USA…where the Shah sat on his throne and all was right with Iran…

I thought and thought until the day turned into night, until the door of my cell opened and Skunk's silhouette emerged, a cigarette hanging from his lips, its glowing tip and furling smoke casting omens of hell and damnation.

"I saw the two faggots." He was breathing heavily as he stepped in, closed the door of the cell, locked it, and tossed his key ring to the far corner. He opened the satchel he was carrying and tipped it to show me that it was full of American dollars. Then he put the satchel down in the corner on top of the key ring, unbuckled his gun belt, and set that on the floor next to the satchel.

"Brother Zaki? What is the meaning of this? What do you mean to do?" I asked as I backed away as far as possible within the cell's close confines.

He didn't answer. Instead, he quickly crossed the space between us, grabbed my arms, and whirled me around, throwing me on the cot.

"What's the matter with you, brother?"

"You have played enough with me, jendeh," he panted and began fumbling with my clothing.

"Please, tell me why you are so upset with me," I begged him, trying to hold tight to the waistband of my pants.

"Upset? I'm not upset. Actually, I am celebrating!"

He lowered his full weight upon me, crushing my chest so that I couldn't breathe. He tore off my scarves, grabbed my hair, and yanked my head around.

"Look at those dollars, Sister Zahra! Your daddy and his blue-eyed bastard son, I took their money and got away. Your stupid father and brother will be waiting for me to bring you to them. But you will never see them again. After I am done fucking you, I'm going to send a few brothers to arrest your father and brother with the rest of the ransom, and I will split it with them. That's right, at nine o'clock tonight, on the corner of the Revolution Square and Imam Street!"

"Please, you're too heavy, I can't breathe!"

It was such a horror. A nightmare replay of Ali's attempted rape. When would these animals with all their supposed religious and political zeal realize that rape was the antithesis of all that their Allah intended for them?

In my panic, my hand hit the floor. I touched one of the pens Skunk had given me. I snatched it up and rammed it point first into the soft skin just behind the hinge of his jaw. Skunk reared up, howling. He was clawing at his face as he tried to get a grip on the blood-slick pen and pull it out. I contracted my stomach, tightened my thighs, and bucked him off me. He fell to the floor as I slid on my belly across the narrow expanse of floor to where his gun belt lay coiled like a snake. I pulled the pistol from its holster and whirled around to point it at his chest.

"Stay away or I'll kill you!" I screamed.

Skunk, who by now had managed to extract the pen from his neck, returned his attention to me. He sat on the cot, eyeing me warily as he tore a strip of cloth from his tunic and held it to his puncture wound to staunch the bleeding.

"Don't be ridiculous, sister. You don't even know how to use that."

"What?" I replied, glancing at the pistol. "You mean I don't know how to use a Sig Sauer nine millimeter? Double action on the first shot; single action, thereafter?"

I wasn't bluffing. The Sig Sauer was a standard issue for the Shah's army, and it was the very model my grandfather, General Omid, had carried as his personal sidearm. I had fired his many times. Now I racked the slide on the pistol to chamber a round, in the process cocking the hammer, so that the gun would go off with just the slightest pressure on the trigger.

Skunk was looking suddenly very pale. "You...you haven't taken off the safety catch," he said, trying to bluff.

"This pistol doesn't have a safety," I said. "Just a de-cocking lever."

"What kind of woman are you?" Skunk muttered incredulously.

"The important question for you is, Have I convinced you that I know the manual of arms for this weapon?"

"Yes." Skunk sulked.

"Good. Then do not, even for a second, let it cross your mind that you can subdue me. Just sit there and don't move while I contemplate ending your life."

The expression on Skunk's face was now a mix of disbelief and absolute panic. "I have a wife and three small children," he began to plead. "In the name of Allah and all sacred prophets, please don't kill me."

"Maybe I won't," I said, standing and grasping the pistol with two hands as my grandfather had instructed me. I lowered my aim to his groin. "Maybe I'll just shoot off your pathetic manhood."

Instinctively he clasped his knees together tightly.

"No!" I shouted. "You spread your legs wide, right now!

Whining in fear, he reluctantly did as he was told. "I...I..." he whimpered.

"I know what you want to say," I reassured him, my aim rock steady, just like when I was a teenager shooting at bottles nested in the sand. "You want to tell me that Satan had deceived you. Or perhaps I have bewitched you, you pious Muslim man? So I will do you a great favor. I will shoot off the miserable little tool that Satan has sewn onto your filthy body so that you won't have the means, no matter how small and how impotent, to assail women. But before that, I have something else to do."

I was out of control, I will admit. I was drunk with the power the pistol clutched in my hands had transferred to me. All the repressed rage and anger I'd felt over what had happened to me almost six months ago in my office with Ali, and how I had so unjustly ended up in this hellhole, to be tormented by this demon, boiled over inside of me. Without even thinking about it, I lashed out with my foot and I kicked Skunk as hard as I could between his spread legs. I felt the toe of my shoe sinking into his soft groin, and I luxuriated in his high-pitched, almost womanly scream. Skunk's face went from pale white to bright red and back again. He contracted, crumbling like paper. He rolled off the cot and curled up on the floor on his side in a fetal position.

For a full minute, all he could do was writhe in the dirt and try to breathe. Then, as his agony lessened, he began to shout for help.

"Weren't you the one who told me that there was nobody around this place except for those two other women prisoners at the other end of the corridor? Who do you think will come to your aid, you fool?"

"Think, Sister Zahra," Skunk gasped as he managed to sit up, still breathing heavily as he waited for the pain in his balls to subside. "I'm a Revolutionary Guard! They will catch you and lynch you. Now just give that pistol back to me."

"Did you ever wonder why I rarely called you by your real name?" I demanded. "It's because you stink, you filthy animal. That's why I named you Skunk. Why are you so filthy? Is it not one of our most important religious instructions to keep clean?"

"Yes...Yes, Sister Zahra!"

"My name is not Zahra and I am not your goddamned sister. If I am your sister, I might ask if it is your religious practice to sexually assault your sister. What has this 'beloved revolution' of yours brought about that you could call me sister and yet, with no qualm, decide to rape me?"

"I understand."

"No, you don't! Your petty brain is not capable of understanding anything. You want an example?" I gestured quickly with the gun to his key ring lying on the floor in the corner, and then just as quickly brought the weapon back to bear on his chest. "Those keys, the use of which you so stupidly explained to me, that's one thing you don't grasp the significance of. And you know what else you don't understand? That Cyrus is my fiancé and not my brother."

"I don't care about any of that," Skunk said, pleading. "Give me back my gun and I promise I will treat you nicely."

"No, Skunk, I am not going to give your gun back to you," I said calmly. "Here's what you're going to do. You're going to get on your knees with your back to me. Facing the door."

He understood the ramifications of what I was ordering—that I was positioning him to be executed.

"Oh, please..."

"Do it!"

Weeping now, Skunk did as he was told. Ready for anything, my finger dancing on the trigger, every nerve in my body singing with tension, I pressed the barrel of the gun against the back of his head.

"Please, please, please. I promise, I swear to Allah—"

"Shut up, you pathetic, hypocrite," I said. "You blemish the sanctity of your religion with your blathering. Shut your filthy mouth and don't utter a word without my permission."

I pressed the gun harder against his skull. "Have you ever really been a freedom fighter as you claim? Yes or no?"

"No, sister, I haven't," he confessed like a sullen penitent.

"So you are no freedom fighter, but you have always been a garbage collector? Yes or no?"

"Yes."

"Now say, 'My name is Skunk.'"

"My name is Skunk," he whispered. I could hardly hear him past his sobs.

"Remember how you wanted to make a pious woman out of me, Skunk?"

"Yes."

"I'm now going to make a dead piece of meat out of you. I'm going to send you to the fires of hell."

"Please—"

The acrid stink of urine filled the cell. Skunk was literally peeing in his pants. Pathetic excuse for a man.

I willed myself to pull the trigger. But I couldn't.

I kept imagining how much harder the already arduous life of his wife and children would be without him. And, besides, who was I kidding? Could I execute a human being, no matter how detestable, in cold blood? No, I couldn't do that. Perhaps Skunk, feral creature that he was, sensed my hesitation.

"Please, please, reconsider, for the sake of Allah, Sister Zahra—"

I corrected him. "Leila Omid is my name." Quickly I reversed my grip on the pistol so that I held it like a hammer. I swung my arm up and around in an arc and brought the butt of the gun down as hard as I could—like I was hammering a nail—against the top of Skunk's skull. When I landed the blow, the vibration from the sickening thud traveled through my forearm. Skunk collapsed to the floor and lay twitching and moaning.

I gathered up my memoirs from beneath my pillow and stuffed them into the satchel that held the money. I fastened my scarves beneath my chin, grabbed the pistol and satchel in one hand, scooped up Skunk's key ring with the other, and left the cell, locking the door behind me.

Whether I'd fatally injured him or not, I would never know. I never saw Skunk again.

The corridor was empty. I put the gun in the satchel with everything else, tied it around my waist under my shirt, and ran down the corridor to the second door—when I remembered the other two women prisoners. I ran back and opened the door of the first cell. There I saw a woman who seemed to be in her sixties, hunched in the far corner of her cell.

"*Ash'hada en la Allah el-Allah*!"—I testify that there's no God but Allah—she recited her death prayer in a shaky voice.

"Come! You must leave now. You are free!" I cried.

She raised her head and looked at me with dead eyes.

"I've locked the guard in my cell. Now run away!"

I had no time to waste. I left her, rushed to open the door of the second cell, but it was already empty. What had happened to that poor woman, I didn't want to imagine. Over my shoulder, I saw the older woman prisoner I'd freed uncertainly following me as I unlocked the corridor door, made my way through the abandoned front rooms of this derelict house, opened the front door, and stepped out onto the street and freedom for the first time in almost six months.

I inhaled the fresh hot summer air. The city, in contrast with my black cell, seemed bright and illuminated. There was a full moon in the sky. The unfamiliar street was empty. If Skunk was not lying, my father and Cyrus would be waiting for me on the corner of Revolution Square and Imam Street. I read the street sign on the corner. It said, Imam Street! I was so close!

I started to run, then realized I had no idea which direction I was going.

I heard a man order me to stop. Hearing his heavy footsteps, I turned around and saw a revolutionary guard approaching.

"What are you doing here alone so late at night, sister?" he asked in a suspicious tone.

"Well…" I hesitated, praying that he would not notice me shaking. If necessary, I was certain I could reach into the satchel and extract the pistol before the startled pasdar could bring into play his rifle slung across his back. This I could and would do. This would not be executing a broken man peeing in his pants on his knees. This would be self-defense—killing for my own survival. Under no circumstances would I be returned to my crypt. I would rather kill, or be killed, if it came to that.

"I was visiting my sister, brother pasdar," I mumbled, making up a story as I went along. "In the early days of the revolution, the Shah's wild dogs killed her husband. You may have heard of him, the famous revolutionary martyr, Mohsen the Lion?"

"Maybe." The guard shrugged. "Yes, I think I have."

"Now my sister, the poor soul, has to take care of her three children single-handedly. I was supposed to spend the night with her, but my husband called and said that our own little boy is very sick. My husband and the baby are waiting for me at the corner of Revolution Square and Imam Street. We have to take my boy to the hospital."

"But Revolution Square is that way, sister," the man pointed in the opposite direction I had been running.

"May Allah bless you, brother! So worried was I about my child, I didn't know which way I was going. Thank you!" I began to hurry away.

"Wait, sister," he called after me. "Do you want me to accompany you?"

"No thank you, brother," I said, "Now I know my way."

A thousand bleak thoughts ran through my mind as I hurried to Revolution Square. I didn't know what time it was.

Was it too early for the rendezvous Skunk has pretended to arrange, or too late? What if Cyrus and my father weren't there? I couldn't loiter in the square without arousing suspicion. Perhaps I could go to Bijan's house—No! He had already escaped Iran! How much time did I have before my escape was discovered? Did I correctly lock the door of my cell? What if Skunk was sounding the alarm on me right now?

There! Among the parked cars! Headlights flashing once! I broke into a run, not caring that I might attract unwanted attention. I saw my father and Cyrus getting out of the car, and I threw myself into my startled beloved's arms.

"Where is Skunk?" Pedar whispered as I held tight to Cyrus. "We have to pay him the rest of the money."

"I escaped," I said. "I knocked him unconscious and locked him in the cell. I have the money you already gave him."

"Quick," my father muttered, his voice shaking as Cyrus guided me to the backseat of the car, a black Chevrolet. Cyrus sat next to me. I noticed there was a driver—a man I did not know. My father sat next to him in the front passenger seat. The car started up and pulled away. As it did, I broke down, crying hysterically, holding my face in my hands.

"Hush, Leila jaan," I heard Cyrus's voice and felt the warmth of his embrace. "Whatever happens now, will happen to us together."

Together…

His voice, his words, warmed me like a fire.

We drove through the night. The man behind the wheel was a member of the Kurdistan Liberation Movement, the same person who had smuggled the rest of our family out of Iran. We would drive all night along the twisting, turning road through the mountains of Kurdistan in northern Iran. From there, on the backs of mules, we would cross into Turkey, where, thanks to my father's garnered passports, and Cyrus's connections, a Jewish refugee organization and our visas to America awaited us.

Soon the three of us would be reunited with the rest of my family in Los Angeles, USA.

My father, my trellis.

Cyrus, my love.

And me, in a place where I could shed my hijab for good.

And my name would always and forever be Leila.

CHAPTER 41

January 20, 1981

"Senator Hatfield, Mr. Chief Justice, Mr. President, Vice President Bush, Vice President Mondale, Senator Baker, Speaker O'Neil, Reverend Moomaw, and my fellow citizens..."

Cyrus and I—husband and wife—sit with our arms around each other on the sofa, watching on the television as the new United States president, Ronald Reagan, begins his inaugural address.

"To a few of us here today, this is a solemn and most momentous occasion. And yet, in the history of our nation, it is a commonplace occurrence."

It has been almost seven months since I held that gun to Skunk's head and escaped from my jail. Our apartment is not far from the house of my mother and father. The homes of my grandparents, my siblings, and Bijan, who has a teaching position at UCLA, are also not far away in this Iranian community in Los Angeles that has come to be called Tehrangeles. It's a stretch of Westwood Boulevard, on the edge of the UCLA campus, next door to Beverly Hills. In some ways, and at certain times, walking about our neighborhood, I feel like I still live in Iran—when the Shah still ruled.

Pop into any shop and you'll hear Farsi. The business signs are all in Persian. The women are stylish in the latest American and European fashions. I am one of the most stylish, I'm pleased to say. Every day as I feel the breeze ruffling my hair and the sun on my arms and legs, I thank God to be in the Land of the Free. I know most of my community's store owners well, and not just from shopping. I have a small CPA practice that I run out of our spare bedroom, keeping the books for them.

Of course, soon, we will need the spare bedroom for a nursery, I think happily, my hand going to my belly. The other day Cyrus and I went to the doctor to confirm what I already knew—that inside me our child is growing. It will be such fun shopping all over again for maternity fashions in a few more months!

"The orderly transfer of authority as called for in the Constitution routinely takes place as it has for almost two centuries," President Reagan was saying on the television. "Few of us stop to think how unique we really are. In the eyes of many in the world, this every-four-year ceremony we accept as normal is nothing less than a miracle…"

Cyrus is a partner at the Los Angeles offices of Jenkins Brothers & Associates. Since our escape to America, my husband and I have been following the tragic events in our country. At times, we talk about all we went through, from Ali to Skunk.

"Not talking about calamities doesn't make them go away," Cyrus says. "But talking about them sometimes can."

We especially follow the fate of the American hostages from the embassy. My husband and I both know so well what it is like to be held against one's will. Our hearts go out to those brave Americans still being held captive.

"As for the enemies of freedom, those who are potential adversaries, they will be reminded that peace is the highest aspiration of the American people. We will negotiate for it, sacrifice for it; we will not surrender for it—now or ever..." Reagan continues in his strong actor's voice. My father, and especially my grandfather, the general, were so pleased when Reagan was elected!

"Above all, we must realize that no arsenal, or no weapon in the arsenals of the world, is so formidable as the will and moral courage of free men and women. It is a weapon our adversaries in today's world do not have. It is a weapon that we as Americans do have. Let that be understood by those who practice terrorism and prey upon their neighbors..."

As Reagan—now the president of the United States for the past half hour or so—finishes his inaugural address to great applause, the newscaster, Walter Cronkite, comes on the air:

"The Associated Press has announced that the Iranian news agency Pars has reported the takeoff of an aircraft with the American hostages, and that's the nearest thing to an official report we have..."

I glance at Cyrus. "Do you think it's true?"

Before my husband can answer, someone offscreen hands Cronkite a sheet of paper from which he reads: "We now have confirmation from the West German Embassy in Tehran that the hostages are out of Iranian airspace...So, I guess we can come to the conclusion that the Iranians, in the last defiance of civilized behavior, have waited until the inauguration of President Reagan before letting the hostages go, ending the unnecessary four hundred forty-four days of their captivity."

"I finally feel like our nightmare is over, once and for all," Cyrus tells me, sounding vastly relieved.

"Our children will never know the repression and terror we endured," I say and press Cyrus's hand to my stomach, where the fruit of our love is blossoming. It is far too soon to feel our baby's kicks, of course. But in the spring, by the time of the first of Nowrooz, Persian New Year, it might be a different story.

God willing, my family—now Cyrus's family as well—will gather around the Nowrooz table to rejoice in our lives and in our good fortune to be together. Then will come the Jewish holidays of Passover and Yom Kippur.

A new year in our new lives

"What do you think, Leila jaan: is it a boy or a girl?"

"Which would you prefer?"

"Well, just as long as our child is healthy," Cyrus says. "But, perhaps, a son, I suppose," he adds shyly.

"It so happens that it is a son," I tell him.

"But how can you say for sure?"

"A woman knows these things."

"But I know you want a daughter," Cyrus says.

I look into my beloved's beautiful blue eyes.

"So a daughter will be next," I manage to say before my Cyrus smothers me with kisses.